THIEF OF SOULS

THE STAR SHARDS TRILOGY

Scorpion Shards
Thief of Souls

THIEF OF SOULS

BOOK TWO OF THE STAR SHARDS TRILOGY

NEAL SHUSTERMAN

TOR®

A TOM DOHERTY ASSOCIATES BOOK
NEW YORK

For Brian Pellar
who always reminds me
to question reality.

This is a work of fiction. All the characters and events portrayed in this novel are either fictitious or are used fictitiously.

THIEF OF SOULS

A Tor Book
Published by Tom Doherty Associates, Inc.
175 Fifth Avenue
New York, NY 10010

Tor Books on the World Wide Web: http://www.tor.com

Neal Shusterman on the World Wide Web: http://www.storyman.com

Tor® is a registered trademark of Tom Doherty Associates, Inc.

Library of Congress Cataloging-in-Publication Data

Shusterman, Neal.
    Thief of souls / Neal Shusterman.—1st ed.
       p.   cm.
    "A Tom Doherty Associates book."
    ISBN 0-312-85507-9 (alk. paper)
    I. Title.
    PS3569.H8645T47   1999
    813'.54—dc21   98-37531
                            CIP

First Edition: April 1999

Printed in the United States of America

0 9 8 7 6 5 4 3 2 1

ACKNOWLEDGMENTS

This novel, more than three years in the making, would not have been possible without the help of a great many people, without whom I would have been overwhelmed in the waters.

My gratitude to Man Susanyatame of the Hualapai, for his wit, wisdom, and wonderful translations. My appreciation to Barbara Potter, Jeanne Hess, Cindy Adams, and other educators who read early drafts of the novel. My thanks to the Fictionaires; the mysterious and insightful cabal that challenges me to push the envelope, and Jennifer Leavitt-Wipf for helping me to keep all the plates spinning. My deepest thanks to Kathleen Doherty, Jonathan Schmidt, and Linda Quinton for their passion, and belief in my work, as well as their friendship, and to Orson Scott Card, for giving me something to aspire to.

Most of all, I'd like to thank Elaine, and the kids, whose endless love and support keep my orbit stable.

"Beware; don't whistle, talk, or laugh into the night. Night eyes are upon you. Guard your soul with light and fear, for you know not what evil lurks in the blackness of that which is, and isn't."
—Hualapai Saying

PART I · KINGDOM GONE

FOUR SHACKLES. CHAINS POUNDED INTO GRANITE BY THE blows of the blacksmith's hammer.

They wouldn't kill him—for they didn't think it possible—so instead, they left him to suffer in agony, stretched across the face of an unfeeling mountain, forever facing east.

The harsh Mediterranean sun would rise day after day, year after year over the island where he was chained, bronzing his ruined skin, and heating his blood until he felt it would boil through his veins. Then, at night, the mountain face would cool, draining the heat from his splayed body as the cold wind passed. The fire of day and the chill of night had taken every measure of his energy—but it had not taken his life. He was not an immortal being, as his imprisoners believed him to be. In fact, death would have been the easier choice—but instead he kept himself alive by the sheer force of his will, and year to year measured the passing time by the steady pounding of waves on the shore below.

Each day, in the hours of twilight, the birds would come. They would pick at him as if he were a corpse, and his only defense was his anguished wail. The chains made sure of that. No amount of struggling could tear his arms or legs free from the anchors that held him tight to the stone.

Then at night, when the birds left, he would will himself to heal, refusing to die—refusing to reveal his own mortality to his captors, who still reveled in the palace far above.

With each sunrise his fury grew—but rather than letting it weaken him, he shaped his anger, and gave it focus. Then he would impel that anger deep into the heart of the mountain. He was a being of profound strength and spirit, and could accomplish such an incredible thing as feeding his anger to the mountain. He was far superior to the high-primates that infested the Earth—superior even to the twelve who dared call themselves gods. He had come to the Earth as a bringer of light. He had gathered The Twelve when they were nothing more than awkward human youths from distant, backward lands. He was the one who had shown The Twelve how to destroy the dark titans that had latched on to each of their bright souls. He had even offered them wisdom from beyond the bounds of this universe, and all he asked in return was that they kept his appetite sated. Yet in spite of all he had done for them, they chose to repay him by shackling him to the mountainside. If there was any goodness in him, it had been maimed by his years of suffering, leaving behind a sinewy scar of evil. And he had learned to wear that scar well.

He knew there was a way out of this Hell they had created for him.

If he could survive long enough, his anger would provide him an escape.

Through thirty years of bondage, he forced his anger into the pit of the mountain, seeing in his mind the dense levels of strata that plugged the mouth of the silent volcano. He picked at that stone with his fury, creating tiny fractures in the volcanic rock . . .

. . . until the day he finally made it erupt.

After years of waiting, the eruption was sudden, quick and violent— the mountain shook with the force of a thousand earthquakes. Immense boulders sailed across the sea and toward the mainland with the force of the explosions.

Still his shackles held.

He heard a boulder pounding down the mountain above him, but couldn't crane his neck far enough to see it. It hurtled past, for a moment eclipsing the bright sun, before crashing into the Mediterranean below.

Then he felt himself move. It wasn't just the shaking of the mountain—it was something more. He felt himself begin to list forward. The force of the boulder smashing past had fractured the stone face of the mountain! The wall of rock behind him heaved, and fell forward.

The sky and Earth switched places, and switched again as he tumbled, still chained to the careening stone, certain it would take a wrong bounce and crush him—but instead the falling stone cartwheeled him down the side of the mountain and to the rocky shore, where the immense chunk of granite shattered into a thousand pieces against the jagged rocks that sur-rounded the entire island of Thera.

Waist-deep in the water, he pulled his hands and legs free from the pulverized stone. The heavy shackles still encircled his ankles and wrists, but now they anchored him to nothing but air.

Far, far above, the sky burned as lava spat forth from the bowels of the Earth, threatening the great summer palace high on the mountainside. It was a citadel of splendor, carved from the stone of the mountain itself, even more extravagant than the palace on Olympus, where The Twelve wintered. He had taught them how to create such a glorious place—as he had taught them so many things. Now that he was free, it was time for the twelve star-shards on the mountain who called themselves gods to pay their debt to him in full.

He set his sights on the great palace, and hobbling on feet ruined from thirty years in shackles, he climbed toward the home of the so-called gods.

HUMAN SLAVES AND *servants scattered wildly, paying him no heed as he hobbled across the grand marble courtyard, his chains dragging on the smooth stone. It was then that he caught sight of the beasts. They were all around. Strange miscreations that had no business on Earth. Something that was half man, half horse galloped clumsily down the palace steps. A winged lion with the talons of a falcon clawed at a wooden door, flapping its wings. The sight of these things inspired his rage to new heights. No doubt these creatures were forged by the hands of the blacksmith—whose talent for shaping flesh and bone must have progressed over the years. But the smith wasn't the only one whose powers had matured. In fact, all around the courtyard was evidence of The Twelve's supernatural abilities. Black scars in the stone spoke of their lightning tempers. Statuary that was human flesh turned to stone filled the grounds, their limbs and necks broken by the shaking of the mountain. A great golden mural attested to the shifting shape of the King—human to eagle, to tiger, and back again.*

To see this place, one would think the so-called gods had been here for eons, instead of a mere thirty years. To glimpse their powers now, one would think they sprang full-grown from the heavens and seas. No doubt the ignorant masses of Earth were already spinning tales that implicated The Twelve in the very creation of the universe. And all because they were lucky enough to be born filled with the luminous soul of a shattered star. What would the masses think if they knew these gods they worshiped were born to the same race as themselves, only forty-five years before?

It had been an amusing-enough diversion to take these twelve, and set them above the rest of mankind—but a diversion was all it was supposed to be. He had not foreseen them turning on him as they had. Now, in the intervening years, their powers had grown unchecked, swelling wildly out of control. They were weeds, and like all weeds had to be torn out at the root.

An arch collapsed behind him as he crossed into the great hall. He barely flinched, for his mind was focused now. Time was short and the task immense. He could not be sidetracked.

He descended a narrow set of stairs toward the forge, as the shaking mountain settled to a slow rumble.

There, in the dungeonlike cavern of the forge, he found the blacksmith, cowering from the heaving force of the mountain. On the table lay the bronze form of a new creation: a hideous thing with snakes growing from its skull, like hair. It did not yet live, its metal not yet turned to flesh by the hand of the smith.

All around were living monstrosities in cages. Creatures clearly too vile to be set free on the island. The cages shook and rattled with the rumble of the erupting volcano. Seeing this place made it clear that this day of reckoning had been too long in coming.

"Hephaestus," he called out to the cowering blacksmith. The blacksmith stood, a full six foot five, but still as hideously ugly as he had been at fifteen . . . on the day Hephaestus had shackled his teacher to the mountain. All that talent in shaping flesh, yet the homely blacksmith did not have the power to change his own unattractive features.

"Prometheus!" wailed Hephaestus. It was a name The Twelve had given him. Forethought. Premeditation. As if he were the divine embodiment of some greater plan. He abided the name, as it served his purposes, although he much preferred to be called the Bringer, for he had brought them all into the glory which they now abused.

The Bringer looked with scorn on the snarling, caged teratisms. "Thirty years of practice, and these monsters are the best you can create? How can you call yourself a smith?"

Hephaestus quaked in his sandals, and spoke in a voice far too weak for such a large man. "They . . . They are for the King's amusement."

The Bringer nodded. "After today the King no longer needs to be amused."

He strode forward, and Hephaestus quickly ran to the other side of the stone table. "We grew afraid of you," he tried to explain. "They made *me build those shackles. They made me hammer you to the mountain. I couldn't go against their wishes . . ."*

"You had nothing to fear then," the Bringer told Hephaestus. "But you do now." He held Hephaestus in his gaze as he moved around the table. "In these years I have come to realize that your species is not only corrupt, but pathetic. Unworthy of the slightest charity or sympathy."

"Let me live!" pleaded the homely blacksmith. "I'll do better! Kill the others if need be, but let me live!"

The Bringer thrust his hand forward, and grabbed the blacksmith by his tunic, pulling him closer. "Your selfishness disgusts me," he said. "But enough chatter. I'm hungry." And with that, the Bringer smiled, and, for the first time in many, many years, prepared to dine.

As he held Hephaestus, he forced an ounce of his true self up from the depths of the human body he wore. He opened his mouth, letting red tendrils of light stretch through the air, probing forward like roots seeking water.

Hephaestus gasped, but could not squirm out of his grip. The hungry tendrils latched on to the struggling blacksmith's face, and the fight drained out of him as the Bringer began his feast.

"No," the blacksmith screamed, but it was already too late. The Bringer cast him aside. Weakened, but still alive, Hephaestus felt his arms and chest. His body was unharmed, but something was different. Something was wrong.

"What have you done to me?" he demanded.

"I've taken from you what you never deserved," said the Bringer. "I've devoured your soul."

As he said it, the Bringer could see the weight of the loss beginning to take effect in the blacksmith. A living, thinking brain suddenly robbed of being. A body going through the motions of life, with nothing living inside. Unbearable emptiness.

The soulless blacksmith fell to his knees, covered his eyes, and wept the dry, anguished tears of the living dead.

SEEKING OUT THE *others was a simple matter. He found most of them in their temples, still playing the parts of gods to the servants who had gathered there, seeking salvation from the erupting mountain. The "gods" must have sensed he was coming, for there was no surprise in their eyes— only fear. They knew of his hunger for souls. In fact, they had helped him gorge on the boatloads of virgins and eunuchs their loyal followers were so fond of sending from the mainland. They helped, that is, until they grew disgusted of the endeavor, and fixed him upon the mountainside. Now it was their souls that would be devoured, and they knew it. Some ran when they saw him coming, but he caught them as they fled. It was their fear of his hunger that gave him the upper hand. Even in his weakened state, the Bringer could latch on to their powerful souls and tear them loose as easily as a human might skin a rabbit. Others held their ground and fought him. Hera, Apollo . . . Yet with each soul he drank in, the stronger he became for the next confrontation. The self-proclaimed Goddess of Love did not resist him. Instead she wrapped herself around him, giving herself to him in one final moment of dark sensual ecstasy. Ares, on the other hand, proud and warlike as always, raised a sword and tried to cut him down, but in the end spat forth his soul into the Bringer's devouring tendrils just as Hephaestus had, and the Bringer set his empty shell free to wander the crumbling halls of the doomed palace. Only Athena, seeing there was no hope, had the wisdom to take her own life before he arrived.*

Finally, only one remained.

The King sat alone in his grand throne room, like a captain going down with his vessel. He must have heard the screams of the others, but did not lift a finger to help them. Even now they could be heard wailing in the crumbling chambers below, their soulless bodies still mimicking life.

The Bringer had dined on the others and was now bloated with power. He had never before dined on such great souls, and felt as if he would burst out of the human host-body that held him. Still he kept all of that energy contained within as he approached the King. He knew that this was his true adversary. The King was the strongest of them all, and would not be as easily defeated.

The King's hair was white. Although he was no older than the others, he looked more weathered. Still his eyes were the same as they had been when he was fifteen. They held depth, and a hint of true greatness.

The King's manner was calm, but the Bringer could feel his fear.

"Get off my island," proclaimed the King.

The Bringer let loose a cold and bitter laugh. "It was not your island until I gave it to you, Zeus. You had nothing until I came to teach you of your powers."

Then the King stood, stepping down from his heavy throne. "We would have defeated our titans, and learned of our powers without you. We would have achieved greatness all alone."

The Bringer felt his lips curl from his own rage. "I see no greatness here. Only decadence and waste."

"And you intend to end it?"

The Bringer smiled cruelly. *"With great pleasure."*

Suddenly the King's form began to change. His particular talent was the shifting of form. It was a formidable skill—something the Bringer himself could not do . . . But the Bringer had a defense against it. He had had thirty years to plan for this confrontation—and for once he would fit the name they had given him, for the murder of the King was indeed a premeditated act. He only hoped the King had become so arrogant that he could be caught off guard.

In an instant, Zeus had transformed into a white tiger that pounced in a single bound across the great throne room. The Bringer felt the animal's hot breath, and then pain as its yellow teeth dug into his shoulder. He tried to reach out and devour the King's soul, but, as he suspected, Zeus was far too powerful and strong-willed to ever be devoured. So instead, he forced an image into the King's mind.

A peacock.

A vain, ridiculous bird. A useless creature whose colorful plumes hid its stupidity.

The thought entered the King's mind through an unguarded path, and instantly the magnificent tiger-king unwillingly transformed into the scrawny, flightless bird. It opened its mouth to roar, but could only squawk.

The moment the transformation was complete, the Bringer grabbed the bird-king by its long slender neck, and looked into its eyes. The eyes of the King, in the body of the peacock, no longer appeared wise. Just frightened.

"A fitting form for you, boy," the Bringer told the King, for he still thought of him as the boy he once knew. Then the Bringer smiled broadly, and with a flick of his wrist, snapped the King's neck.

He hurled the dying bird onto the throne, and the King reverted in midair, back into his white-haired self, before smashing down on the throne, neck broken. The light of his great soul left him as he released his last breath. Nothing remained of him but his broken body, slumping limply in the chair, his royal-blue robe now a shroud around him.

With the King dead, the Bringer focused his energy on the final deed to be done. He turned his thoughts to the center of the island, and spat forth all the energy he had collected from the devoured souls of the others, sending a shattering force to a single point beneath the island.

And something tore.

Although it could not yet be seen, the Bringer knew what he had done—he could see it in his mind's eye. He had created a tear in the fabric *of the world beneath the island—a rip he stretched wider and wider with every last ounce of his strength, until the entire erupting island was poised above the hole like a stone about to fall through a sheet of cracking ice. The entire island rumbled with greater urgency, as it began to sink into the great abyss.*

As the island dropped, the ocean began to spill back into the bay. The lush green lowlands were flooded first, swallowing man and beast. The many servants of The Twelve drowned as the sea washed over them.

There must be nothing left of them, *thought the Bringer.* No memory, no evidence. There must never be an artifact found, or a site unearthed. This place had to be cut out of the Universe forever.

With the palace collapsing around him, the Bringer dragged himself up the King's private stairs, to the high stable. He was bloody and crushed from his battle with the King, but he knew the rift he had created beneath the island left him little time.

He found the King's mount in the high stable; a white, winged horse, kicking and neighing in terror. The flying horse was another one of Hephaestus's creations to amuse the King. With no other way off the island, the Bringer climbed onto the back of the Pegasus, kicked it with his shackled feet, and the horse leapt off the ledge of the high stable, frothing at the mouth as it struggled toward the sky.

Down below, the size of the rift was clearer, and much more impressive. The island was sinking faster than the ocean could rush in to fill the void. It was as if a great sinkhole had opened in the ocean floor, and, as the entire island plunged through the hole, the Bringer caught a glimpse of the place he was sending it. Through the hole, he could see distant red sands far, far below. The hole had opened above a strange alien sky. A place of nothingness. An "unworld" that existed between the walls of worlds. This is where he had consigned The Twelve, their servants, and their miscreations. He watched from high above, as the island plummeted out of this world.

Now all that remained of where the island had been, was a circular waterfall, miles wide, pouring down, through the hole in the world, and into the strange sky of another. The hole quickly healed itself until the waters met, becoming a whirlpool, and then the simple crashing of waves as the tear sealed itself closed. The ocean would rage for days from the cataclysm, and people on far shores would say that Poseidon was angry. But the truth was, Poseidon was gone, along with the King and the Queen, the Blacksmith and the Beauty, the God of War, the Goddess of Peace, and the rest of their accomplices. In spite of their vain pretensions, and their powers, they were not the gods they claimed to be. In spite of their luminous souls, they were hopelessly human after all.

It was now that the Bringer realized his own folly—for the Pegasus, however beautiful, was a useless beast, like so many of Hephaestus's creations. Although it had wings, its stallion's body was too heavy to stay aloft for more than a few minutes at a time. Time enough to amuse the King, and to generate a host of overblown tales among humans, perhaps, but not enough to reach the mainland. The Pegasus flapped futilely above the raging sea, already exhausted. A few moments more and it lost the battle. The beast and the Bringer plunged from the sky into the churning ocean.

The Bringer might have found the strength to swim, had he not used everything he had left to tear the island of Thera from the world. He might have floated on ocean currents if he didn't still have shackles on his ankles and wrists—heavy shackles that weighed him down like anchors.

The roar of the ocean became the muted churning of water as he sank beneath the waves, dropping toward the ocean floor.

The winged horse lost its battle as well, and drowned, its heavy mass sinking into the depths with him.

No survivors, *thought the Bringer.* Nothing left.

Perhaps there would be stories of this place, but nothing more. The legends would become twisted and confused, the tales divided and reformed age to age until not a single truth remained. The short reign of The Twelve would be remembered as curious invention from an ignorant time—excised from history and dropped into the boggy depths of myth.

He had finally destroyed them, and his satisfaction was so immense, that it almost didn't matter that he was sinking into colder, darker waters. The Bringer held his last breath of air until it was crushed from his lungs by the building pressure around him as he sank, and he felt the human body he wore begin to die. So he shed it.

Tearing free from the human host-body he had used, he struggled to create a rift in space through which he could escape back to the universe he came from . . . but such a feat would take more strength than he had left. As the body drifted away from him down into darkness, he fought a battle to hold on to life. He needed a new host—some sea creature large enough to hold his being—for he had no flesh of his own—not in an earthly sense—but survival in this world required a body to live in. It was inconvenient and impractical, just like everything else in this universe of matter.

He reached his mind out, but found no large sea creatures he could inhabit, and he knew he would die in this awful, awful world.

It was the fault of The Twelve. It was their fault and the fault of every human infesting this place. His sole consolation was that the twelve star-shards—the only ones ever born to the undeserving human race—had been squelched. And soon, he imagined, this entire race would no doubt destroy itself with its petty and selfish ways.

If it was in his power, he would do the job for them. He would draw out the soul from each human that ever lived, and cast their weak bodies to the red sands of the Unworld. He would blot out this world from creation, just to make sure no star-shards were ever born to humanity again.

He held on to his anger and his hatred of human kind as his life slipped away. As he died, his spirit dissolved into the ocean depths, and his thoughts were carried by the currents to the far corners of the Earth. Lost in the waters of death . . . for three thousand years.

PART II · SPHERES OF INFLUENCE

1. THE REPAIR MAN

DILLON'S ARMS HAD GROWN STRONG FROM HIS LABORS.

At first, his back and shoulders had filled with a fiery soreness that grew worse each day as he worked. His biceps would tighten into twisted, gnarled knots—but in time his body had grown accustomed to the work. So had his mind.

He dug the spade in the soft dirt, and flung it easily over his shoulder.

The chill wind of a late-September night filtered through the nearby forest, filling the midnight air with the rich scent of pine. He shivered. With knuckles stiff from gripping the shovel, he struggled to zip his jacket to the very top. Then he resumed digging, planting the spade again and hurling the dirt, beginning to catch the rhythm of it, giving in to the monotony of spade and earth. He made sure not to get any dirt on the blanket he had brought with him.

He realized he should have worn heavy workboots for the job, but his sneakers, though caked with mud, never seemed to wear out. None of his clothes ever wore out. He had just torn his jeans hopping over the wrought-iron fence, but he knew they would be fine. Even now, the shredded threads around the tear were weaving together.

The fact was, Dillon Cole *couldn't* have a pair of faded, worn-out jeans if he wanted to. He called it "a fringeless fringe benefit." A peculiar side-effect of his unique blessing.

The shovel dug down. Dirt flew out.

"I got a scratch."

The small boy's voice made Dillon flinch, interrupting the rhythm of his digging.

"Carter," warned Dillon, "I told you to stay with that family until I got back."

"But the scratch *hurts*."

Dillon sighed, put the shovel down and brushed a lock of his thick red hair out of his eyes. "All right, let me see your hand."

Carter stretched out his arm to show a scratch across the back of his hand. It wasn't a bad scratch, just enough to draw the tiniest bit of blood, which glistened in the moonlight.

"How'd you do this?" Dillon asked.

Carter just shrugged. "Don't know."

Dillon took a long look at the boy. He couldn't see the boy's eyes clearly in the moonlight, but he could tell Carter was lying. *I won't challenge him just yet,* Dillon thought. Instead he brought his index finger across Carter's hand, concentrating his thoughts on the scratch.

The boy breathed wondrously as he watched the tiny wound pull itself closed far more easily than the zipper on Dillon's jacket. "Oh!"

Dillon let the boy's hand go. "You made that scratch yourself, didn't you? You did it on purpose."

Carter didn't deny it. "I love to watch you heal."

"I don't 'heal,' " reminded Dillon. "I fix things that are broken."

"Yeah, yeah," said Carter, who had heard it all before. "Reversing Enter-P."

"Entropy," Dillon corrected. "Reversing entropy," and he began to marvel at how something so strange had become so familiar to him.

"Go back to those people," Dillon scolded Carter gently. He returned to digging. "You're too young to be here."

"So are you."

Dillon smiled. He had to admit that Carter was right. Sixteen was woefully young to be doing what he was doing. But he had to do it anyway. He reasoned that it was his penance; the wage of his sins until every last bit of what he had destroyed was fixed.

The blade of Dillon's shovel came down hard, with a healthy bang.

Carter jumped. "What was that?"

Dillon shot him a warning glance. "Go back to the house."

"That woman won't stop praying," Carter complained, shifting his weight from one leg to the other, and back again. "It makes me nervous."

"You go back there and tell them I'll be back in an hour. And then you sit down and pray *with* them."

"But—"

"Trust me, Carter. You don't want to see this. Go!"

Carter kicked sullenly at the dirt, then turned to leave. Dillon watched him weave between the polished gravestones and slip through the wrought-iron fence.

When Dillon was sure Carter was gone, he took a long moment to prepare his mind for the task of fixing. Then he brushed away the dirt, and reached for the lip of the coffin.

LITTLE KELLY JESSUP, wrapped in a blanket, clung to Dillon Cole, shivering. Dillon braced himself as he carried her through the door of the Jessup home. Mrs. Jessup stood in the hallway, not quite ready to believe what her eyes told her, until the little girl looked up and said, "Mommy?"

The woman's scream could have woken the dead, if the job had not already been done.

DILLON'S DREAMS THAT night were interrupted, as they always were, by the green flash of the supernova—a memory that had seared its way deep into his unconscious. It was the first flash of vision that there were five others like him out there . . . and the first inkling of what they truly were; the most powerful and luminous souls on earth. Shards of the fractured soul of the scorpion star, incarnated in human flesh.

From there his dream took a turn into nightmare, and he knew where he would find himself next. The throne room of a crumbling palace, on a ruined mountain, within the red sands of what he could only call "the Unworld." That non-place that existed between the walls of worlds.

And before him stood the parasitic beast that had leeched onto his soul for so many years, its gray muscles rippling, its veiny wings batting the air, and its face an evil distortion of his own. It was a creature that would never have grown so powerful, had Dillon's own soul not been so bright.

I will be fed! It told him. *You will destroy for me. I will feed on the destruction you bring.*

In the dream, Dillon saw himself raising the gun to shoot it, knowing what was about to happen, unable to stop it. He pulled the trigger, the beast stepped aside . . . and there was Deanna.

The bullet struck the chest of the girl Dillon himself would die for.

He ran to her, took her in his arms, while his beast flexed its muscles, absorbing this act of destruction, feeding on Deanna's dying breaths.

"I'm not afraid," coughed Deanna; "I'm not afraid"—for after she had purged the parasite of fear from her own soul, terror had no hold on her.

Suffer the weight, Dillon, the creature said, as Deanna died in his arms. *Suffer the weight of destruction . . . and every moment you suffer is a moment I grow strong . . .*

Dillon was shaken awake by small hands on his shoulders. He opened his eyes to see Carter standing above him. By now this had become a regular routine.

"The monster again?"

Dillon nodded. The thing was still alive out there, Dillon knew. Both his beast and Deanna's still stalked the sands of the Unworld. The other four shards had killed their parasites, and Dillon suspected that if his were dead too, it wouldn't invade his dreams with such alarming regularity.

"My dog had worms once," said Carter. "They got to his heart and ate him from the inside out. Was that what it was like having that thing inside you?"

"Something like that," said Dillon. He sat up, taking a moment to orient himself. Where was he this time? What had he done here?

He was in the Jessups' home. Yes—that was it. Kelly Jessup had been dead almost a year now, and her parents driven insane. Dillon had undone all that damage.

Dillon looked at his watch. Three in the morning. "Get back to bed," Dillon told Carter. "We need an early start tomorrow."

Carter returned to the couch across the guest room. "Who do we see tomorrow?"

"A family called the Bradys. There'll be more work than here."

"What about my father?" asked Carter.

Like so many others, Carter's father had gone insane, and died a nasty death last year. Dillon's failure to find his grave was something Carter loved to hang over Dillon's head, and was a constant reminder to Dillon that there were still a million and one things and people screaming to be fixed.

"I'll find him," said Dillon. "And I'll fix him, just like I promised."

Carter shrugged. "No rush," he said, far too pleasantly. "I like being called Carter instead of Delbert anyway."

The thought unsettled Dillon. When the boy had been found, last year, wandering the streets, he had been a mumbling, maddened lunatic, just like everyone else left alive here in Burton, Oregon. He hadn't even known his own name.

"Carter was the tag on your T-shirt. Do you want to be named after an underwear company?"

"I don't care."

And that was the problem. Since Dillon had fixed the boy's mind, he had latched on to Dillon like a puppy. Dillon didn't mind the company, but he knew it just wasn't right. Life with Dillon was a poor substitute for life with his real family.

Dillon, knowing he would not sleep again tonight, turned to leave the room, but Carter stopped him.

"You were calling her name out in your sleep," Carter said.

Dillon sighed, wishing he could forget the dream. "Was I?"

Carter rolled over on the couch to face him. "You know," said Carter, "you could bring her back now . . ."

Dillon grimaced to hear the words spoken aloud. When Deanna had died, Dillon had had no skill in bringing chaos from order, life out of death. All he knew was how to see patterns of destruction and act upon them. But a year had honed his skills.

Now it would be so easy to take Deanna's broken body in his arms and bring her back to life, cell by cell. He imagined that moment when he could gather her life back and see her smile at him again. Hear the gentle forgiveness in her voice.

But he could not get to her. She was sealed away in the Un-world—a place Dillon could not reach. He was trapped in the here-and-now, and the people around him were constant reminders that he didn't deserve Deanna. All he deserved was the endless, exhausting task of fixing the disasters he had created—because he'd never be able to forgive himself for willfully feeding his parasite—until he had repaired every last bit of his decimation. From the moment the other four surviving shards had left him, he knew what his job was going to be. And one of the first things he bought was a shovel.

"Yes, I know I could bring her back," he told Carter. "Now go to sleep."

Carter rolled over, and in a few moments, he was sleeping peacefully. *And why not?* thought Dillon. He had repaired the boy's psyche so well, he never had nightmares, in spite of the horrors he had been through.

Dillon slid noiselessly out of the guest room. Downstairs he found Carol Jessup sitting in the family room. The air smelled of sweet cocoa and smoke from the smoldering fireplace. The woman lovingly held her sleeping daughter in her arms, absorbed in stroking the little girl's hair as she hummed a lullaby. She had been doing this for hours, unable to believe that her daughter was alive again. She stopped humming the moment Dillon stepped into the room. It took her a few moments until she could speak to him.

"I'm afraid to ask who you are," she said, "or how you did what you did."

"It's just patterns, Carol," Dillon answered. "My mind can see patterns no one else can see, and my soul can repair them. That's all I can do."

"That's all you can do?" she said incredulously. "That's everything. It's creation. It's reversing time!"

"Space," said Dillon calmly. "Reversing space."

The woman looked down at her daughter and her eyes became teary. "Maybe I don't know *who* you are," she said to Dillon, looking at him with the sort of holy reverence that made him uncomfortable, "but I know *what* you are."

Dillon found himself getting angry. "You don't know me," he told her. "You don't know the things I've done."

But clearly she didn't care what Dillon had done in the past. All that mattered to her was what he had done here, today. "When the virus came," she said, "my husband and I got lost in the woods, wandering insane like all the others in town. When we finally came out of it, we were told that Kelly had drowned in the river. I wanted to die along with her."

"What if I told you there was no virus?" Dillon said to her. "That they call it a 'virus' because they don't know what else to call it? What if I told you that *I* destroyed this town last year— shattered everyone's mind—and that, in a way, I was the one who killed your daughter in the first place?"

Dillon thought back to the time of his rampage. It had taken so little effort for Dillon to shatter the minds of everyone in town. All he had to do was find the weakest point in the pattern, then simply whisper the right words into the right ear to set off a chain reaction, like a ball-peen hammer to a sheet of glass. Just a single whispered phrase, and within a few short hours, every last man, woman, and child in town was driven insane.

"In fact, what if I told you that I was responsible for the deaths of hundreds of people . . . including my own parents?"

"If you told me that," said Carol Jessup, "I wouldn't believe you. Because I know that a spirit as great as yours isn't capable of such evil."

"Bright light casts dark shadows," he told her, and said no more of it.

Dillon looked around the room. The furniture that had been well worn a day before was now in brand-new condition, and the carpet was thick and lush where it had once showed heavy tracking. Dillon wondered if Carol Jessup and her husband had noticed. He hoped they hadn't. Lately it wasn't a matter of him *willing* these things to happen anymore. Now they happened whether he wanted them to or not. He could sense his power was growing, and now his presence had its own sphere of influence, which affected everything around him. It made him not want to linger anywhere for long.

Little Kelly Jessup's eyes fluttered open for a moment, then closed again as she snuggled closer to her mother. She had already had a bath, but the child still had the faintest smell of the grave lingering behind the baby shampoo. But that, too, would be gone in a day or two.

"You need to leave here," Dillon told Carol Jessup. "Before anyone sees your daughter, you have to go somewhere where no one knows you. Where no one will ask you questions. You can never tell anyone what I did here today." Dillon knew there was still so much confusion in Burton, that one more abandoned house would not raise the questions it might raise elsewhere. It was that confusion which kept Dillon safely hidden from the view of the authorities . . . but the more he repaired, the less disorder there was to hide behind. Dillon knew his corner was getting tight.

"What if we do tell someone?" the woman asked. "What will happen?"

"You don't want to know."

The woman shrank back, and paled.

In truth, nothing would happen to *them* if she told . . . but if word of Dillon's deeds got out, he didn't want to think about what would happen to him.

"We'll pack our things, and leave in the morning," she told him. "And we won't tell a soul."

But it was clear from her tone of voice that she already had.

TWO HOURS LATER, the town of Burton was swarming with police and state troopers, and Dillon knew they were looking for him. He had slipped away from the Jessups' at dawn, already sensing the world closing in around him. As always, they had decided to drive along the back roads. Carter sat silently in the passenger seat, impassive and unconcerned as Dillon managed to evade one police checkpoint after another, until he finally slammed the brakes on his Land Rover, and slammed his fists on the steering wheel.

"What'sa matter?" asked Carter.

Dillon shook his head to clear his thoughts. There was no way out of town—every road was crawling with troopers. The news of his feats must be more widely known than he had suspected, to mobilize so many troopers to ferret him out. Bringing back the dead must have been an offense as serious as mass murder in the eyes of the law.

A hundred yards ahead, the officers at the Harrison Street checkpoint took notice of Dillon's car stopped suspiciously a hundred feet away from them.

Carter yawned and brushed some morning crust from the corner of his eye. "We'll get away from them," said Carter. "You can get out of anything."

But it wasn't that simple. Dillon silently cursed his luck. His talent for seeing patterns in the world around him was as acute as ever, but when it came to his own life, he was blind. He knew someone would eventually give away his secret, but he had thought he would have more time. And it probably wasn't just the Jessups who had blown the whistle; other families must have come forward, too. He could imagine the most hardened of police investigators turned into blubbering morons when they saw the resurrected dead with their own eyes. No, they couldn't catch him, or he'd never be able to complete his repair work. He had to get away.

"We're smarter than them!" said Carter. "They'll never catch us!"

Dillon took a good look at the boy. Dillon couldn't remember ever being that innocent. That trusting.

"We're going to run, aren't we?" Carter's eyes were bright and eager. "Aren't we? You won't let them break us up—we're a team, right?"

Dillon knew what he had to do. Carter deserved more than an apprenticeship to a freak—Dillon owed him at least the *chance* at a normal life. And so, as the troopers approached, Dillon made no move to escape. Instead he quickly whipped up a new plan. A brilliant, brutal plan that would leave everyone better off.

Well, almost everyone.

THE TROOPERS DRAGGED Carter, kicking and screaming into one police car, and took Dillon off in another. Dillon offered no resistance. The two cars drove off, away from Burton, toward a saner part of the world where, presumably, Dillon would be "held for questioning."

The two state troopers in the front seat smelled of morning breath doused with black coffee. The older one, who drove the car, his graying hair cut in a tightly cropped butch, kept glaring at

Dillon in the rearview mirror. His name tag read WELLER, Dillon had noted. The stripes on his sleeve made him a sergeant.

"You've got the folks around here in one mighty uproar, son," he said. "We don't need any more uproars around here—the virus was enough trouble to last a lifetime."

"What are you charging me with?"

Weller laughed smugly. "Does it matter? You're obviously a runaway, and we're well within the law to bring you into 'protective custody.' "

Dillon broke eye contact and gazed out the window.

"Are you listening to me, son?" said Sergeant Weller.

Dillon still didn't answer him, but he did turn to catch Weller's eyes once more as Weller watched him in the rearview mirror. Dillon studied Weller—the way he moved, the cadence and inflections of his voice. Dillon noticed the way the man held his shoulders, and judged the way he aggressively changed lanes. To anyone else, it wouldn't have meant a thing, but to Dillon, the tale couldn't have been clearer if it were painted on the man's forehead. *I can see patterns,* he had told Carol Jessup. *That's all.* And the patterns of Sergeant Weller—each action, every word—betrayed to Dillon who this man had been, who he was, and who he was destined to be. It was not a pretty picture.

"Don't you talk, son?" Weller asked. "Or are you one of them idiot savants?"

Weller chuckled at his own words. Dillon paid particular attention to the methodical but nervous way Weller rubbed the fingers of his right hand, then clasped the hand into a fist. To Dillon, this man's life was easier to read than a street sign.

"Your wife wishes you would stop smoking," Dillon told him. "She wishes you would stop drinking, too."

Catching Dillon's intrusive gaze in the rearview mirror, Weller's cold demeanor took a turn toward winter. "Watch yourself, son," he said. "You make up stories about people, you may find people making up stories about you."

For the first time, the trooper riding shotgun turned around. His name tag read LARABY. He was younger than Weller and to Dillon didn't seem nearly as unpleasant. He did, however, seem troubled. "People are saying you bring back the dead," Officer Laraby said. "You got anything to say about that?"

"It's all a bunch of voodoo talk," Weller sneered. "Mass hysteria—these people all think they got over 'the virus,' but I say some of their marbles are still lost in the drain pipe."

Officer Laraby turned to him. "So how do you explain all those people who turned up alive?"

Weller brushed a weathered hand over his butch and threw a warning glance at his young partner. "It's all hearsay. That's how a hoax works—hearsay held together by spit and tissue paper, isn't that right, son?"

Dillon smiled, all the while thinking how much he hated the way this man called him "son". "I suppose so."

The grin made Weller more irritable. "You think you're pretty smart, don't you? What did you do—take money from folks who didn't know any better, then bring back people who weren't even dead? That's the way you worked it, wasn't it, son?"

Dillon let the grin slip from his face. "You hit your wife one more time, and she's gonna leave you, you know?"

Panic flashed in Weller's eyes. His jaw twitched uncomfortably. Laraby watched the two of them, his head going back and forth like it was a game of Ping-Pong, to see who would speak next.

Weller hid his uneasiness behind an outburst of laughter. "Oh, you're good," he told Dillon. "You put on one heck of a show— but the truth is you don't know a thing about me."

Dillon found himself grinning again—the way he did in the days when the wrecking hunger had consumed him. "I know what I know," he said.

Dillon sensed the younger cop's growing discomfort, his confusion and uncertainty. Dillon also noticed the particular shade of the rings beneath Laraby's eyes, the faint smell of mild perfumed soap, and a handful of bitten fingernails. Dillon, his skill at deciphering patterns as acute as ever, understood Laraby's situation completely.

"Sorry your baby's sick," Dillon told Officer Laraby.

The man went pale. Dillon noted the exact way his chest seemed to cave in.

"Heart problem?" asked Dillon. "Or is it his lungs?"

"Heart," Laraby said in a weak sort of wonder.

"Don't talk to him!" Weller ordered Laraby. "It's tricks, that's all."

"Yeah," said Laraby, unconvinced. "Yeah, I guess . . ."

In front of them, the car that carried Carter had pulled out far ahead of them. If Dillon's plan was to work, he knew he would have to strike now, with lethal precision. He leaned forward, and whispered into Sergeant Weller's sun-reddened ear, hitting him with a quiet blast of personal devastation in the form of a simple comment.

"Sergeant Weller," he whispered, *"no matter what everyone says . . . it* was *your fault. Your fault, and no one else's."*

A subtle hammer to glass. Dillon could feel the man's mind shatter, even before there were any outward signs. Weller gripped the steering wheel tighter, his knuckles turning as white as the cloud-covered sky. Dillon could hear the man's teeth gnash like the grindstone of a mill, and then, with a sudden jolt, Weller jerked the wheel.

The car lurched off the road and careened down a steep wooded slope. Pine branches whapped at the windshield, and a single trunk loomed before them. Then came the crunch of metal, and the sudden *PFFFLAP!* of the air bags deploying in the front seat, while in the backseat, Dillon's seatbelt dug into his gut and shoulder. The car caromed off the tree, skidded sideways another ten yards, until smashing into another tree hard enough to shatter the right-side windows before coming to rest.

Dillon was stunned and bruised but he didn't take time to check his own damage. He climbed through the broken window, falling into the thick, cold mud of the woods, and for once the deep, earthy smell was a welcome relief. He stood, and quickly pulled open the passenger door of the ruined car. Officer Laraby was pinned between the seat and the firm billow of the air bag. The bag had knocked the wind out of him, and his gasps filled the air like the blasts of a car alarm. Dillon pulled him out of the car, and he fell to the ground.

Meanwhile, Sergeant Weller didn't seem to care about any of it. He just sobbed and sobbed. Dillon didn't dare catch his gaze now, for Dillon knew how his eyes would look. One pupil would be wide, the other shrunken to a pinpoint. They always looked like that when Dillon drove them insane.

"Wh-what's going on?" asked Laraby, still dazed from the crash.

"It's my fault," sobbed Weller, deep in a state of madness that went miles beyond mere guilt. *"It's my fault my fault my fault my fault . . ."*

Laraby turned to Dillon, just beginning to recover his senses. "What's his fault?"

"I don't know," said Dillon, "But it doesn't matter now." And he really didn't know—all Dillon knew was that every pore of that man's body breathed out guilt that he was trying to hide. Very old guilt, and very potent. All Dillon had to do was tweak it to shatter his mind.

Up above, the other car, which had doubled back, had pulled to the side of the road. Doors opened and closed.

"Listen to me," Dillon told Laraby. "The boy in the other car—he says his name is Carter, but it's really Delbert. Delbert Morgan. You and your wife are going to take him in as a foster child. You're going to volunteer to do it."

The officer squirmed. "But—"

"You *will* take him in, and take care of him until his father comes for him someday"—and then Dillon added—"or else."

"Or what else?"

The answer came as another incoherent wail from the insane cop, still in the driver's seat pounding his fist mindlessly against his air bag. It was evidence of the destruction Dillon was still capable of when he chose to destroy—his ability to create chaos still every bit as powerful as his ability to create order.

Dillon could hear shouts on the hillside above them now, and people hurrying toward them. He tried to run, but Laraby, still on the ground, grabbed Dillon's shirt as if he were sinking into quicksand.

"Can you save my son?" asked the officer. "Can you fix his heart?"

The look in Laraby's eyes—a clashing combination between hope and terror—was something Dillon had seen before. In recent months, people would cling to him, asking him to fix things he hadn't broken in the first place. People begging him to change the patterns of their destinies.

"If you do," bribed Laraby, "I'll take care of that Carter kid. I swear I will."

Time was short, and Dillon needed to know that Carter would be cared for. Dillon nodded. "Agreed. I'll come back someday and fix your son—"

"Not someday. Now!" demanded Laraby. "They say he's gonna die, so you gotta do it now!"

"It doesn't matter if he dies," Dillon told him. "I'll come back later, and fix him anyway."

The cop had no response to that. The very idea tied his tongue.

Dillon broke free, sliding the rest of the way down the wooded slope until he could see the Columbia River through the trees far up ahead. He could hear the officers from the other car on his tail, but the image filling his mind was that of Laraby's face; the desperation as he had gripped on to Dillon's shirttail; those eyes staring at him in fearful, hopeful awe as if Dillon held both salvation and damnation in his fingertips.

And then there was Weller.

Dillon had shattered the man. He had sworn he would never shatter anyone ever again. Dillon had been so certain that his destructiveness was in the past. *But I had no choice,* he reasoned. *I had to escape.*

Dillon told himself that he would come back and fix the man someday, although he knew it would be a long time before he could surface in Burton again.

He continued down the slope, bouncing off trees like a pinball, stumbling through the mud and peat.

It was foolish of Dillon to think the people of Burton could keep quiet. It was human nature to whisper the things that no one should hear, and it was only a matter of time until all of those whispers grew loud enough to bring out a swarm of badges from a dozen government agencies. And despite what Weller had said—they *did* believe in what he could do. Otherwise they wouldn't have sent out a posse of state troopers to find him.

Now they'd be on the lookout for him everywhere "the virus" had hit. Foolish, because it was their meddling that would prevent him from fixing the mess.

The dense wood suddenly ended, and he stumbled over a gnarled root, to the muddy edge of the river.

"Down here—this way!" his pursuers shouted.

Dillon leapt from the bank into the raging torrents of the river, swollen by a storm upstream. The cold hit him instantly, sucking the heat from his limbs. His muscles seized into tight knots, but he stretched his arms and legs out so he wouldn't cramp. He was quickly spirited downstream, pulled away from those chasing him. The opposite bank seemed much more distant than it had from shore, but he willed his arms to move. Yes, his limbs had grown strong from his work. Even in the cold waters, he could force his arms to stroke and legs to kick, long after many would have drowned, until he finally collapsed on the far shore.

His mind hazy, and his body leaden from the cold, he tried to catch his bearings as he knelt on all fours, coughing up lungfuls of river water. He tried to stand, but moved too quickly, and a wave of dizziness brought him back to the ground. He rolled over onto his back, forcing deep breaths, trying to will a steady flow of oxygenated blood back to his head.

He never heard them approaching. He didn't know they were there until their silhouettes eclipsed the light of the gray sky.

"He's all right," said a voice just above him. A female voice.

Dillon gasped through his chattering teeth. The voice was familiar, and in his confusion, he felt sure he knew who it was.

"Tory?" he said. There were others around him now. "Winston? Lourdes? Michael?" He had hardly known the other four shards, and yet for months they had occupied most of his thoughts. Only now did he realize how much he needed them—to talk to, to be with. He thought he saw their faces before him, and it filled him with comfort and gratitude.

He sat up, and as his blurred vision cleared, his heart sank like a boulder in the furious river.

"No," said the voice. "It's me, Carol Jessup."

There were more gathering around him now. He was mistaken—these were not his friends, they were all residents of the town. He knew them all—the Kendalls, the McMillans, the Schwartzes. He had spent time with each of them, restoring the life of a loved one. He had entered each of their lives, and returned them back to order.

"We're glad the police didn't take you away from us," said Carol.

Dillon began to feel his gut slowly churn and he knew it wasn't just the cold.

"Don't worry," said her husband, taking his hand. "We'll protect you."

"We'll take care of you," said one of the others, rubbing Dillon's sleeve.

"We won't let them hurt you," said another, reaching out and touching Dillon's hair.

This is wrong, Dillon thought. *This is terribly, horribly wrong.*

"We'll follow you," said another voice. "And we'll help you do your wondrous works."

"We'll tend to your needs," proclaimed another.

"We'll be your servants."

"Because we've seen your glory."

"We've been blessed."

"And you'll bless us again."

"And again."

More hands. Dozens of hands, reaching out, touching his skin, his hair, his clothes. He felt himself raised from the ground, and as he looked into the clouded sky, he realized why this all felt so wrong.

His unique talent for making connections showed him a new pattern emerging in the world around him now. There were always a million possible roads, and a million possible futures, but now, every road focused toward one end: a murky darkness of chaos and ruin.

A year ago, during his own dark time, Dillon had sought to trigger the ultimate act of destruction. A quiet whisper that would precipitate a massive chain reaction, eventually shattering every relationship, every connection, every mind until the entire world became like the maddened mobs in Burton. Dillon had thought he'd failed to achieve that final act . . . but now he wasn't so sure. What if his "great collapse" had simply taken a different course? The swarming patterns of destiny he saw when he looked at these people around him seemed to scream back the same answer.

The destruction never ended.

It just hid, dormant until now—and all the fixing he had done would soon be overshadowed by a new threat. Some bleak chain of events spreading forth from this moment, that not even he could foresee.

He wailed again in the pain of this revelation, but the crowd ignored all his protests, as they carried him off in the cradle of their happy, needy hands.

In the random rush of water, a pocket of stillness formed where the Columbia River had caressed Dillon Cole's body. With Dillon's passing, the entire river slowed . . . and a tiny portion of the river ceased its swirling, defied entropy and came to order, touched by Dillon's unique gift. It became an oasis of focused calm, beneath the surface of the raging river.

The calm pocket carried within it the simplest of bacteria, born from rotting leaves and dead salmon farther upstream. Only, now those bacteria didn't swarm and divide haphazardly. Instead, the single-celled organisms drew toward one another, aligning and dividing in unison; positioning themselves in a choreographed mitotic dance—a perfect pattern, as if the millions of bacteria were all of a single mind.

Farther downstream, where the river spilled into the Pacific, plankton fed on the aligned bacteria, and in turn tiny shrimplike krill devoured the plankton. Farther from shore, a school of fish, ten thousand strong, gobbled up the krill with ease and swam south, their tight formation suddenly becoming more perfect, and more orderly than it was possible for a school of fish to be, as it headed south, toward shark-infested waters.

2. WAKE-UP CALLS

AT NINE A.M. EASTERN STANDARD TIME, WINSTON PELL
bolted awake from a chilling dream to the sound of breaking glass.
He knew the sound well by now—it came as regular as clockwork.
If it wasn't his window, it was Thaddy's, or his mother's, or the
window in the living room.

Thaddy, who should have known better, came scurrying into
Winston's room. "Stone! Stone! It happened again!" He yowled
as his feet came down on the broken glass.

"Thaddy, your brain's gotta be off in orbit."

Thaddy hopped onto Winston's bed. "Ow, ow, ow," he
whined, but let Winston look at his bleeding feet. Thaddy trusted
his big brother's judgment, now that his big brother had grown
taller than him again.

"You'll live," said Winston.

"How'm I gonna walk?" Thaddy asked angrily. He frowned
as if it was Winston's fault. Winston sighed. Maybe it was. He
patted Thaddy's soles with a balled-up corner of the sheet. He
wished he could heal Thaddy's feet, but his own repertoire of gifts
didn't include Magical Suture.

Their mother walked in, turned on the light, and shook her
head. First at the broken window, and then at Thaddy's feet.

"We're gonna make the glass-man rich," she said, then carefully stepped over the glass toward Thaddy, examining his feet. "I
just hope it won't need stitches."

The suggestion made Thaddy groan. She took Thaddy off to
the bathroom for Bactine and butterflies.

Winston stepped into his slippers and gingerly crossed the floor
toward the broken window.

A heavy branch had punched through the window like an
elbow. Winston noticed that the tip of the elbow-shaped limb held

new growth that hadn't been there yesterday. The tree would have to be cut down to save the house. Just like the tree which had rooted up the septic tank, and the one which had lifted the home off its foundation.

The fact was, ever since Winston had come home from his mysterious journey west, he wasn't the only thing growing like a weed. He stood five foot eight now, and while his predicted height was expected to top out at six foot one, the plants and trees around their home had no such limit. These days, his mother's garden coughed up blueberries the size of tomatoes, tomatoes the size of cantaloupes, and cantaloupes the size of pumpkins. The grass had to be mowed on a daily basis, and you couldn't see the house for the trees.

"Some green thumb you brought home with you," his mother had said when they first began to notice how profound Winston's effect was. "Guess we're gonna get lifted to the clouds by a bean-stalk one day."

As he contemplated the tree invading his bedroom window, a feeling came to Winston's limbs, like a fugitive breeze.

A cold river. A wail of agony. A cry for help.

What had he been dreaming about? It was coming back to him now, and the memory made the tight curls of his short-cropped hair feel as if they were curling tighter.

He was dreaming about Dillon Cole. Something was wrong in the dream; Dillon needed help. There were hands all around him. The hands meant to comfort, but did not. One thing more . . . Winston knew this was not a dream. Dillon had cried out, and Winston had heard it—it was not his imagination. It had to be a pretty nasty bit of business going on, if Winston could feel it this far away.

He's in trouble, thought Winston. *Well, good. He deserves it. I won't go help him.* Winston had seen the damage Dillon had done. Buildings destroyed, people turned mad. When they had parted ways, Dillon claimed to be repentant—claimed that it was all be-cause of the dark parasite that had leeched onto his soul. But how much of it was the beast, and how much was Dillon? Winston found it hard to have any sympathy for him.

In the bathroom, his mother bandaged Thaddy's feet. Winston watched her, marveling. She had been out of her wheelchair for almost a year now. Winston's touch, which had once been the cause of her paralysis and all forms of stunted growth, was now responsible for making her get up and walk. His curse under the tyranny of his parasite, had turned into a blessing once that thing was dead: a gift of growth in every sense of the word.

"Heard you thrashin' in your covers even before the window broke," his mother said, finishing up on Thaddy. "Must have been some fright you were having."

I won't go help Dillon, Winston told himself.

"Just a dream," he told her.

"Guess that's what you get for sleeping in." His mother never probed for details. Winston had never spoken of his experiences out west to her, and she had the wisdom not to ask.

They ate breakfast quietly, Winston's mind full of heavy, distracting thoughts. He knew his mom could read the troubled look on his face.

"You know, I've been thinking of putting the house up for sale," Mom said. "Too much bad blood between us and the neighborhood, anyway."

Winston shook his head sadly. Folks around town hadn't known what to make of him before, and now they surely didn't. But that was okay. Winston had grown to understand them a bit better now. Their fears. Their superstitions.

"Momma," he said, before he knew the words were coming from his mouth. "Momma, I gotta leave."

His mother took a deep breath. It had become her habit to take Winston's pronouncements in stride.

"I suppose it was only a matter of time till you outgrew this place," she said. "Although I didn't think it would be so soon."

"Stone ain't outgrown it," chimed in Thaddy. "His feet don't hang off the end of the bed or nothing."

Winston chuckled. "That's not what she means, Thaddy."

In the year since coming back home, Winston had found himself driven to think. To learn. He had pulled down all of his father's dusty books—the ones his father had treasured—and he read them all. "Education is a black man's greatest ally against injustice," his father had been fond of saying. He kept a fine library that was left to his wife and sons when he died. Books of science and art, great literature and world history. Volumes on philosophy. Great thinkers, with grand thoughts. Winston downed all he could at home, at school, at the library. He hadn't come up with any grand answers to the mysteries of life yet, but now at least he felt he knew some of the questions. He had grown to know how much he didn't know.

But that wasn't why he had to leave.

I won't head west. He struggled to convince himself. *I refuse to help Dillon Cole.* But there was a gravity pulling on him now. He knew he could resist it, but didn't know if he should.

Thaddy just looked down, his thoughts buried in his cinnamon toast. Winston's mother took a long look at Winston, with a certain wonder in her eyes. He let her have her moment. To be honest, he felt kind of teary-eyed himself.

"I know you'll do great things for this weary world," she said. "I've got faith in that."

A few hours later, he kept her faith cloaked around him as he boarded the bus alone toward all points west, and Dillon Cole.

THREE HUNDRED MILES away, the yolks of a dozen eggs oozed through their smashed shells, blending with the milk, Gatorade, and maple syrup that spilled forth from their ruptured containers. Everything in Tory Smythe's arms had fallen to the ground in the wake of her sudden vision, and now the polished white floor of the spotless convenience store was a disaster of running colors and wildly clashing aromas.

Max, Tory's boyfriend, surveyed the mess. "That's not good," he said lamely. "I told you we should have taken a basket."

The clerk ran out from behind the counter, his face stricken, as if someone had unexpectedly died in the aisle. "Look at this!" he shrieked. "How could you be so clumsy, you stupid, stupid girl!"

He ran to the back room to get a mop. Tory was pale, unsteady. She gripped the handle of the glass refrigerator case to keep her balance.

"Are you okay?" Max asked.

She was shivering from the cold, although it wasn't cold.

She was recoiling from the touch of their hands, but no one was touching her.

She was screaming, but it wasn't her voice she heard—it was—

"Dillon!"

Her boyfriend eyed her uncomfortably. The clerk returned with the mop, bucket, and about a gallon of Lysol. "Stupid, stupid girl," he said again, in case Tory hadn't heard him the first time.

Tory grabbed Max's hand, hoping his steady fingers would keep hers from shaking. "Let's go."

"But . . . the shopping list," he said, "Your mom can't make breakfast without—"

"Just forget about the damned list!"

Max gasped, and ripped his hand from hers. "Tory!" he said. "What's wrong with you?"

Tory sighed. "I'm sorry," she told him. She grabbed his hand again, and he reluctantly clasped his fingers around hers.

Behind them the clerk had mopped up much of the mess, yet continued mopping at the same, maniacal pace, as if the spill were acid that would eat through the linoleum. Tory knew he would mop and mop until nothing was left to mar the purity of his clean white floor. It reminded Tory of the way she bathed. Compulsively scrubbing to pull away dirt she knew wasn't there, but still felt all around her. These days, her skin was cover-girl smooth, instead of oozing with open, infected sores as it had been a year ago. Now her hair had a fine blonde sheen, instead of being a matted greasy mess. She had been cleansed beyond any shadow of doubt, but sometimes she could still feel the filth, like a ghost, and the only way to get rid of it was to wash and scrub. The way this ridiculous man scrubbed at his clean floor.

Tory couldn't watch, so she left, pulling Max along with her.

The Sunday-morning streets of the neighborhood were full of people walking hand in hand. Children played games, the elderly sat on benches feeding exceptionally healthy pigeons. A Cuban couple smiled at a group of African-American teens on the corner, and they waved back. A Korean man walked a little Anglo girl across the street.

"It's a nice morning," Max said.

"Yes," said Tory. "Nice." The fact was, every morning was "nice" in her neighborhood. The streets were clean, the alleys were free of grunge, and anyone who didn't pick up after their dog was reported by the Neighborhood Watch—which everyone belonged to. The neighborhood was safe, spotless, and uncorrupted. Strange, because this part of town was called "the Miami Miasma" and was the worst neighborhood of the notorious Floridian metropolis.

"What happened back there?" asked Max.

What happened? thought Tory. *I think I got a wake-up call from an old friend.* But all she said was, "I guess I slipped on the floor wax."

A policeman strolled past them, grinning. But when he took a look at Tory's feet, his expression changed to one of suspicion.

"Hmpf," he said, eyeing Tory warily as she passed.

"Maybe you ought to roll down your socks," whispered Max, "so people won't see how dirty they are."

Tory glanced down to see a few stray spots of egg yolk splattered on her socks and Nikes. Normal people, she knew, wouldn't care about how clean her socks were, but the people who now resided within her extended aura were not exactly normal. They were . . . clean.

"I don't care if people see," she muttered.

Max bristled. "Whatever."

They turned down an alley that had once been full of fetid cardboard and rags—a place where the destitute took shelter. But there were no homeless here anymore. No one was exactly sure what happened to them, and apparently no one in the neighborhood cared.

Tory stopped walking, overcome by a wave of cold nausea that dragged her back to her vision of Dillon. She leaned against the brick of the alley, and Max looked at her with concern, trying to make sense of her odd behavior. He gently touched the smooth skin of her face "You're cold," he remarked. "Tory, are you sure you're okay?"

Tory closed her eyes and thought back to the day she arrived here, in November—almost a year ago—in search of her mother, who had vanished from her life years before. Back then, this part of town had been the armpit of civilization, aspiring to even less attractive regions of the anatomy. There was no discrimination in the Miami Miasma. The dregs from all nationalities were drawn here equally.

She had found her mother in a welfare hotel, destitute and wheezing with bronchitis. Tory had nursed her back to health remarkably quickly. And, amazingly, the woman began to find in herself the qualities of a good mother. Before long, Tory noticed other things changing around her as well. Actions and attitudes of the neighbors began to slowly shift. The evidence of it surrounded her even now as she walked with Max. A group of small children ran through the street picking up litter as if it was the best game to play. From across the street came the caustic hiss of a shop owner sand-blasting decades of soot from his building. Strolling all around them were sparkling-clean men and women oozing an almost Victorian refinement. The whole neighborhood had become a strange mix of accidental *übermenschen*—an anomalous set of people suddenly rising above the random violence and lewd behavior that had once been a part of their lives, repulsed and mortified by the sights and smells of urban decay. Turns out, the Miami Miasma cleaned up real good; now, not even the garbage smelled.

It was still hard for Tory to understand and accept that she was the cause of all this. Not by anything she did, but by her mere presence. It was an aura that penetrated the streets around her like radiation, cleansing it, body and soul.

Of course, just a few blocks away, the wretchedness still lived on in the places where her light did not reach.

"Tory, are you sick? Do you have a fever or something?" asked Max. "Maybe you're getting the flu." It obviously hadn't occurred to him that no one in this part of Miami had come down with the flu this year.

"Max," Tory dared to ask, "do you remember what you were like before?"

Max blinked at her in total innocence. "What do you mean?"

"I mean, when I first met you?"

Max's shoulders twisted in a shiver. "I was awful. Let's not talk about it."

The fact was, he had been worse than awful. He was a gang-banger with neither conscience nor remorse for any of the brutal things he did. He bragged about his gun, and longed for the day it would take a life. Tory had despised him. The way he and his cohorts would hang out on the corner, shouting rude, lusty comments at her as she passed had made Tory hate leaving the small apartment she and her mother shared. She had feared that one day the verbal assaults might turn physical when those thugs were too drunk or aroused to care.

But then Max began to change. The gun went away first. Then his attitude. He became caring, and good, without even noticing the change in himself. His gang slowly turned as innocuous as a team of eagle scouts, and their street-corner greetings became a caress rather than an assault.

There was a time several months ago, when Max's hair was still long, and his spirit still untamed, that Tory loved him deeply. That's when the newfound goodness of his heart was tempered by mischievous unpredictability.

But the changes continued. He cut his hair short and neat. His fun-loving grin became the blank smile of total innocence. And every single word he thought to utter was pure and wholesome. Tory had sanitized him.

Tory realized she was crying. She wondered if Dillon, wherever he was, could feel her cry, the way she had felt him scream. She thought of the other shards, who were suddenly at the forefront of her mind, and for the first time in many months, began to feel herself being pulled toward them, as she had been pulled that first time, when the light of the supernova had filled the night sky, filling them all with the overwhelming need to find each other. But this time it was Dillon's call beckoning her to come west.

Max regarded her tears with deep concern. He was so clean it made her feel dirty. It made her feel like slipping into a scalding bath.

"Tory, I'm worried about you," he said.

Tory looked deep into the eyes of this handsome, wholesome boy. There was no question he was better off than before—after all, it was far worse to be unconscionably bad, than to be pathetically good. Still it saddened her.

Tory leaned toward him, wanting to kiss him, but he leaned away, shocked and embarrassed.

"Tory, no! We're in public!"

"Please," begged Tory. "Just this once."

"Oh, all right." Max leaned forward and endured the public kiss. There was tenderness in the kiss, but nothing more. No passion or urgency. No hint of mystery. No spice of unknown intentions. His thoughts were as pure as the smell of his breath and taste of his kiss—flavorless as distilled water.

"Good-bye, Max," she said sadly, then strode away from him without looking back, heading west toward Dillon Cole, and to escape the effects of her own scouring presence.

3. COAST TO COAST

THAT SAME MORNING, TOWARD THE EASTERN END OF LONG Island, Lourdes Hidalgo concentrated on the five girls around her as the volleyball arced over the net toward them. None of these girls were on the volleyball team, and yet, over the past month, they had become a curiosity in their phys-ed class, and had gained the attention of the volleyball coach—enough of his attention, that he helped schedule today's challenge match against the *real* volleyball team of Hampton Bays High. No spectators were officially invited, but word of mouth had brought at least two dozen.

The ball cleared the net, and Andrea, the girl to Lourdes's right got under it, passed it to Lourdes, who was the setter of their unofficial team. Lourdes passed it to Patrice in the front row, who spiked it to win yet another point. Cheers from the sidelines. The coach shook his head. "Incredible!"

Meanwhile the real volleyball team scowled in disbelief. "Who are you rooting for anyway?" shouted the team's Amazonian captain.

Coach Kline scowled right back at her. "If you're a team, then play like one."

Lourdes smiled. Now she and her friends controlled the court like a team that had trained together for years. They functioned with the precision of a Swiss watch, as if they were all being controlled by a single will.

The truth is, they were.

As setter, Lourdes was the leader of the squad, but rather than merely positioning the ball for the net players to spike, Lourdes set the players themselves. She gripped each of them with her will, subtly pulling their strings and manipulating the movements of their bodies. She could adjust their metabolisms in microseconds, causing adrenaline to flow, and muscles to contract faster, with added en-

45

ergy, as if they were all part of a single being, with Lourdes at the center. It was a gift Lourdes was learning to brandish well.

She forced them to work as a perfect team, and as volleyball was ninety percent teamwork, no one could beat Lourdes's machine.

Her team served, and the real volleyball players fought valiantly, returning the ball over the net in a powerful spike—but Lourdes was ready. She raised Patrice's hands to save the ball, then got under it herself for the second tap. Next, she willed Andrea into position to slice it over for the final point. It couldn't have been easier if all twelve hands, and all twelve feet, were hers.

The ball was still in the air when Lourdes got the mind-blast from Dillon Cole. Her head swam, her vision faded, as if she had stood up too quickly. He was calling for her—for all of them. He was being smothered by a crowd. . . . She felt faint, but only for a moment. When her vision cleared, the team on the other side of the net was suffering the agony of their humiliating defeat.

"That's match," said Coach Kline.

As the players cleared the court on both sides, the coach pulled Lourdes aside. She reigned in her frazzled thoughts and emotions, refusing to be befuddled in this moment of victory.

"I have to admit, Lourdes," he said, with deep admiration, "you've really come into your own this year. You've come a long, long way."

Lourdes had heard that a lot, but she never tired of being reminded. She had gone from being a 350-pound outcast, to one of the most admired girls in school, at half the weight. True, her figure wasn't exactly that of a model—the large bones of her frame wouldn't allow for that—but she was as slim as she needed to be. She felt comfortable in her clothes; her many chins had melted away; and when she looked in the mirror, she liked what she saw, from the front, and from the side. Ralphy Sherman told people that she had undergone a high-risk experimental liposuction technique at a Swedish clinic—and since no other explanation surfaced, people actually believed him. In any case, "fat" was not the word that came to people's minds when they saw Lourdes Hidalgo, these days. "Impressive," maybe even "powerful," but not "fat."

"You've surprised me, Lourdes," said the coach. "I never thought you'd turn out to be so . . . athletic."

"Where there's a will, there's a way," answered Lourdes. By now, even the defeated players began to gather around her. Such was her new gravity—it no longer attracted stray paper and lint as it had in the days when she was hideously fat. Now people were drawn to her instead. She was wildly popular, and everyone wanted to finagle their way into her circle of friends.

Well, almost everyone.

"Good for you, Lourdes," said Cathy Burns, her insincerity painted on like lacquer. She had always been one of "the beautiful people," and had watched the game from the sidelines with several of her debutante friends. "Hope you've enjoyed your fifteen minutes of fame," she said, with a cutting snideness in her voice that had taken years to cultivate.

"I'm still in my first minute," said Lourdes, not allowing the girl a moment of satisfaction. "Happy dieting."

Cathy frowned and strode off with a flick of her hair, adjusting a belt on jeans that were growing too tight. Cathy and her friends were the few hold-out hatemongers, whose attitude of disdain was strong enough to resist Lourdes's magnetic personality. They were social butterflies and beauty queens who longed for the good old days when tormenting Lourdes was a school pastime. Well, their reign wouldn't last for long, because those girls had already found themselves gaining a pound a week, as Lourdes slowed down their metabolisms to a crawl. Soon *they* would know the social joys of obesity. For Lourdes, revenge wouldn't be sweet; it would be fat.

In the aftermath of the volleyball game, her thoughts went back to Dillon, and the certainty that he—and maybe all of them—were in trouble once more. And yet the more she thought about it, the more she was excited by it—for she realized the opportunities it suddenly opened.

It was a chance to see Michael again.

Just thinking of him filled her with potent anticipation.

Michael had told her she was beautiful, even when her body was wrapped in dense rolls of flab. And when she had grown too large to move, he refused to leave her side, even when it would have meant his own death. But things had changed once they returned home—as if being in Hampton Bays brought back to Michael the old pain of his life there. Soon after, Michael and his father moved to the West Coast.

Perhaps Michael wanted to escape his old life, but Lourdes wasn't interested in escape. She wanted to conquer, to become the victor of Hampton Bays High, instead of the victim—to be the one that everyone looked up to; the center of attention and admiration.

Certainly, as she reveled in the victory of today's game, all eyes were on her; but it wasn't enough, because Michael wasn't there to share it with her, and she found herself longing for him more and more. Now Dillon was calling them all together again, and Lourdes was more than happy to go, if it meant Michael would be there, too.

"I'd like to start you and the other girls on a training program," the coach told Lourdes. "I think you'd be great additions to the team." Although Lourdes knew he meant "replacements" rather than "additions." It was a tempting offer, as it was one more step in that conquest she so desired. But there were other considerations now.

"I can't do it now," she told him. "I'm going away for a while."

"Not for long, I hope. You're not leaving Hampton Bays High, are you?"

"No," answered Lourdes. "Just a short trip."

"To finish her treatment," she heard Ralphy Sherman whisper to a friend.

She chose to let it go at that. *Let them wonder,* she thought.

THE NEXT DAY, she had her parents buy her an airline ticket west.

"I have to visit Michael," she told them. The mention of his name always filled her parents with an apprehensive awe. They knew that somehow that strange boy, Michael Lipranski, had played a major part in the miraculous transformation of their daughter. Her father was dead set against letting her go, yet he found himself lifting the phone and making the reservations, as if his hands were not under his own control.

Her brother and sisters were devastated by the thought of her leaving.

"You can't leave!" her brother and sisters cried, for so much of themselves revolved around Lourdes now. She had slipped deep into the center of all of their lives. Lourdes was going to help Lita choose a college, and Gerardo buy a car, and Monica pick which boys to go out with. Although they were all older than her, they now looked up to her as if she were the eldest in the family.

"This is a good thing," Lourdes told them. "I'll be back. You'll see."

The next morning, with little more than Michael's street address, Lourdes said good-bye to her family at the gate, and boarded a jet. As the plane lifted off from JFK, Lourdes filled her mind not with thoughts of finding Dillon, but with images of Michael.

MICHAEL LIPRANSKI WAS not obsessed by images of Lourdes. He had far too many thoughts and feelings to maintain these days, without sorting through his feelings for the girl who had shared his misery.

He stood at dawn in a flurry of snow, on a beach in southern California, which hadn't seen snow during his lifetime, until this week. As he stood at the edge of the pounding surf, Michael slipped on his Walkman's earphones, and listened to the rhythms and riffs of *Insurrection*, one of his favorite bands. The music helped him to dig deep within himself and find the bright, warm emotions that had been chased away by his nightmares. He thought of peaceful days stretched out on the beach. He thought of cycling down Pacific Coast Highway, and feeling the warm, ocean-scented breeze on his face. Then he turned his eyes upward, and as his spirits began to lift, they punched a hole in the dense cover of clouds.

A pinpoint of blue appeared, and as the clouds peeled back, the hole widened. The last of the snow wafted down through the air, and a chill breeze blew, but it rapidly turned warm.

Michael brushed a lock of dark hair out of his eyes, and looked toward the horizon. He didn't have to push back the cold that far—only about five miles, for that was as far as his mood reached. He pushed forth strong, sun-filled thoughts, and struggled to roll back the cold layer of clouds pressing in on him.

Those clouds had first rolled in on the morning of his dream about Dillon. That was three days ago—and even though Michael did his best to ignore it, each night the dream would replay itself over and over, with greater urgency, bringing a morning snowfall that he had to chase away.

Well, what am I supposed to do about Dillon?

Michael knew there was an answer, but he chose to roll that away with the clouds as well, keeping it far from his thoughts.

Soon the retreating clouds were forced back to the edge of Michael's reach, leaving a narrow rim like a smoke ring, ten miles wide, in the middle of clear skies. He could already feel his new mood begin to infuse not only the skies, but the people in the neighborhood around him. His gift was one of emotional resonance—a resonance so strong it seized the very skies around him, putting them in his control, forcing them to mimic the weather patterns of his own powerful emotions. It was a force so strong, it affected the nature of anyone he came in contact with, filling them with joy, or consternation—whatever was in Michael's heart at the time.

The sun climbed out from behind Saddleback Mountain, and Michael turned to let its rays warm his face.

"What's with you?"

Startled by the voice, Michael stumbled, nearly falling into the high-tide surf. He ripped the headphones from his ears, and turned to see the face of his friend and running partner, Drew Camden. Had Drew seen him change the weather? How would Michael explain it if he had? "How long have you been there?" Michael asked.

"Long enough to see you staring at the sky like a psycho," said Drew casually. He didn't seem concerned or confused; he just stretched his arms and legs, preparing for their morning run. *Good,* thought Michael. *He didn't make the connection.* Michael glanced at his watch. It was already seven o'clock. He always lost track of time whenever he futzed with the sky.

"So what's the deal with this weather?" said Drew, zipping open his running jacket. "It was freezing when I left my house. How did it get so warm?"

"It's called the sun, Einstein," said Michael.

Drew began jogging in place. "So, are we running or not?" he asked. "Let's go; it's time to get some color into that pasty face of yours." Which was easy for Drew to say. Years running track had left Drew well tanned, and the sun had worked his hair enough to leave it various shades of bronze. It was a look Michael would have wanted to duplicate, but his own hair never lightened, and his pale skin just burned. Drew loved to rub it in. "C'mon, get moving," he said. "Just because you *look* embalmed doesn't mean you have to act like a corpse."

Drew took off across the sand, toward the paved path that ran the two miles between Newport and Balboa Piers. Michael followed, filling his lungs with the fresh air, and his mind with the pleasant sights and sounds of the morning.

It was good to have a friend like Drew, who arrived like clockwork to drag him out to run. It was good to have any friends at all. The parasite that had laid waste to his soul since sixth grade, had left him friendless for four years. It had twisted people around him, turning them into bubbling cauldrons of their own most base natures. Girls lost themselves in a lust for him so powerful he had to fight them off, and guys became angry and aggressive, wanting little more than to beat the crap out of him.

But now his life had filled with others who actually thought he was worth having around. Even his father liked him. Both Drew and Michael were juniors on the track team, and although Michael had no real aspirations in track, he didn't mind the comradery.

The beachside path was already becoming crowded now that the weather had changed. Rollerbladers in skintight Lycra wove around men and women propelling their babies in jogging-strollers. Bicycles sped past joggers and power-walkers.

This was where Michael wanted to be—not beating the bushes looking for Dillon again. He had seen enough of Dillon in the short time he knew him, and there were the constant reminders to boot: like news reports on the cleanup in Boise, and expert opinions on the mysterious "virus" that had driven people insane in the Pacific Northwest. No, Michael had no desire to think of his soul mate Dillon Cole—or for that matter, any of his other soul mates. Life was good without the Scorpion Shards. Life was a walk on the beach.

"I'm feeling prime today," Drew said, picking up the pace as they neared Balboa Pier, and Michael kept up with him. *This is a good day,* thought Michael. And he was determined to keep it that way.

MICHAEL DID A pretty good job of holding up the sky that day, through the rigors of school. Afterward, at the mall, he worked his part-time job with a smile and a pleasant air that brought joy to everyone who came to the Dog Kabob.

It was around five that he began to give in to the crushing weight. The skies beyond the atrium windows were beginning to clog with clouds. Michael still felt pretty good, if somewhat tired— but his resistance was low, and he wasn't expecting a "customer." At least not one like this man.

"It never rains in southern California," the man whispered to him over the counter of the Dog Kabob. Michael nodded in understanding. This was one of his *real* customers.

Michael wasn't sure how it all got started. Perhaps it had been that suicidal housewife he had hugged in the supermarket once, completely reversing her depressive nature—or maybe word got out when he shook the hand of the guy who smacked his kids around, permanently melting his angry temperament into a cool, even disposition. Or maybe it was his father, who kept bringing Michael into his sales office, knowing that Michael could, with a single grin, woo people into feeling it was a pleasure to buy anything. In any case, a few months after moving to California, troubled people began to secretly seek Michael out, and ask for favors.

"How can I help you?" Michael asked the man at the Dog Kabob counter.

"It's not me," the man said. He looked around to make sure no one else was nearby, then he leaned in closer. "It's my son who needs your help."

The man looked to be fairly well off. A tailored suit, Armani tie. Michael wondered how much he'd be willing to pay for Michael's services. Sometimes his customers paid very well. Well enough for Michael and his father to buy the beach house, and the sports car, and all the other trappings that made Newport Beach what it is. His father, having glimpsed Michael's special talent, decided not to ask too many questions when money seemed to appear in the bank account. Besides, Michael had tweaked his father's nature, turning the man into an incurable optimist, so how could he be anything but thrilled?

Usually people would show up at the Dog Kabob with melancholy tales of disappointment, depression, or despair. Some requests were heartbreaking; others were merely self-indulgent. *"Make me feel better,"* was always the bottom line, and Michael delivered. By now he was single-handedly putting the local shrinks out of business.

"Go on, I'm listening," said Michael.

"My son's a good kid," the man whispered. "He does well in school—a shoe-in for the Ivy League . . ."

"So what's the problem?" Michael asked, a bit impatiently.

"He's got a problem with the girls."

Michael felt his own toes start to get cold. A wind began to buffet the windows of the food court.

"What kind of problem?"

"Well, you see—it's like this . . ." The man stammered, and gestured with his hands, fumbling to spit out what he was trying to say. "My son . . . he doesn't entirely appreciate them—girls, that is. He doesn't . . . he doesn't have the requisite feelings for them, so to speak," whispered the man desperately. "In fact his feelings are decidedly . . . off. Do you see what I'm saying?"

Michael cut him off curtly. "I'm sorry, sir, all we sell here are lemonade and hot dogs."

The man reeled, confused. "But . . . but I was told—"

"You were told wrong." Michael handed him a corn dog. "Take it. It's on the house. May I help the next in line, please?"

The man, corn dog in hand, gazed at Michael despondently, then turned to leave. But even after he was gone, Michael couldn't relax.

There had been others like this man. Too many. People who came in wanting to change their own natures, or the nature of someone they loved.

Michael knew it was in his power to do it, but a cold front always seemed to blow in whenever he considered it. Switching winds and easing depression was one thing—but altering a person's sexual desire? His thoughts would instantly fill with the memory of the libidinous parasite that had violated his soul. The thing was a succubus, thriving on his member, driving him mad with desire for every woman around him, and filling those girls and women with the same desire.

But it had been dead for a year—and since it was gone, he no longer remembered how that felt. There was no one who aroused him anymore; his sense of passion—his sense of *love*—was stripped from him entirely, leaving him emotionally castrated. Yes, it might have been in his power to alter a person's nature—but how dare he change the shape of someone else's desire, when he felt no desire of his own?

It was easy to ignore when the world was a sunny day, and no one asked him questions . . . but a wind was blowing now, and stormclouds flowed in from all directions.

HE WAS DRENCHED by a relentless downpour on his way home, and when he got there, Drew was sprawled on the sofa, freeloading leftover Chinese food.

"What are you doing here?"

"Political asylum," said Drew. "My parents go ballistic at least once a month, and today they took it out on me. So I launched a major counteroffensive."

"You had a blowout?"

"We're talking megatons. I doubt we'll be able to resume diplomatic relations anytime soon." Drew held out the leftovers to Michael. "Kung pao?"

Michael shook his head and deposited himself like a bag of laundry on the plush leather sofa.

"C'mon, Michael," Drew taunted. "Hot and sizzling, fresh out of the microwave—I know it's your favorite."

Michael ignored him, trying to sink into the sofa as far as he could go. He wanted to disappear—not think, not feel—and he didn't care if his mood brought in a season of monsoons.

Drew finished off the last few chunks of kung pao chicken, as he watched Michael.

"Tough day at the Dog?" he asked.

"Not in the mood," Michael answered.

Drew picked up the remote, muting the annoying blasts of laughter from the sitcom he was watching, and Michael closed his eyes, listening to the rain on the skylight.

"You know, you oughta quit the Dog," suggested Drew, "and spend some time out, you know? I hear Wendy Holt's got it bad for you. Hey, if you ask her out, I'll ask her friend, what's-her-name. Sound like a plan?"

"No." Michael closed his eyes tighter and tried to sink farther into the sofa. The rain was sliced by a crosswind, and its tattered edges pummeled the window.

"C'mon, what's wrong with you anyway? You're starting to make *me* feel depressed."

Michael still had nothing to say.

"Hey, talk or I walk," said Drew, " 'Cause I'm not hanging unless I know why you're pissed."

Michael turned to Drew. Although he never had had a brother, he suspected Drew was what a brother might be like on a good day. Michael wasn't gifted with words, but he didn't want his silent storming to send Drew packing.

"My brain got a little fried before I moved here," Michael began. "And now I don't . . . *feel* things the way I'm supposed to. Certain things I can feel so intensely, you can't imagine, but the things I want to feel—the things I *need* to feel—I get nothing but dead air."

Drew shook his head sadly. "Drugs'll do that to you, man. Sauté your brain, and leave you impotent to boot."

Michael dug his fingertips into the arm of the sofa, pushed himself to his feet "I can't talk to you. You have no clue what I mean."

Michael propelled himself out the back door, into the downpour, but Drew followed, and although Michael tried to run, Drew was faster. They were both drenched by the time Drew caught up with him and grabbed his arm, angrily forcing him to turn around.

"I don't know what bolt you busted in your head," shouted Drew, "but whatever it is, it's not worth getting struck by lightning."

Michael laughed ruefully. "Trust me, I won't," he said, and then added, "You might, though."

"Yeah, well, screw you too."

"Listen, you don't know enough *about* me to help me with this."

"I know enough," said Drew. "I know about baseball. Y'ever play baseball?"

"Huh?" It was a non sequitur so far out of . . . well, left field, that it caught Michael off guard. "What are your lips flapping about?"

"You heard me," said Drew. "Baseball. Did you ever play?"

The rain suddenly stopped, leaving the wet beach in a low-pressure silence.

"Once in a while."

"Yeah, well, my grandfather played baseball," continued Drew. "So did my father. Now my brother plays in college, my sister's captain of her goddamn T-ball league, and for all I know, my mother was a slow-pitch softball star. So all my life, baseball oozes out of my parents' ears like friggin' earwax, but the thing is, I don't *feel* the game. Sure, I played Little League. I've sat and watched it on TV. We've got season tickets at Edison Field for God's sake! But I still don't feel what my family feels. No matter how much I want to, no matter how much I kick my ass to enjoy it, all I can feel is bored. When my friends talk baseball, I pretend like I care, all the time smelling my own bullshit."

Drew stared Michael in the eye, determined to hammer his point home.

Michael shook his head. "Drew, that's really pathetic."

"All I'm saying is that you don't have a monopoly on feeling disconnected."

Michael looked down. The rain had left pockmarks on the sand like the face of the moon.

"So how about you?" asked Drew. "What's your pathetic story?"

Michael considered it, and realized that letting Drew in on the Big Picture was something he had to do; something he needed to do, because he couldn't bear being alone with it anymore.

"Maybe it's better if I just show you," answered Michael.

Michael turned his eyes to the thick clouds that hid the evening stars, and prepared for a demonstration. There were no good feelings left in him just then, so instead he let the faces of the shards fill his mind. One by one he opened his memory to the terrible beasts they had harbored, turning each of them into untouchables in their own way. He imagined himself as he had been then: lascivious and lecherous; consumed by lust. As he thought about it, fear filled him and became an icy wind. Up above, the clouds began to boil, and in an instant the wind shredded them apart, dividing the clouds north and south. They peeled back like a curtain until they were gone, and all that was left were the stars, the moon, and the cold.

When it was done, Michael turned to Drew. Even in the dim moonlight, he could see Drew's eyes wide with disbelief.

"Sorry. I guess I should have prepared you for it."

But Drew wasn't looking at him. Drew was looking past him, to the sea, where the pounding waves had suddenly taken on a new, furious sound. "Michael," he said pointing toward the ocean, *"MICHAEL!"* he screamed.

Michael spun to see a gaping mouth bearing down on him, teeth sharp as daggers, as if some new beast were leaping up from the depths to devour him.

LOURDES SAW IT more clearly. Drenched from the downpour but undeterred, she had spent over an hour searching for Michael's home in Newport Beach. The streets were confusingly arranged, and although people were happy to give directions, Lourdes found herself wandering up and down one blind alley after another.

Finally she had resorted to walking along the beach, for she knew from the single letter Michael had sent her, that he had a beachfront home. She put her trust in her own ability to feel his presence.

In the aftermath of the storm, the moon made an appearance, and the waves gleamed its blue light. Lourdes imagined she saw shapes in the foam, like huge sleek serpents. But there was nothing imaginary about it. The shapes hurled themselves from the water, skidding on the sands. Huge things with shiny black eyes. Lourdes backed away from the edge of the surf, then screamed as a shark lunged at her from the surf, mouth open, gills flaring. It hit her like a car skidding to a stop, and she fell over its slick body, a dorsal fin digging into her side. Suddenly there was another, and another. She scrambled to her feet, and ran from the beached sharks as their jaws gnashed futilely at the sand. Only when she got far enough away from shore and her own screaming stopped, did she hear two other voices screaming: two boys far off, running from the writhing frenzy of beached beasts. She had heard enough of Michael's screams before, to recognize them now, and she ran across the beach toward him.

MICHAEL AND DREW dragged themselves away from the waterline and watched the sharks die.

"Did you do this, too?" Drew asked weakly.

"No!" said Michael. "I couldn't have!"

They stood up to look at the shoreline. "Tiger sharks," said Drew. "I think this one's a great white."

But it wasn't only sharks. There were swordfish, and marlins, deep-sea groupers . . .

"Man," said Drew. "It's like mass aquacide."

And he was right—it was as if a conglomerate of great fish had chosen to end their lives in a single chaotic lunge. *But it isn't chaotic at all, is it?* thought Michael. *The way they're lined up, it's almost orderly. Orderly?* . . .

"Michael!" It took a moment for him to recognize her voice. It no longer seemed wrapped in cotton, the way it had sounded when she was fat. "Michael, it's me."

She ran to him and pulled him close in her strong arms, planting a kiss on his cold lips.

"Lourdes?"

"Who's she?" asked Drew.

People were starting to flood onto the beach. In the moonlight, they had spotted the freakish beaching from their homes.

"I knew you wouldn't have left yet!" said Lourdes. "I knew you wouldn't leave without me!"

"Huh? What?" Michael had yet to get over the sight of the sharks, and the sudden appearance of Lourdes. She might as well have been speaking Swahili.

Michael turned his attention back to the death scene by the shore. It was all beginning to fall into place for him. The way these creatures had beached themselves wasn't haphazard, it was meticulous. They were lined up and spaced in precise intervals. In a perfect pattern. There was only one shard who could bring such order out of chaos.

"Dillon!" he shouted. "Dillon did this!"

"Who?" asked Drew.

"He called out for help the other day. You heard it, didn't you?" said Lourdes. "Something's gone wrong."

Michael nodded. He couldn't deny it anymore. He couldn't pretend it didn't matter. Yes, he had heard Dillon's scream. It had echoed through his sleep for three days now. Running from Dillon's call was no longer an option, and now he realized it never had been. The five of them were too tightly bound to ever escape one another.

"How will we find him?" wondered Michael.

"The same way we did before," answered Lourdes. She gently

took his hand, and started leading him away. "We'll find him to-gether."

But Drew grabbed Michael's other arm firmly "What is this? You part the sky, and you think you can just leave?"

Lourdes turned to him. "Whoever you are, this doesn't concern you!"

"Like hell it doesn't. I'm coming with you!"

"You can't," snapped Lourdes. Then Drew went pale, and fell to his knees, gripping his chest.

"Who says he can't?" asked Michael. "Let go of him!"

Lourdes turned to Michael, embarrassed. Clearly it had been a knee-jerk reaction to take hold of his heart with her mind. She let the blood return to Drew's head, before he could faint out cold. Drew stayed down on his knees, as he caught his breath.

"Sorry," said Lourdes.

"Lourdes, meet Drew. Drew, meet Lourdes," said Michael, hoping to get them to shake hands, which they didn't.

Drew stood up, still trying to shake off his dizziness. "Michael . . . who are you? *What* are you?"

"Well, it's like this," said Michael. "Our souls are the shattered fragments of the star Mentarsus-H, which went supernova, at the moment each of us was conceived. That makes us pretty damn impressive, if you haven't already guessed."

Drew stared at him completely baffled.

"It'll make more sense in the morning," Lourdes told him.

"No it won't," Drew answered. But he went with them anyway.

LIFE SLIPPED FROM the sea creatures that had cast themselves on the shore, their last breaths gurgling out through their gills in unison, just as the birds came. Dozens upon dozens of them. Not nearly as many as there were sea creatures on the shore, but enough to pick hundreds of holes in the softer parts of the carcasses. The birds drifted in randomly, over a period of hours, yet left as a single flock at dawn, well fed for a long, long flight.

They took to the air, flying in a single perfect wedge; cutting through the sky and heading east. It was a living vector, propelling itself on five hundred wings flapping up and down in perfect order.

Above the coastal ranges, over the dry hot sands of the California desert, the birds traveled without rest. They were long beyond their endurance by

*the time they crossed into Arizona airspace, but something beyond mere
muscle pushed them forward.*

*A faint awareness propelled them now. Faint, but growing, like a mind
sliding out of sleep. As the flock followed the path of the Colorado River,
the angle of their wedge narrowed from thirty degrees, to twenty, to ten,
until they were a slim arrow of movement across the sky. Moving directly
toward a bird much larger than themselves.*

*The thing before them roared dangerous and loud, but still the flock
willed itself forward . . . until it was devoured by the spinning mouth of a
jet engine.*

*The 767, outbound from Phoenix, was filled with thrill-seekers, on
their way to win and lose fortunes in the smoke-filled casinos of Las Vegas—
but they had not bet on this particular thrill. Although the plane's engines
often inhaled stray birds that got in their way, the plane wasn't designed to
withstand an entire flock ramming down the throat of a single engine.*

*The right engine, fouled by the remains of the birds, blew out with
such force that the wing caught fire. Inside the cabin, there were a few brief
minutes of panic as the plane slipped out of the pilot's control and plummeted into the jagged depths of the Grand Canyon.*

There were no survivors.

Not from the passenger list, that is.

*However, of those passengers, several of them had packed their pets into
the cargo hold—in fact, more than the usual number—and the jet harbored
more than the usual number of rats, as if the confluence of coincidence had
now evolved a structure beyond mere randomness. With the cabin burning
above, and their travel kennels shattered by the impact, several dogs and cats
followed the rats—sixteen animals in all—bursting out through the shredded ruin of the cargo hold, each filled with a new life force gleaned from the
Osterized birds. Rather than scattering, they traveled from the crash in a
tight and orderly pack, their minds filled with a limited but powerful awareness that their journey was not yet complete. And so they pushed deeper into
the canyon, where hungry predators searched for a night's meal.*

4. FUSION

IN A RUSTED MOBILE HOME WITH NO WHEELS, LARA AND Jara watched smoke rise in the southern sky, and waited for their parents to return.

Hours after it had crashed, the downed jet still blazed in the canyon.

Not many exciting things occurred in Hualapai land, and it seemed sad to both Lara and Jara that it was only disasters that brought excitement. Most of the village had headed off into the canyon toward it. Surely the media would want to talk to witnesses. Only a few actually saw the plane soar past on its way down, as it was way past midnight, but plenty were willing to tell every last detail of the crash.

Jara and Lara would have none of that. They had no heart for wallowing in the misery of the dead—and they did *not* want to face the media. They were of one mind when it came to that. And so, while their parents had gone off with the others to view the spectacle and search for survivors, Lara and Jara stayed put in their trailer, as was their way, and they started a new game of chess. They were always starting new games—the problem was finishing them. It was that way with so many things in the twenty years they had lived, that their lives felt little more than a collection of unfinished business.

Still, they started a new game, always hoping for some miracle of completion.

Tonight their concentration was finally broken by the melodic chants of the Shaman next door. He was, by trade, an electrician, but every once in a while, when some earth-shattering event stirred up the town, he would wrap himself in the old skins, and old traditions. Then he would spend hours filling his yard with sand paintings, and singing the chants that few remembered. When Radio Joe began his chants, and cast sulfur into the flames, Lara and Jara would almost believe that somewhere within the heart of the poverty that gripped the town, there truly was magic. The town scoffed at him in the light of day. But when someone was deathly ill, it was always Radio Joe they wanted spilling sands on their floor, and evoking the ancients in the secret dark of night.

At times like this, when the distant sky burned, and Radio Joe called on the spirits, Lara and Jara began to feel that eerie sense of magic, thick as the smoke on the wind.

"He's louder than usual," said Jara.

Lara turned to look out of the window where they could see Radio Joe, sitting before the small fire on his lawn. He shook the ceremonial spices to the left and right; he wailed and invoked; he danced and stomped around the flames, and it *did* seem as if the flames grew higher as he tended them with his ritual.

"The crash must have really spooked him."

The fact was, it was hard not to be spooked by it. The plane had come roaring right over their heads, before it disappeared over the canyon's edge. And although Jara and Lara rarely left the confines of their home, tonight the brother and sister strode out to speak to Radio Joe, leaving behind the strange, twisted footprints that can only be made by conjoined twins.

IT WAS RARER than rare. Impossible, if you believed the experts. Siamese twins born male and female. In every other way they were identical. The survival of conjoined twins usually depended on their level of conjunction. Jara and Lara were severe thoracopagus. They had four legs, but the two central ones were withered and useless. The bones of their hips were fused, and they shared a liver, a pancreas, and a confused intestinal tract. Both their hearts were separate and strong, free from defects; but since their bloodstreams were connected, the two hearts often fought one another, like two drums beating out disparate rhythms.

Hospitals had offered to separate them for free years ago, but their parents both feared the dangers of the operation, and despised charity, so they refused those early offers. Then, as the twins grew, all those excited surgeons found other projects, and so Lara and Jara ultimately fell into the canyon of the forgotten. In times past, conjoined twins were killed at birth. Western medicine used to call them "monsters" before the advent of modern compassion. In spite of it Jara and Lara always tried to see beyond their hardship. Sometimes it was a blessing, to be able to be so close. To almost know the other's thoughts. To share more than most others on earth. But there were only three people who could look at them and not see freaks. Their mother, their father, and Radio Joe.

"THE SPIRITS SPOKE to me tonight," Radio Joe told them, as they warmed themselves around his fire. Lara and Jara grinned at one another.

"Was it AM or FM?" asked Jara. The old man often told tall tales to local children, of spirits that spoke to him through the radios and TVs he repaired.

"No. This time for real." He closed his eyes and offered an open-palmed chant to the flames.

"What did they sound like?"

"They came in the voice of the mountain lion," he told them. And even as he said it, they heard the guttural roar of the great cat somewhere close by.

The twins pulled themselves up quickly, but Radio Joe didn't stir. He opened his eyes, and turned slowly to look up at them. The fire painted a stroke of madness in his ancient eyes. "They called for you," he said. "You did not quest after your spirit. So your spirit has quested after you."

In truth few of the teenagers in town went on vision quests anymore. Radio Joe never missed an opportunity to rebuke them for it.

The roar came again. It sounded strange—different from roars they heard before. It sounded more powerful than other lions. There was a lion that had attacked a woman a few weeks before; surely this was the same one. With most of the neighborhood gone, the twins knew they would have to take care of it. How surprised the others would be when they discovered that the freakish pair had dispatched the troublesome cougar.

"Are you going to shoot it?" asked Radio Joe.

"Once it's had a taste of human blood it won't stop," said Jara. "It has to be destroyed. I know it's not what you believe but—"

"Use my rifle," Radio Joe said. "It's in the shed."

★　★　★

TONIGHT THE WORLD seemed to end at the rim of the canyon. As the twins stood there, gazing out across the great expanse, they could still see an orange glow far below, on the canyon floor. Smoke from the smoldering wreckage had blown to the canyon wall, filling the space beneath the cliff with a haze lit pale blue by the gibbous moon.

They had followed the strange roars of the mountain lion to this spot—and although they could catch hints of its gamy scent, the smell of smoke masked it as they neared the rim.

They looked down into the pit of the canyon.

"Do you think it went back down?" asked Lara. And the answer came as a single earth-shaking roar behind them.

It awakened in them a searing terror, and they realized at this awful, vulnerable moment that they feared death far more than they had imagined.

They turned in a ballet-smooth motion to see not one, but four mountain lions stalking toward them, out of the shadows of the Arizona night. Their mouths were covered with the fur and blood of their latest kills.

Jara raised his rifle but did not know which creature he should aim at. "Don't move," Jara said.

There was something about these beasts that was not right. It was the way they walked—their paws stepping in perfect unison as if they were all reflections of the same beast. And it was common knowledge that mountain lions did not hunt in packs.

The quartet of beasts opened their mouths to roar, and only now did the twins understand why the sound had been so strange. It had been the sound of *all four of them roaring at once.*

Backed against the half-mile drop to the canyon floor, Lara and Jara knew their lives were about to end one way or another. But the lions stopped ten feet away and held their position. Dark eyes fixed on the twins. Perhaps they were confused by the sight of Siamese twins, or perhaps it was something else. Out of nowhere, a voice spoke to them.

"I understand now."

The twins heard the voice, but it was as if the voice had originated deep within their own minds.

"I understand." This time the thought had come from the direction of the great cats. Although Lara didn't pretend to under-

stand all the mysticism of the old ways, she felt sure this was a vision—the kind Radio Joe often spoke of. The kind of vision that opened the door to one's destiny.

Jara, on the other hand, wasn't so convinced. He held the rifle on one of the creatures, unwilling to let his guard down.

"What do you want?" he asked.

"Completion," said the four voices. *"Mine* and *yours."*

"We don't believe in animal spirits," said Jara.

"I don't think that's what they are." Lara raised her hand and pushed down the barrel of Jara's gun.

"What are you?" demanded Jara.

"I am nothing," said the voices. *"I am nothing without you. Because you are the point of focus. You are the one."*

Although the twins did not yet understand the full implication, the truth of it rang deep within them. The suggestion of them being at the focus of anything was a powerfully charged notion. They had lived so much of their lives in hidden anonymity, that it was more than just their curiosity that was piqued. It was a call to their souls.

"What do you mean?" the two asked in unison.

But they didn't need to ask, because they implicitly knew. Jara and Lara were the point of focus. That meant that these creatures had not arrived here by random means. They were directed here by an ordered series of events. Then an image flooded the twins' minds, and they instantly saw how these creatures came to be.

The bacteria aligned.

A powerful force injected perfect order into the river's current, and the bacteria aligned!

The same order flowed its way up the food chain until the alignment of those billion bacteria had distilled down into the alignment of these four dangerous predators.

"And you . . ." said the four voices again. *"You are the point of focus."*

If it were true, thought the twins, then it was something more than fate, and more than destiny. It meant that the unknowable forces of nature had not spat the twins out as freaks, but as vessels for something greater than themselves.

"I can give you what you need. What you long for," said the voice. *"I can give you completion."*

As they heard those words, they finally knew what it would mean to be the point of focus. They had lived lives of incompletion—from their own bodies, to the games of chess they never finished. They were like a tune, straining on the penultimate note, waiting for resolution. They *were* incompletion, and nothing was more desirable than to finally be complete.

"What do we have to do?" the twins said simultaneously.

"You already know," came the answer.

Yes, they did know.

Jara raised his gun at the beasts . . . and released four deadly blasts.

The cats did not flinch, or shy away. Instead they each received the bullet through the brain, and collapsed to the dust, one after another. The twins realized what was about to happen next even before it began, and the knowledge made it even more joyous. The moment the creatures were dead, and their spirits were released, Lara and Jara could feel the four dissolve together, funneling into them. Now the twins could truly hear each other's thoughts, feel each other's beings. The four incomplete spirits that had inhabited the cougars, meshed together, weaving into a single great spirit that wound itself around the twins like a cocoon.

The strange force of order that had touched the distant river was now reversing in the twins what never should have occurred, and all at once, they knew what their innermost wish had always been.

To be one.

There, standing on the rim of the canyon, Lara and Jara—the two halves—merged together into a single being, brought into perfect focus—flesh, mind, and soul.

When it was done, two legs stood where there had been four. Two hands were raised in joy to the heavens, and one mind held the singular human being that had once been sister and brother.

The powerful spirit that had united them, allowed them to linger in their joyous moment of completion. And then that same spirit descended upon them on all sides with such violent ferocity that the twins' soul imploded.

THE BRINGER STOOD in the cold night admiring his new body. It suited him just fine. It was young, it was strong—and like the

Bringer itself, this body was neither male nor female, but a perfect synthesis of both.

"Sleep," he told the twins, as he felt their soul collapse in upon itself. They had experienced their completion, which was more than most did. And although he spared their soul the indignity of being eaten, he had no remorse at having buried it beneath the heavy weight of his own spirit.

He took the four mountain lions that, for a brief time, had housed his quartered soul, and one by one cast them off the cliff and into the dark mist of the canyon.

This was not an ancient Mediterranean empire. That was a world and many ages away. Having stolen the twins' memories, he knew the year and the ways of the modern world. But what was he doing here? He remembered the circumstances of his death: the drowning of the old human shell he had worn; the dissolution of his spirit into the sea. Who had coaxed his fragmented spirit back from the waters of death, causing it to congeal once more into a glorious whole? Who in this world had that kind of power? Instinct told him it must have been a star-shard who had done it, akin to the ones he had destroyed so many years ago. . . .

He peeled from himself the strangely tailored clothes the twins had worn. Clothes sewn by their mother, the Bringer recalled from his usurped memories; arm and leg holes cut at absurd angles that no longer fitted the single symmetrical body the twins had fused into. A perfect human body. He discarded them over the canyon rim, then strode toward the lights of the nearby village, already feeling the pangs of a three-thousand-year-old hunger.

RADIO JOE HAD heard the fours shots go off like the monotone chime of the old church bell, ringing a spirit into the earth.

He waited for the twins to return, tempering his own anxiety with the steady hypnotic spill of sands between his fingers, contemplating the ancient patterns on the hardpan of his yard.

When he saw a figure coming toward him out of the darkness, he thought it must have been the twins, but this figure moved in a steady gate. It was naked, and when Radio Joe looked into its face, he thought for a moment he had slipped into some terrible half-sleep, for what he saw was impossible.

The old man felt his aging heart attempt to stop, but he willed it to sustain his life—if only long enough to know the nature of the monster before him.

"Radio Joe," said the figure, with the slyest of grins, "don't you recognize me? Or should I say, 'us.' "

The old man stood in the center of his sand paintings, studying the figure before him. Firm, hairless pectorals that could have been breasts. Hips that were smooth like a woman's, yet thighs as muscular as a man's. And a dark wedge of venereal abomination, with two distinct organs, one wedged loosely within the folds of the other.

"What have you done with Lara and Jara?"

"They sleep," it said. "For I may yet need them."

Radio Joe reached down, grabbed a handful of black powder, and hurled it into the flames. The fire spat forth a bright green flame.

"Giyá Bachál vomga," he chanted. "Return to the dark place. I command you to fall from the living world!"

But it only laughed. "Empty words," it said. "I had thought it was you who had called me back from the dead—but you are no star-shard. You are barely a man anymore."

The thing that had been Lara and Jara took a step forward, and Radio Joe took a step away, keeping the fire between the thing and himself.

"Who has drawn me back from the waters?" it asked, with a force that could not go unanswered.

"No one has!" said Radio Joe, knowing this more surely than he had known anything in his life. "No one would knowingly call such a creature as you to the living world."

The creature considered his answer. "You're far wiser than you know," it said. "Perhaps my life is an accident, then. How fortunate for me!" It looked at its arms, studying the gooseflesh that had risen there. "Clothe me!" it ordered.

"I will not help you with your dark business," Radio Joe told it, finding one more moment with this creature unbearable. "Either kill me or leave."

It stalked slowly toward him, stepping over the sands, unbothered by the strong magic of their patterns. It stepped over the flames, ignoring the heat, until at last it was face-to-face with Radio Joe.

"Do you have any idea who I am?" it asked.

Radio Joe refused to look away, even though he sensed the depth of the danger he was courting. "At first I thought you were the one who caused the crash . . . but now I see I was wrong. You *are* the crash. You are the death of all you touch. You are the darkness that swallows light. You are *Quíkadi Bp; páa Misma Ga Máa*. The Bringer of Shadows. The thief of souls."

The creature let him go, for a moment taken aback by his words—which clearly hit far closer to the mark than this creature wanted. *Perhaps,* thought Radio Joe *my words have earned me respect enough to be spared.* Or maybe there was some power in the sands yet.

"Your life force is too old to be worth the effort of devouring," it told him. "Aged into vinegar. I leave it with you." And then the thief walked off into the shadows. Radio Joe followed it as far as his open gate, where it had dropped his rifle. He picked the gun up, aimed it at the creature's back as it left, his fingers aching to pull the trigger . . . but he could not—for he knew that he would be also killing whatever was left of the twins as well. Still, he held his aim until it vanished into the night. Then he turned to the flames and cried to his ancestors, knowing that it would take more than a gun, and more than the strength of a hundred generations, to purge the world of this thief of souls.

THE BRINGER WAS clothed by a woman elsewhere in town, claiming to have been robbed and left that way. Then he set out from the Hualapai nation, first on foot, and then in the bed of a hay truck. By now, he was sure that his new life was an accident—an unexpected side effect, of a star-shard's passage—and he marveled at the power of such a shard, whose very presence could line up enough random events to give the Bringer's life impetus against three thousand years of death. Order out of chaos! It was a power more awesome than that of the shape-shifting king, so many years ago. It was a power worth harnessing. Perhaps there were no worthy pupils here, but there was plenty to exploit. Plenty of things to *use*, and a world full of souls to devour.

In the great expanses of Arizona desert, where imprints of life were scarce, sensing the direction of the shards was as easy as listening for cicadas in the dead of night. These shards were separate from one another now, but converging.

Star-shards on Earth once more!

If that were so, he would not make the same mistakes he had made the first time. He would no longer be a Bringer of Wisdom for this dim world, giving his gifts freely to the undeserving. This time he would serve his own voracious appetites.

And as for these new star-shards—he would find them, and he would bend them to his will . . .

. . . and if they would not bend, he would simply destroy them.

PART III · SIMEON SIEGE

5. THREE'S A CROWD

SHIPROCK ROSE FROM THE DESERT FLOOR OF NORTHWEST-
ern New Mexico like a massive sentinel just off of U.S. 666. From
a certain angle, the towering sides of the dead volcano appeared to
be the wings of a great dragon, folded around something dark and
unseen, and more than one local culture saw the end of the world
rising one day from its hidden heart. Tory Smythe had come into
the shadow of this dark sandstone basolith earlier that day, and now
tried to wash away the day in a scalding bath. Yet, no matter how
hard she scrubbed, she couldn't strip away the strange feeling that
had plagued her all afternoon.

A feeling that something was wrong in the town of Shiprock.

—wrong with the quiet couple who tended to the little gift
shop.

—wrong about the woman who offered her a ride.

—wrong about the cluster of teens pumping gas into their van.

And as the late-afternoon sun cast the shadow of the rock over
the town, the feeling got worse, and Tory felt the disquieting sense
that her life was about to take a brand-new turn for the worse.

With exhaustion tugging at her limbs, she decided it was just

71

fatigue, and figured that one night's layover on her journey to Dillon wouldn't kill her.

The town of Shiprock was no Shangri-la. Hardworking but impoverished people populated the flat-roofed homes that were sun-baked by day, and sandblasted by night, courtesy of the merciless desert winds.

She took a room at the only motel that had a room. Although it wasn't the cleanest place, she knew every corner would be pretty well sanitized by the time she woke up in the morning. The way her influence had grown, she figured a single night in one place would fry every germ within a hundred yards—not to mention purify the minds of quite a few overnight guests.

As Tory soaked in the tub, she thought back to the woman at the reception desk. She seemed pleasant enough, and yet, there was something vacant about her expression. *Something wrong, something wrong, something wrong, something . . .*

"I'll take whatever you have," Tory had said, spreading out some crumpled bills on the counter. The woman presented her a key on a cracked plastic chain.

"Checkout time is at ten, and there's a continental breakfast at eight. Aren't you a bit young to be on your own, miss?"

"Is that a problem?" Tory had dropped an extra ten dollars on the counter, and the woman snatched up the ten-spot like a frog catching a fly. "You get yourself a good night's sleep, honey."

Although she was already looking like a parboiled lobster, Tory added more hot water to the tub. It wasn't just the wrongness now. There was an uncanny feeling of presence. An unsettling sensation, like the powerful magnetic field around a high-voltage transformer. Even in the bath, Tory felt her skin fill with gooseflesh.

She tried to shake off the feeling by watching TV through the open bathroom door. There was a report on the news about dead fish in California, then an update on yesterday's deadly plane crash. Tory sighed and sunk down until her chin touched the water. More bad news for a beleaguered world—Tory couldn't stand it. She kicked the door closed, and reached up for a bar of soap . . . but as she did, something caught her eye.

On the counter sat a sorry potted plant. Overwatered and yellow, the little plant was not long for this world. But now as Tory looked at it, she was certain it looked different than it had just five minutes ago. The old, dying leaves had fallen off, and the plant had sprouted new shoots. Tory could swear she could see it growing in tiny spurts.

The exhaustion she felt suddenly seemed unimportant.

"Winston?" she called. "Winston!"

And from the room on the other side of the paper-thin wall came a voice a bit deeper than she remembered, but still familiar.

"Tory?"

WINSTON HAD ALWAYS been a champ at guarding his emotions, but he couldn't contain his excitement at seeing Tory. At last he could talk to someone like himself—someone who understood what it was like to change the world by your very presence, and yet have to hide that light so no one else would know. Someone who understood what a handicap true power could really be. They talked for hours—there was a year of strange tales to tell one another. . . .

"You won't believe all the things I know," bragged Winston. "Medicine, law, philosophy, I'm like a walking encyclopedia."

"You can't believe how I change people just by being around them," said Tory. "I've turned hardened criminals into model citizens!"

Then, somewhere in their conversation, Winston asked the question that had dominated his thoughts since he had stepped foot into Shiprock. "Did you feel something strange when you got here?" he asked. "Something about the people?"

Tory nodded. "It's like . . . they look fine on the outside, but on the inside, they're black-and-white, while the rest of the world is color, you know?"

So it was a sensation they had both felt!—But neither knew what it meant.

At midnight, they ventured out to an all-night coffee shop down the street, sparsely populated by truckers and tired travelers. As they sat at the counter, devouring greasy burgers, a planter just outside the window became clogged with weeds and cactus, and at the table behind them, a grunged-out biker suddenly began cleaning his fingernails with his pocketknife.

"Our powers keep growing," Winston told Tory. "No telling where it's going to stop."

"What if they don't?" whispered Tory.

Winston, in all his newfound wisdom, had no answer.

Just then, a customer who had been sitting alone in a booth, sauntered to the counter and slid onto the stool beside them. Their chatter stopped abruptly.

"You can keep on talking, I don't mind," said the intruder, who seemed to be about twenty or so. "My name's Okoya." Like most people in town, Okoya was Native American, with long, black hair, and dark eyes. It was those eyes that caught Tory and Winston. They were deeper than a person's eyes ought to be.

"Do you mind?" said Winston, taking the defensive.

"Can't I sit here?"

Tory shrugged. "Sit wherever you want."

The intruder seemed far more comfortable than they were.

"You both seem excited but worried at the same time," Okoya noted. "I wonder what that could be about?"

Winston shrugged. "What, do you poke your way into everyone else's business?"

"Only when it's interesting," said Okoya, pushing a ketchup-covered plate of fries to share with them. "The truth is, I'm just passing through town. I was hoping I could travel with some interesting people."

"I don't think so," said Winston uneasily. But Tory touched Winston's hand, a signal for him to step down from red alert.

"Where are you headed?" asked Tory, beginning to munch on the fries.

Okoya looked out the window, gazing into the dim, dusty street. "Wherever you are."

Great, thought Winston. *The last thing we need is some asshole tagging along on our trip to find Dillon.* And yet . . . Winston suddenly felt a pang of loneliness—as if this Okoya person had all at once created a space in their company that needed to be filled. Having a third party to talk to—to take their minds off of things for a short part of the journey might make the trek more interesting. And then again, this stranger might want nothing more than to rob them, or kill them or both. But considering where they had been, and where they were headed, such a threat seemed minuscule and easily dealt with.

"We're not leaving until morning," Winston explained.

Okoya shook his head. "Why not leave now?"

Because we're exhausted, Winston was about to answer, but suddenly he didn't feel tired at all.

Tory turned to Winston. "We really don't *have* to stay overnight."

When their meal was done, they left together, to gather what little they had from their motel. As they slipped their keys into the night drop, Winston turned to Tory.

"Interesting guy. Do you think he's Navajo or Hopi?"

Okoya stood by the curb, looking west; as if knowing their direction better than they did. Tory stared at Winston as if he were out of his mind.

"What do you mean 'he'?" said Tory. "Okoya is a girl!"

Winston took a second look. The Indian's long hair blew with the night wind—but long hair didn't mean anything these days. Okoya's voice was a gentle tenor . . . could it have been contralto instead? "Try again!" said Winston. "He's a guy. You think I can't tell the difference?"

"Apparently not." said Tory. And so to prove it, Winston ran up to Okoya, fully prepared to ask the question point-blank: *What the hell are you?*

But when Okoya turned to him, Winston found that he didn't have the nerve to ask. "Uh . . . Okoya," stammered Winston. "That's a very interesting name."

Okoya smiled proudly. "It's Hualapai," Okoya said. "It means 'Bringer of Fire.' "

EIGHT HUNDRED MILES to the west, the Newport Beach Festival of Dead Fish had attracted massive media attention, but even as the media crews were arriving at the beach that night, Michael, Lourdes, and Drew were racing toward the marina to Michael's boat.

It wasn't all that spectacular a craft compared to the million-dollar yachts that graced the Newport marina, but the price was right.

"I made a suicidal lawyer see the joys of life," Michael explained to Lourdes. "He was so thrilled that he gave me his boat, turned his house into a bed-and-breakfast, and now he serves poached eggs instead of lawsuits."

Lourdes was amused, and Drew could only shake his head in

utter amazement. "If you can do all that, why work at the Dog Kabob?" Drew asked.

"Because it's normal," answered Michael, and normality was something in short supply in Michael's life.

He powered up the boat and piloted it out of Newport Channel to the open sea. As Michael suspected, a cold ocean current ran down the coastline about a half mile from shore. It was like a river in the middle of the ocean. Waves died as they hit the smooth ribbon of water, only to be reborn on the "river's" other side—and all the while the mid-ocean stream remained so flat, you could see every detail of the moon reflected in its glassy surface.

"Dillon's order," Lourdes commented when she saw it. The ill-fated fish had traveled down this serene thread of water from somewhere up north. They could follow this ocean river straight to Dillon, if it lasted long enough. It was as easy as tracing the ashen trail of a burnt fuse.

"So who's Dillon?" Drew had asked.

There was the long answer and the short answer, and Michael had no patience for long answers. "He's the best of us, and the worst of us," Michael said. Drew, who was generally too cool to admit cluelessness, accepted the answer, and didn't ask again.

A day later, nightfall found them off the central California coast. They fueled in Morro Bay, and dropped anchor in the shadow of Morro Rock, its massive dome growing out of the ocean like the skull of a giant.

The boat had only one cabin, with a single, triangular bed beneath the bow. It was comfortable for one, livable for two, and impossible for three. Their ears practically touched as they all lay face-up, looking at the low ceiling of the cabin.

"I've never slept in a boat," said Lourdes, to Michael's right.

"It's kind of cozy," said Drew, to his left.

"It's like a coffin," said Michael, the only one who seemed bothered by the tight space. To him it felt like trying to sleep in the tip of a pointed shoe.

Outside, a mild wind blew, gently rocking the boat.

Lourdes sighed contentedly, and the sound irritated Michael no end. There was nothing about this journey that was the least bit blissful, but to listen to Lourdes, you'd think they were all on a pleasure cruise.

"I'm really starting to worry about how unworried *you* are," Michael told her.

"What's to worry about?" she said gently. "You and I can beat anything." She kissed him on the cheek, and a few minutes later, Michael heard her breathing slip into the relaxed whistle of a deep sleep, leaving Drew and Michael to stare at the beige-carpeted ceiling.

"So," whispered Drew with a sly smile. "Is she the mystery woman you've been saving your moves for?"

"I don't have any moves," answered Michael.

"But she is your girlfriend, right?"

Michael had to consider the question. He had never thought of Lourdes as a girlfriend. More like cell mates than soul mates. "I don't know," said Michael glancing at her to make sure she was still asleep. "I guess."

Drew shifted so he could look at Michael. "You must love her a lot."

"Yeah, sure," said Michael, wishing he would just shut up about it.

"That's good," said Drew. "There are guys I know on the track team that think girls are only good for one thing—and love is only as big as their hard-ons. Which in most cases offers no wind resistance, if you know what I mean."

Michael laughed in spite of himself. "You have all the answers, don't you, Drew?" he said. "I wish I had my head together half as well as you do."

"You must *really* be screwed up if you think *my* head's together." They laughed a bit longer, and when it got quiet once more, Drew slid out of the cramped space.

"You'll never sleep while I'm in your face," said Drew. "I'll go up and pilot the boat. No sense losing a night of travel time."

Michael quickly filled the space where Drew had been, and was already dozing when he noticed that Drew had not yet left. He was still standing there, watching Michael and Lourdes sleep, like he had nothing better to do.

"Not that it really matters," Drew said in that offhanded way of his. "But you remember that baseball story I told you? . . . Well, it wasn't really about baseball."

Michael yawned. "That's nice," he said absently.

Drew lingered a moment longer. Then Michael heard him up on deck as he raised the anchor, and started the engine. In a few moments, Michael was asleep, his back toward Lourdes, and his face to the windowless wall.

TORY AWOKE TO an unsteady world, uncertain of where she was or why she was there. It was a large space around her, rectangular and rusty. Light poured in from an open door, and the whole world rattled.

A boxcar. Yes, that was it. They were heading west from New Mexico. It had been past midnight when they had reached the train yard, and found a train bound in their general direction. The white noise of the rolling stock had lulled her to sleep. The boxcar had been filled with the stench of decay and urine when they had hopped on, but now any unpleasant odor was gone, washed away by more than just the wind pouring in through the huge open door.

Curled up beside her, still in the deepest of sleeps was Winston. And a few yards away sat the stranger, Okoya. She was staring at Tory, as if she could have been staring that way throughout the night.

"Sleep well?" Okoya asked.

Tory rolled the kink out of her neck. "Better than I expected."

"You looked like you needed it." Okoya grinned, but only slightly. It was unsettling, because Tory couldn't discern what the grin meant.

"It's been a long few days."

"It's more than just a few days, isn't it?" Okoya asked. "There's weight on the two of you far heavier than this journey."

"Long story."

Then that grin again. "I imagine it would be."

Tory looked to her fingers. They were still numb from the cold night. The skin around her cuticles was frayed. She had been picking at them in her sleep again. Her hands, her whole body felt sticky, unpleasant, and unclean; even though she knew the feeling was only in her imagination, it didn't make her feel any less uncomfortable.

"What I wouldn't give for a nice hot bath," said Okoya, practically reading her mind.

"Same here." But Okoya couldn't know how much Tory longed for that bath, especially now that the thought had been put in her head.

Okoya glanced over at Winston, who still slept, fine slashes of morning light cutting across his face, from the many cracks in the boxcar panels.

"This Winston," said Okoya. "He always has a chip on his shoulder, doesn't he? Always negative."

Tory shrugged. "All show. He's a real sweetheart once you get to know him."

Okoya considered this. "Maybe," she said. "Still, you could do better."

The train began a wide turn. Tory felt her whole body shift to the left with inertia. "Better than what? Winston and I are just friends."

Okoya reached for her pack, then fished for something inside. "Yes, I can see that." She pulled out a small bottle of cologne. "But friends can often bring you down."

Tory found herself bristling. "Not my friends."

"Really? And how about this friend you travel toward?"

"Dillon?" Tory looked away. "That's different."

Okoya turned the bottle in her fingers. The pale fluid within refracted a crescent of light across the wall. "Are you friends by choice, or by circumstance?"

"Why should that matter?"

"Best not to put your trust in circumstantial friendships," Okoya said. "Because circumstances change."

"I can trust Winston . . ." But as she said it, she felt her own conviction waver.

Okoya stood and moved toward the open boxcar door. The bright rugged terrain of the Arizona desert sped past, a red dusty blur. Okoya opened the bottle of cologne, and dabbed some on the nape of her neck. The wind caught the scent, and brought it back to Tory, who breathed in the scent deeply. It was an aroma that Tory could not identify. Neither flowery nor musky. It simply smelled . . . clean.

"We'll be in California soon," Okoya said.

Tory tried to get another whiff of the cologne, but could not, and found herself angry that the scent seemed to fade so quickly.

When Okoya came back from the open door, Tory could not even smell it on her, even when Tory moved closer. She thought to ask Okoya if she could try some herself, but thought better of it. Tory had never been one to wear perfume. Okoya slipped the vial into the dark hole of her pack, and pulled the drawstring tight.

"You said your story was long."

"Excuse me?"

"Your story. Your reason for this journey. You said it was long, but as far as I can see, we've got nothing but time."

Tory shook her head. "You wouldn't believe it."

"Then that will make it all the more enjoyable to hear." Okoya tossed back her flood of black hair, revealing high, square cheekbones. Tory thought for a moment that perhaps Winston was right about the gender of their traveling companion. Then Tory laughed, more at herself than anything else. Why would it matter what Okoya was, when they would part ways in just a few short hours, once the novelty of each other's company wore thin. And did it matter what Tory told this stranger they would never see again?

"Sure I'll tell you," said Tory. And maybe confessing all of it to this drifter might unburden her own soul. She began with her days as an untouchable in Alabama, when her flesh-sores were so virulent you could tell neither her sex nor the color of her skin. "The Scorpion star went nova the moment each of us were conceived," she explained, "but it took sixteen years for its light to reach the earth. When we finally saw its light, it made each of us realize our connection to one another . . . that we were luminous in a way we never knew . . . and that same brightness had attracted parasites like a flame attracts insects . . ." Then Tory told of all they had endured since the supernova lit up the sky. It was remarkable how easy it was to unload the tale on a patient, receptive ear. And Okoya was nothing if not receptive.

A FLIER WAS circulated in Peach Springs, Arizona, and surrounding communities, featuring a picture of the missing conjoined twins. Those who did not know them thought the absurd picture must have been some sort of prank. Those who did know them, did not expect them to turn up alive—least of all their devastated parents, who knew that Lara and Jara never dared to venture far from the safety of home.

Radio Joe cooperated with police, insofar as he told them half the story, ending it upon hearing the distant four shots, and saying no more. There were no footprints to corroborate his story, as the wind had dusted the hardpan clean, but bloodhounds had tracked the twins' movements as far as the canyon rim, where they recovered their clothes, shredded but bloodless. Snagged at various points down the canyon wall were the bodies of the four cougars, as well as Radio Joe's rifle, which Joe had hurled into the canyon, not wanting to be near anything the *Quíkadi* had touched. It was confiscated as evidence. At the canyon rim, however, the hounds became feral, howling and frothing at the mouth as if the scent had taken a turn into canine nightmare. They were of no use beyond that.

The fringe element in town spoke of alien abductions and police complicity, which mired the investigation further.

Through the first night and day, Joe performed his rituals, asking the spirits for guidance. He used to perform his rituals more out of respect than anything else, for there was a peace in carrying on a tradition, but now it all took on the type of mystical power it had in his childhood. The spirits were very real again. The only question was, how was he to act upon what he knew—what he had seen? He listened for voices in the wind and in the calls of birds. He forced his dreams into lucidity, remembering their images, and a sense of purpose began to take shape. Two days after the plane crash and the twins' mysterious disappearance, Radio Joe began to visit the neighbors.

"ALL THIS FUSS over those two," Mary Wahomigie said to Joe through her screen door. He had approached her under the pretense of looking for work. "TV repairs, air conditioners, any gadget that's giving you trouble," Joe had said. "I'll give you my preferred-customer rate."

Mary laughed. "I thought I already was a preferred customer, Joe."

The woman had no need of repairs, and so the conversation had slipped to the air crash, and then to the missing twins.

"All that fuss," Mary said. "But maybe what happened to them is for the best. Those two never belonged here to begin with. A miracle they survived as long as they did."

"So you think they're dead?"

Mary hesitated for just an instant. Radio Joe imagined that if this were a polygraph test, the needle would be pinned in the red. He could almost feel the electric charge of her lie. "Yes, they must be, don't you think?" she said.

Joe took off his baseball cap, revealing his thin, sweaty hair. He brushed his hand across his forehead, wiping off the sweat.

"Would you like something to drink, Joe? Maybe a piece of berry cobbler?"

She swung open the screen door, and as she did, Joe stole a look into her eyes—the same look he had stolen from each of his neighbors today. Although several had invited him in, he had turned them down. Until now.

"Yes, Mary, I'd appreciate that."

Mary Wahomigie's house was both spotless and cluttered. The shelves and walls were polished and dusted, but several lifetimes' worth of dime-store trinkets sprouted from every surface like fungus on a stump. No shelf space remained for future memories— perhaps because all of Mary's memories were behind her. Phil, her husband, had died of a heart attack five years before, and their only daughter lost her battle with breast cancer shortly thereafter.

Mary had had her eye on Joe for a few years now, but Joe had no interest in her. His solitary life had always suited him fine. However, now he turned to whatever charm he had, complimenting her on her sun tea and cobbler.

"I grew the berries myself. Only enough for a couple of cobblers a season, but every bite's worth a dozen."

Joe took the last bite, and set down his fork. "I see you still keep Phil's guns out."

He was referring, of course, to the glass showcase cluttered with a preponderance of hunting weapons and accessories.

"Never dream of selling them," Mary said. "He'd roll over in his grave"—which was a curious expression, considering the man had been cremated.

"Ever consider loaning them to a friend?"

"Planning a hunting trip, Joe?"

"Been thinking of it."

She unlocked the case for him, and he pulled down a shotgun. "Phil's pride and joy," she told him. "I'm sure he wouldn't mind it being used again."

It was a Winchester 1300—a sleek, 12-gauge pump, far superior to his own.

"My shotgun's evidence now, you know."

Mary shifted uncomfortably. "So I heard. The twins went to kill those cougars."

"Did the job, too."

"Imagine that."

"The police wonder if I had anything to do with their disappearance."

Mary came over to him, and put a hand on his shoulder, as if she had been waiting for an excuse to do so. "I know you didn't, Joe."

"No," admitted Joe. "But I *do* know more than I tell. . . . Just like you."

She recoiled for a moment, but he smiled, and she softened, smiling back. "Just what does that mean?" she said coyly.

"You tell me, Mary . . . and then I'll tell you what I know."

Mary glanced out of her living-room window, as if they might be under surveillance, then she pulled the shades. "If you know about the cousin," she said, "then you know it's for the twins' own good."

"The cousin," said Joe. "Yes, I know about the cousin."

"Spitting image of them, don't you think?" Mary sat down on her couch, patting the space next to her. Joe stayed where he was.

"And you helped him?" Joe prompted.

"He was robbed, you know. They took his car, the clothes off his back. He said he was here to take the twins away to a special hospital where they could be taken better care of."

"You believed him?"

"Why shouldn't I? Anyway, I gave him some of Phil's old pants, and a shirt. He was practically busting out of them, but they had to do.

Radio Joe's eyes wandered back to the gun case. He strode over, and grabbed the rifle that was her dead husband's pride and joy. He opened a drawer beneath the case, and as he expected, found boxes of shells in various calibers. Phil Wahomigie never kept his ammunition too far away.

"They're five years old," Mary said. "You might want to get new ones."

"They're be fine as long as they're dry."

"So you saw the cousin, too, didn't you?" asked Mary. "Now it's your turn—tell me what you know. Did he go to your place after he left here?"

Joe slipped cartridges into the shotgun. Eight, and it was full. "Actually, he came to my place first."

Mary looked up at him, confused. "You didn't help him? Joe, that's not like you."

"I offered him nothing and he took nothing from me. Because he was nobody's cousin. Nobody's child. It was a Quíkadi."

She stood up. "What are you talking about?"

There were tears now clouding his eyes, but he quickly flipped them away. Then he pumped the gun, loading the chamber. "It took more from you than your clothes, Mary."

The woman began to back away. "Joe, you're scaring me. Are you drunk, Joe? Put that rifle down."

Joe looked at the rifle. "Perhaps you're right," he said. He leaned the rifle gently against the sofa. Then he advanced on Mary with his bare hands.

"No! Stop!"

But there was no sense in responding to Mary Wahomigie now, because she was not there to hear. She had been dead for three days now, her soul devoured, leaving behind an empty shell to mimic life.

Radio Joe grabbed the slight woman, and hurled her to the ground, breaking the coffee table, sending knickknacks scattering across the faded green carpet. She tried to scream again, but he wedged his boot firmly under her chin, cutting off her cries. "I mourn Mary Wahomigie. She was a good woman," he said. "Her body deserves the peace of the grave." He turned his ankle and shifted his weight forward onto her neck. The body of Mary Wahomigie struggled, but that, he knew, was merely a reflex, like the twitching nerves of a fly on the face of a swatter. This body would have continued to twitch and talk and mimic life for years. It could not be allowed. With a grimace, he lurched forward, feeling the crumbling of glottal cartilage, and the final crunch as her neck snapped beneath the weight of his heel.

The body stopped struggling, and came to rest. Then, when he looked in her eyes, he knew he had done the good and proper thing, because they looked no different now than they had five minutes before. Death was death, even when it walked.

He gently laid Mary on her bed, covered her with one of her handmade quilts, then returned to the living room, taking as many weapons as he could carry.

Although he didn't know where the Quíkadi had gone, he knew he'd have more luck than the bloodhounds in tracking it, for he knew what he was searching for. And if he listened, attuning his soul to the dark, his ears to the silences, and his heart to the void, he would be able to trace its footsteps.

6. HOUSE OF THE RISING SUN

SOMETIME BEFORE DAWN, FIVE BUSES SNAKED SOUTH DOWN the Pacific Coast Highway, hugging the cliffs of California's central coast.

By the time the sun made its appearance, the buses were pulling into the large Visitors Center of the area's most celebrated tourist attraction. The night guard stepped out from his shack to greet the buses. To him the situation was obvious; some overeager tourists must have gotten it into their heads that this was a twenty-four-hour attraction. Not so. The Visitors Center was closed, and the first tours didn't begin for three more hours. He felt sure he'd be able to convince them all to come back later, and if he couldn't, the iron security gate would.

He approached the dark-tinted windows of the first bus, and the door opened to admit him.

Turns out he had misdiagnosed the entire situation.

Ten minutes later, the night guard emerged from the lead bus, bewildered and rubbing his chest. Although he had never told his employer, he was, in fact, a dying man . . . but the redheaded kid who led this group had changed that. Now the cancer that had been devouring his right lung was leaving him. He could almost feel the malignant cells collapsing in upon themselves, the genetic mutation corrected—his body fixed from the inside out. He didn't know what all this meant, but he did know that, even though it broke the rules, he was going to open the gate, and allow these buses to pass.

What was the kid's name? Darren? Devin?

The buses rolled through, and he closed the gate behind them, wishing he could be in there with those people—because he knew that this had been the most important moment of his life.

Dillon! Yes, that was it.

Whoever he was, the guard sensed that Dillon was not coming here as a tourist, and he realized that his own sense of loyalty was no longer with the department of Parks and Recreation. Now he worked for the boy.

He marveled as he watched the buses wind their way inland, amazed by the way they moved in perfect, orderly formation, spaced precisely one bus-length apart, as they drove east down the lone road, and toward the solitary castle in the distance, which stood silhouetted against the rising sun.

7. ECLIPSED

MICHAEL AWOKE WITH AN OVERWHELMING URGE TO JUMP off the back of the boat. That's how he knew they had gone too far. He climbed out of the cabin to find Lourdes at the controls. They were a few hundred yards from shore, and while the flat stream of water still stretched out ahead of them, Michael knew it would only lead them to a place Dillon had been, not the place he was now. The sky, which had been a sunny blue just a moment ago, was already weaving with clouds.

"I took over for Drew at around midnight," she told him with a smile.

"We've passed him, Lourdes," Michael said. "We passed him sometime during the night."

"Or he passed us," Lourdes said calmly.

"Then why are we still headed up the coast?"

"I was waiting for you," she said. "So we could decide together what to do." She turned off the engine and the boat quickly slowed and began to drift.

"You could have woken me!" he said.

Lourdes smiled again. "Maybe I just wanted to let you sleep." She gently brushed his hair out of his eyes. "You looked too peaceful to wake up. . . . I knew when you woke up you would be worried. So I let you sleep."

There was warmth and concern in her words, but Michael couldn't echo back her warmth. All he could do was stare at her emptily. Lourdes leaned just an inch or two closer.

"No kissing in front of the children," said Drew. Their shipmate sat in the corner of the deck, as unobtrusive as a barnacle on the hull.

While kissing hadn't been on Michael's mind, apparently Lourdes had been considering it, because she backed off the mo-

88

ment Drew spoke, leaving Michael to take control of the boat. He brought them around to a southerly heading, while Drew, under the glaring eyes of Lourdes, inhaled Chee-tos.

"Drew," said Lourdes, "if you keep on eating like that, you're going to get fat. Believe me, I know."

Drew shoved another Chee-to in his mouth. "I'm a growing slug," he said.

Michael had to admit that Drew was playing his third-wheel role to a tee—but the fact was, Drew and Lourdes had more in common than they cared to admit. To Michael, it seemed both of them were far too content for their own good.

"Can't you just close your eyes, and figure out exactly where Dillon is?" asked Drew.

Lourdes laughed at the thought, and shook her head. "Better yet, why don't we just teleport ourselves there?"

"Yeah," said Drew. "Why don't you?"

"Just because we can do *some* things, that doesn't mean we can do *all* things," Michael told him. "As far as finding Dillon, it's not like we've got navigational computers in our brains. It's more like playing hot-and-cold. All I know, is that we were getting hotter last night . . . and now we've gotten colder."

Now only about a hundred yards from shore, Michael kept them hugging the coastline as he tried to pick up a sense of Dillon's position . . . and all the while Lourdes watched him—Michael could practically feel her eyes boring into him. She was waiting for a tender gesture, he knew, and when she didn't get it, she came to him, and put her arms around him. He knew he should have been flattered by her attentions, but instead felt caged. So he shrugged himself out of the grasp of her comforting, protective arms.

"Let's just think about solving the problem."

Lourdes gaped at him as if he had hurled mud in her face. Her cheeks flushed with humiliation—but she soon recovered, finding some of her old stoicism to cool her eyes and cheeks. Then she surrendered.

"San Simeon," she said.

"What?"

"I looked at a map, and there's not much between here and Morro Bay—just San Simeon. Dillon could be there."

Michael nodded. "San Simeon it is." He kicked up the engine, and turned his eyes forward. He could tell Lourdes was waiting for more from him—a hug, a grin . . . anything—and when Michael didn't deliver, she stormed down to the cabin.

"Who wants to find Dillon Cole anyway?" She pulled the cabin curtain shut behind her. Closest she could come to slamming a door, Michael supposed.

So, if this trip wasn't about finding Dillon, then what was it about? Michael wondered. But he already knew the answer. It was about the old times. It was about being so alone that they needed each other more than they needed their next breath. But it wasn't like that anymore for Michael—and although he still needed many things, he wasn't sure Lourdes was one of them.

None of this was lost on Drew. He remained a silent observer as Michael cold-shouldered Lourdes down into the cabin, all the while crunching Chee-tos while he watched, like popcorn at the movies.

Now Drew spoke up as the last trace of sun fell behind cloud cover. "Hey Michael!" he said. "You'll screw up my tan—why don't you do that trick with the sky!"

"Not in the mood," Michael told him. For months he had mined his own depths, and forced a happy face onto the world around him—but now that they were headed toward Dillon, there wasn't a single vein of good cheer left to mine.

Drew, on the other hand, seemed as comfortable as could be. The world could end, and Drew would wisecrack his way into oblivion.

Michael was as envious as he was irritated. "Drew, this is serious shit here. I felt Dillon scream—and when Dillon screams, it doesn't mean he stubbed his toe. Something major is going down, and I don't know what the hell it is yet."

"Hey, I have faith in you, man," said Drew. "You can do no wrong."

Michael had to smile. Drew's trust was a powerful thing; something absurdly stable in the madness they were sailing into. But as far as doing no wrong, Drew was sorely mistaken. "You didn't know me back east," answered Michael.

"Yeah, yeah, I know—you were a monumental asshole," said Drew.

"No. It was worse than that." Michael put the engine on idle, and went over to sit beside him. "I had this parasite living inside me. . . . It drove me nuts . . . and kind of *twisted* everyone around me—"

"—And so you all took a trip to Oz, killed a few of your Flying Monkeys, and then realized there's no place like home," said Drew. "Lourdes told me the whole story while you were asleep—but that was like another lifetime. Who you *were*, and who you *are*, are two different things. I won't hold all that other stuff against you."

Michael glanced at the closed curtain of the cabin. "I just want you to understand why Lourdes and I get so weird at each other. It's like you said—we were all different people. But Lourdes still wants us to be the same."

"So, how do you feel about her now?" Drew asked.

"I don't know," Michael whispered. "When I try to dig down and pull up feelings about Lourdes, all I get are rocks." Michael took a deep breath, and the smell of diesel fuel and seaweed cut a stinging path through his lungs. "I don't think I feel anything anymore."

"Maybe it'll come back," suggested Drew.

"I don't think so."

Drew nodded. "Good."

Michael snapped his eyes to Drew curiously. "That's good?"

"Well . . . yeah. I mean, how are you two ever going to deal with this Dillon dude if all you can think about is each other? This way you'll be able to give it all your attention, right?"

Michael had to admit it made sense. "I wish we had you on our first trip," Michael told him. "It would have been a whole lot saner with you around."

"I would have gone, if I knew you back then."

Michael laughed at that. "If you knew me then, you'd probably be first in line to swing a bat at my skull."

But Drew shook his head. "No matter how screwed-up you were, I would have still been your friend."

Although he appreciated the sentiment, Michael knew it couldn't have been true, but still, it was nice of Drew to say so.

Drew put his hand on Michael's shoulder in a gesture of friendship. "And whatever happens now," continued Drew, "I'll still be your running partner."

In a moment the disk of the sun seemed ready to pierce the

dreary sky, and Michael felt a bit embarrassed that his emotions were as easy to read as skywriting. He wanted to tell Drew what it meant to have a friend so true—so devoted. But before Michael could offer his thanks, Drew's face eclipsed the light of the clearing sky like the face of a full moon.

A full moon on a collision course.

Michael realized what was about to happen, and he tried to say something—anything—but suddenly found his lips otherwise occupied.

. . . It did not feel right. . . .

. . . It did not feel wrong. . . .

It just felt . . . odd. Like stepping onto an escalator that wasn't moving.

Michael just sat there, too stunned to respond to Drew's kiss. It went on for a slow moment, and a moment more, before Michael's reflexes kicked in like an emergency generator. He grabbed Drew's shoulders and pushed him away so hard, Drew nearly fell off the boat. Michael should have known what would happen next—but his brain was lagging way behind his gut in reacting to the new spin that the world had taken on. He began to *feel* long before he had the chance to think, and what he felt was *not* flowers and sunshine.

Drew must have seen it in his eyes.

"Michael, I'm sorry! I didn't mean that!"

Michael wiped his lips with the back of his hand, never taking his eyes off of Drew. The air around them began to thin, as hot air shot up through the clouds, and cold air spiraled down around it, picking up speed.

"It was stupid. It was a mistake!" said Drew, his tan cheeks taking on a deep-red embarrassment.

The boat was moving now. Not forward, not backward . . . but clockwise. The boat had slowly begun to spin, and the thin air around it gave way to a sudden horizontal wind beneath a sky that had turned a strange shade of green.

Is this what Drew had been moving toward all this time? Not running partners. Not friends—but *this*?

"Please forget it, Michael," Drew begged. "I *need* you to forget it."

"Shut up!" Michael screamed, beyond hope of control. "You're not my friend! You're not anything!"

Lies—everything he and Drew shared as friends was a lie! But worse, it wasn't just Drew. Somewhere down in a place his own thoughts didn't reach, Michael *knew*—but Michael had let it happen.

His confused rage drilled a hot tunnel through the clouds, while a chill funneled down to the very place they stood, and the boat began to tilt as its slow, clockwise spin picked up speed.

Lourdes stumbled up from the cabin. "What is it? What's happening?"

But Michael couldn't speak to her, he could only stare at Drew, not even knowing who he saw anymore when he looked at him.

"Michael, don't!" shouted Drew. "Please, don't!"

The boat shuddered and tipped. Water began to slosh over the side, and they were all thrown to the wet deck. Michael, suddenly understanding what was happening around them, tried to take control of the swirling winds, but they were too far gone now, taking on a life of their own . . . and through the seawater that spat into his face, he could see the dark funnel of a full-fledged tornado.

"Grab on to something!" screamed Lourdes, just as the floor fell away beneath them, and the boat was plucked out of the sea. Lourdes locked her strong arm around the steering wheel, Michael grabbed the base of the driver's seat, and Drew was hurled down into the cabin. The boat was dragged at least thirty feet out of the water. The waterspout spun it around its waist twice, and then hurled it like a slingshot at the California coast a hundred yards away.

ON PACIFIC COAST Highway, a businessman in a brand-new Lexus sped down the winding coastline road, imagining himself the lead driver in the Grand Prix. So focused was he on hugging the random curves, that he didn't see the cyclone a hundred yards beyond his tinted side windows. He thought the salt water hitting his windshield was just a sudden downpour. He thought the wind was just the resistance his powerful car created as it sped down the coast. And so he had no warning at all when the cabin cruiser hit the pavement in front of him, skidding toward him on the wet asphalt. He stomped on his brake and heard an awful crunch, which became the sound of an inflating air bag.

★ ★ ★

BATTERED AND BRUISED from the short but violent flight, neither Michael nor Lourdes dared open their eyes yet. They just listened as car after car screeched to a sudden halt, and the violent, offshore winds finally died.

Michael turned to Lourdes. "Are you okay?"

"I'm alive," answered Lourdes.

Michael's wind-reddened eyes began to blink back into clearer focus. The world around him began to take shape again.

The boat rested on the smashed, starboard side of its hull. At this angle, its deck was closer to being a bulkhead than a floor. Before them, motorists stood by their cars, stunned and confused by this anomalous sight before them. It would have been funny if they didn't hurt so much from the brutal ride.

And then Lourdes asked, "Where's Drew?"

Michael felt a wave of nausea, chased by a wave of dread. Where *was* Drew?

He had a vague memory of seeing him fall through the flapping curtain of the cabin, before their boat was flung to shore. Michael quickly climbed up the buckled deck, and flung himself into the cabin.

All was not well down below.

The fiberglass hull had crushed down to half its size, and there was the twisted, gold-plated grille of a luxury car, where the bed should have been. The driver tried to catch his breath . . . while steam spewed from his ruined radiator, into Drew's half-open eyes. His body had been crushed against the bulkhead, pinned between the remains of the car and the boat. His chest had collapsed like the shell of an egg, and the life had been pressed out of him in an instant.

The image kept hitting Michael's brain and then bouncing right out, his mind refusing to accept it.

"Noooo!" he screamed. It came out more like a squeal—the kind of awful sound Drew himself might have made if he had the chance.

Lourdes began to warble something in incoherent Spanish when she saw him, paling and turning away.

"Lourdes, help me! *Help me!*" screamed Michael.

Together they wrenched Drew free from the grille of the car.

"He's breathing!" shouted Michael. "He's . . ." But it wasn't air bubbling out of his nose; it was blood. And even that flow quickly stopped, making it all too clear that there was no heart pumping. His chest was little more than a concave crater in his torso.

There were other voices now—motorists who had left their cars to inspect the wreckage. They tried to peer in through the gap where the Lexus had shattered the hull.

"We have to get out of here!" Lourdes tried to pull him away, but he violently shrugged her off.

"I can't just leave him!" Michael knew he was responsible for this. He had brought swift judgment on Drew, and had executed that judgment in a blink of an eye. Thanks to Michael, Drew had been crushed with the same unforgiving brutality of an old-fashioned stoning.

As he held Drew, Michael began to weep, and the heavens answered with a silent rain, lamenting all the things that were lost in the span of ninety seconds.

8. BOOK OF WISDOM

"YOU MOVE LIKE ONE UNACCUSTOMED TO HIS OWN LIMBS," Okoya told Winston. "I was wondering why."

"I thought Tory already gave you the story." Winston brushed the sweat from his brow, and looked around. "We're not getting anywhere." The three of them had left the train more than a day ago, and had since given up on hitchhiking, for the rural roads they traveled only zigzagged in pointless directions. They had taken off on foot, certain that Dillon was just a few miles west, across the bushy hills of central California; but it was more than just a few miles. They were met by endless wastelands where tumbleweeds gathered against neglected barbed-wire fences. They hiked for a good part of the night, and yet the morning landscape seemed no different from the scenery they saw at sundown.

They had come across a stream a few hundred yards back, where Tory had insisted on bathing, and so Winston and Okoya went on ahead, scouting out the next hill. Winston was not looking forward to the view, because he was sure of what it would show them: more hills, and mountains for as far as the eye could see. No Dillon. No anything.

Halfway up the hill, he decided to rest. His legs ached. In truth, they always ached from growing pains as his muscles and tendons fought to match the pace of his bone growth.

"I'd still like to hear your side of the story," said Okoya.

"I don't know why I should tell you anything."

Okoya sat down on a boulder and pulled out a book from his back pocket. A thin, maroon volume, hard-bound, but small, like an address book. "Then don't." He flipped it open, and gave it his attention. Winston found his indifference more irritating than his nosiness.

"A year ago I was the size of a six-year-old, and growing backward," Winston told Okoya. "My touch could numb you—paralyze you. And Tory—she was a human petri dish, covered with open sores that could probably spread every disease there is. That's what we were like when we found each other."

"And then you both destroyed your titans," prompted Okoya. "Tory told me about it."

"Whatever you want to call them; yes, we killed them. And now there's a whole new problem."

"Problem?"

"Yes. You saw our campsite this morning, didn't you?"

Okoya laughed, but Winston failed to find the humor. They had gone to bed on an open plain, and awoke in a forest of weeds that had grown so high you couldn't see the color of the sky. Winston's bedroll had been snared, and it took both Tory and Okoya to pull him free. What amazed Winston was that Okoya had taken the event in stride—as if he had already come to accept their powers at surface value. If there was one thing about Okoya that Winston liked, it was his refreshing lack of awe.

Winston glanced down at the little book Okoya held. "So, you going to write all this down?"

Okoya shook his head. "It's not a book for writing, it's one for reading."

"Hualapai Wisdom?"

"There's only one kind of wisdom," answered Okoya.

"Can't fit much in a book so thin."

"You'd be surprised."

Winston thought Okoya might give him a glance at it, but instead Okoya just slipped it into a back pocket. Winston grabbed his ankle and pulled his foot up behind him, in a hurdler's stretch. The stitching at the tips of his sneakers popped open. Winston sighed, wondering what size his feet now were.

"How much more do you think you'll grow?" Okoya asked.

"I'll be six foot one, according to the doctors, and they're usually pretty accurate."

"That's not what I mean."

Winston let his foot go, and sat down on a boulder a few feet away, studying Okoya.

"Intellectually, you've moved beyond most of the people in your life, haven't you?" Okoya continued. "Tory must bore you to tears—you're way out of her league."

Winston had to laugh at that. "I'll tell you something, Okoya," he said. "When I was in sixth grade, I had the word 'sycophant' in a spelling bee. Couldn't spell it worth a damn then. But now I could spell it, define it, give you its etymology, and its usage in classic literature. So you might say I'm a little too smart to be won over by flattery."

But Okoya only grinned. "Are you telling me you read the dictionary?"

"Only when I can't sleep."

"You're right, Winston. That's not impressive, it's just strange." And then Okoya became serious, taking a long, invasive look at Winston. "A flatterer thrives on telling lies," Okoya said, "but I observe the truth. So what does that make me?"

Winston thought about the question. Wasn't truth what he quested in everything he read, in all the things he learned? And was it true that he had outgrown Tory, and perhaps all the other shards as well?

"Dangerous," he answered. "It makes you dangerous."

"Truth is never dangerous in the right hands," Okoya said.

They both turned at the sound of skittering pebbles. Tory, still buttoning her blouse, hurried toward them, her pocket radio in hand.

"You have to hear this," she said, turning up the volume.

"Bad news?" asked Winston.

"Just listen."

The radio spat forth a strange news report between bursts of static: *BZZZ BZZZ* . . . *"freak tornado hurled the cabin cruiser"* . . . *BZZZ BZZZ* . . . *"multiple injuries"* . . . *BZZZ BZZZ* . . . *"Pacific Coast Highway"* . . . *BZZZ BZZZ* . . . *"closed in both directions."*

Okoya beamed. "I'll bet your friend Michael did that."

Winston had to admit, it did have all the signs of a Michael Lipranski weather pattern. But what troubled him was the fact that Okoya was so quick to figure it out. Now their companion knew everything about them, but they knew nothing about Okoya. If there was any skill Okoya had perfected, it was that of being a mirror, reflecting back at Tory and Winston their own sordid histories, while evading most conversations about himself.

They continued their journey, cresting the rocky hill ahead, to reveal yet more hills before them, as Winston expected . . . but this time, something was different.

"Looks like we're getting somewhere," Okoya said.

On the ridge of the next hill stood a high chain-link fence, far more daunting than any of the halfhearted barbed-wire they had climbed through. This fence meant business.

"Great," said Tory. "What's next? The Great Wall of China?"

But Winston wasn't listening to her; his eyes were focused ahead on a distant hilltop covered with dense trees far different than the dry scrub that claimed the land around it. There was a building within those trees as well. A large one.

"I know where Dillon is," said Winston, trying to catch his breath from the climb.

"In that house over there?" Tory asked.

"House?! Don't you know what that is?"

"Maybe you should tell us," said Okoya.

Winston kept his eyes locked on the distant hilltop, letting the shiver have its way with his spine. "That's Hearst Castle," he said. "Dillon's in Hearst Castle."

9. SIDESTROKE

NEWSPAPER TYCOON WILLIAM RANDOLPH HEARST BUILT A shrine to himself in the golden hills of San Simeon, California: a glorious castle rising on a hilltop, ten miles from the Pacific shore.

In this palace, the billionaire wined and dined the stars of the twenties and thirties, as well as European royalty. He filled the place top to bottom with million-dollar trinkets . . . and when he died, he didn't take it with him. Now the bizarre sprawling expanse of Hearst Castle fed the tourist economy of California's central coast.

But as of today, it served a completely new purpose. And tourists would not be getting in.

Dillon Cole paced the floor of William Randolf Hearst's private suite, thinking and reviewing, calculating and obsessing, focusing and refocusing all of his attentions on the events exploding around him.

It had been five days since he had been carried from the Columbia River, in the hands of those he had fixed . . . and yet somehow he felt he had never left the river. He was still caught in its waters, floundering—drowning in a current out of his control. What he wanted—what he *needed*—was to get in control of the events spinning around him. He did not want to be worshiped by the stifling crowds drawn to him. He did not want them spreading word of his miraculous acts, and gaining converts to a cult dedicated to the service of Dillon Cole. But his power of cohesion was all too strong, and these people had enveloped him like a tidal wave.

Then a simple lesson in survival came to him.

You never swim against a current.

To survive, you forge a diagonal, slicing sideways until you're clear from danger. So he stopped fighting the needy souls around him, and instead began a slow, sideways crawl.

Once again, he focused his attention on fixing, with a renewed passion. He didn't resist the followers pressing in around him. He let them do what they wanted to do, and when they told him they were taking him to a worthier place, he allowed this siege of the castle—for if his current of followers was determined to carry him to higher ground, fighting them would do no good. *Sidestroke.* He had to keep reminding himself that regardless of what they did, his own focus could not be compromised. He had to keep his energies trained on his repair work. Only by diligent repair could he hope to stave off the insidious downward spiral he now sensed everywhere in the world around him. There were times he prayed to have that burden of sight lifted from him; for to be able to feel all those hairline fractures spreading in the fabric of civilization, was a prescience no one should have to endure.

This morning like every morning, he scoured the newspapers brought to him by his followers, with hopes of finding the nature of the reckoning to come. Although he could sense those fractures in the bulwarks, he still didn't know their cause. There had to be clues—a series of smaller events that might point out to him the form that the great unraveling would take. Would it be a wound that slowly leaked out the world's lifeblood, or would it be a massive hemorrhage from which there could be no recovery?

If the great unraveling had a face—if it had a form—he knew he could beat it. If it were a creature that flew in on dark wings, like his own spirit of destruction, Dillon would find a way to grapple with it . . . But this new sense of doom had no form—it was just a feeling that colored everything he saw in a deepening shade of gray. How could he fight a feeling?

He wasn't quite sure, but at least he knew he wouldn't have to fight it alone. The others were coming. All four of them. He could see their faces in his mind so clearly—he could almost hear their voices. They were close now—he was certain of it. Their help would buffer his own growing sense of futility. With the five of them together again, it would be almost like having Deanna alive again. Almost.

The piles of newspapers were of no help today, and so he dared to take a look at the sports pages—not because he expected to find something earth-shattering there, but because it was something enjoyable, and as he looked through the stats and articles of a hundred teams he had lost track of over the past year, it occurred to him that he could not remember when he had last taken the time for simple human pleasure. He had once been an athletic kid, but he hadn't as much as put on a pair of Rollerblades since he was thirteen. He used to live on Rollerblades before the world had heaved itself onto his shoulders. Days when his hair was a brighter shade of orange, and his parents were alive to worry about the stupid things he did.

A knock resounded from the heavy wooden doors of his museum gallery of a bedroom, and he snapped the sports pages closed, as if taking some time for himself was a criminal activity. The door creaked open, to admit Carol Jessup—the woman whose daughter Dillon had "fixed." She carried a tray of food, and although she was at least ten years his senior, she acted as if Dillon were the elder.

"I brought you something to eat," she said. "We thought you might be hungry."

A chorus of anguished wails blew in the door from elsewhere in the castle. People bellowing in pain. The high stone walls drained the life out of those screams, turning them into the hollow baying of ghosts.

Carol forced a smile, despite the awful sounds.

"More work for you," she said. "They're being brought to the Gothic Study—would you like to see?"

"No!" snapped Dillon. "I'll see enough of them later."

The woman put down the tray. "If there's anything you need—anything at all . . ."

"Yeah," said Dillon. "How about a pair of Rollerblades, and a retake of the last four years?"

"Excuse me?"

"Never mind," he told her. "Thanks for the food. You can go now."

She nodded her head respectfully and quietly turned to leave, then turned back to him. "Oh, one more thing," she said. "Three youngsters arrived, claiming to be friends of yours."

Dillon snapped his eyes to the woman so severely, she gasped and took a step back.

"What?! Where are they?" He had sensed they were close, but hadn't realized how close.

"Well . . . uh . . . we've been questioning them," she stammered. "They do seem suspicious . . ."

Dillon stormed toward the door. "Where are they?"

"We only wanted to protect you."

"Just tell me where they are!"

"The Assembly Room."

And since Dillon had no idea where that might be, he had her lead the way, ignoring the mournful moans escaping from deeper in the castle.

THE ASSEMBLY ROOM was a great hall festooned with gold statues and exquisite tapestries. Flames filled an immense fireplace, large enough to be the mouth of a cavern, and the moment he entered, the flames wavered, and the two figures standing before him seemed to sway, as if suddenly blasted by the power of Dillon's presence. He recognized them right away, in spite of how different they looked from when he had last seen them: Winston so much taller; Tory's skin so clean.

He approached them cautiously, as if the creak of every floorboard could be the trigger of a mine.

Winston spoke up first. "I was going to ask how you managed to take over Hearst Castle, but, hell, you're Dillon Cole," he said with a sneer. "You can get away with anything."

Dillon offered him the slightest grin. "Almost anything."

He was met with an uncomfortable silence. They were waiting for an explanation. Why had he called out to them? What were they doing here? Dillon didn't know where to begin.

"I know this is going to sound strange," Dillon finally said, "but you can't imagine how much I've missed you."

They didn't answer to that; the feeling was clearly *not* mutual.

"That's all right," said Dillon. "After what I've put you through, I'm surprised you came looking for me at all." Then a third guest who Dillon had not noticed before, stepped forward from the dim shadows of the corner. This wasn't one of the shards. It was a stranger with dark eyes, high cheekbones, and black hair that ran smoothly from his head and down his spine. "Do I know you?"

"You will," said the dark-eyed stranger.

"Okoya hooked up with us in New Mexico," said Tory.

He reached out and shook Dillon's hand, keeping those dark eyes locked on his. The stranger's grip was firm, but the skin supple.

Dillon felt the bite of fingernails that were a fraction of an inch too long against the back of his hand. "I've become a big admirer of yours," said Okoya.

"I have too many of those." Dillon turned to the Jessups who guarded the door. "I'd like to be left alone with my friends," Dillon told them, but the couple was reluctant to go.

"Are you sure that's wise?" said Mrs. Jessup.

"We don't know these people," said her husband.

"They're not respectful of you."

"They're not in awe of you."

"What if they mean to hurt you?"

"We could never allow that."

"Just shut up and go," Dillon told them.

"We'll be right outside," Mr. Jessup said. "If there's anything that you need—anything at all . . ." Then the couple left, swinging the huge wooden doors shut.

"Some group of happy campers you got here," said Tory.

Dillon chuckled ruefully. "Happy Campers. Yeah, that's exactly what they are."

"So if everyone's so thrilled to be here," asked Winston, "where's all that moaning coming from? And don't tell me it's just the wind."

Dillon thought about how he might answer that question. He could try to explain it in a calm, rational way, and sort of ease them into it . . . but decided it was best to let them see it with their own eyes. Then maybe they'd understand how badly Dillon needed their help.

"I'll take you there," Dillon said. Winston and Tory didn't seem too keen on the idea, but they went along. Unfortunately Okoya thought this was an open invitation. Dillon had to step into Okoya's path to stop his momentum.

"I'm sorry, but you can't come."

There was a flash of ice in Okoya's gaze that was quickly replaced by an apologetic smile. "Of course not," Okoya said. "Actually, I was hoping to explore the castle."

Dillon nodded, relieved. "If anyone tries to stop you, tell them you have my personal permission."

"Your name strikes fear into their hearts," said Okoya with a grin. "I like that about you."

Dillon laughed, thinking it was a joke. But when he thought about it later, he wasn't so sure.

10. DEATH'S DOORSTEP

THE GOTHIC STUDY WAS A STEP BEYOND NIGHTMARE. THE dark arches of its vaulted ceiling gave one the uneasy sense of being trapped in the hull of a capsized ship. The walls were lined with aging, dust-coated volumes, and the entire room had become an ad hoc repository of misery: the diseased; the dying; the ones hopelessly broken by life. The floor was filled with almost thirty desperate souls suffering in pain and anguish.

Winston and Tory turned their eyes away, but Dillon did not. He had surrendered his disgust long ago.

"Every day, my 'Happy Campers' bring me people to fix," he told them. "There's more and more each day."

There was a man before them with multiple leg fractures, who appeared to have been hijacked right from the scene of an accident. "I suppose I've made some converts of the local paramedics, and emergency-room doctors. They've started to secretly divert patients my way."

The wounded man looked up at them in weak terror, not even knowing why he was there.

"There's some people I can help, and others I can't," Dillon said. "Because there are some things I just can't do . . . That's why I need you."

Winston shook his head. "I . . . I can't do things like that—I can't."

"You can, and you know it," said Dillon. "I'm sure you helped a lot of people back home."

"By accident," snapped Winston. "Never on purpose!"

"Somehow," said Dillon, "I thought you would have grown wiser. Wisdom does come along with your gift, doesn't it?"

"Maybe I'm wise enough to know not to screw with things I don't understand."

Tory's eyes drifted to a man across the room whose hacking, liquid cough spoke of tuberculosis.

Like Winston, she had never actively sought to cure the ills of the world around her—as if she had no right to willfully use her power. But faced with the misery before her, it seemed selfish and cruel to stand there and do nothing. And maybe it would make her feel better about herself. Cleaner.

She made her way across the room to the coughing man, and began gently massaging his fiery throat and inflamed chest. "Am I doing this right?" she called back to Dillon, but Dillon had no answer, because he had no idea. In less than a minute, however, the man was breathing easier, as the disease drained from his lungs.

Dillon led the reluctant Winston across the room. "They keep bringing me people with lost limbs . . . but I have to send them away," Dillon told him. "I can fix broken bones, but I can't fix something that's not even there."

They stopped before a man with bandages on his knees, and nothing but air where the rest of his legs should have been. His dressings had already been removed.

"A human being is not a tree!" Winston shouted. "You don't just regenerate a new limb out of thin air. It's against the laws of nature."

Dillon took a step closer. "So break the law."

Winston shuddered out a sickened breath, then knelt down to the legless man, realizing, as Tory had, that his own conscience left him no choice. "Dillon, have I ever told you how much I hate you?"

Dillon nodded. "Maybe we can fix that, too."

"Please," begged the man. "Please take me back to the hospital."

Winston looked at the raw stumps, where swollen flesh was pulled tight by heavy sutures. "What happened to you?"

The man grimaced. "I need morphine!"

"Was it an accident?"

"You kids are crazy! What are you doing here? What are you doing?! I need my medication!"

"Shh." Winston bit back his own revulsion, and pressed his hands forward. He had seen his share of charismatic evangelists lay hands on the infirmed, pronouncing them healed to the cheers of a wide-eyed flock. But this—this would be something very different. Because not even the most brazen of faith healers claimed the ability to put back that which the good Lord had taken away.

Winston focused his attention on the man's left stump, where his fingertips gently touched it. It took about a minute to see the flesh begin to swell—the stump to elongate almost imperceptibly. The skin gathered by the sutures began to stretch as new growth pushed on them from the inside. The sutures burst, but rather than spilling forth gore, new folds of flesh unfolded from within the wound, slowly inflating with bone and muscle. And Winston suddenly found himself smiling, no longer repulsed, but rather thrilled with himself and this ability he had never dared to tap; consumed by the magnitude of his own power.

TEN MILES AWAY, crowds of angry tourists packed around the ticket booth at the Hearst Castle Visitors Center, when a weather system bore down on them from the north. In moments, the sky turned gray, and the wind blew bone-cold.

Three teenagers drove up in a stolen car. The two in the front seemed anxious. The one in the back was dead.

"The castle's closed for repairs," the parking attendant told them. "You can take the garden tour, but you can't get inside the castle."

Lourdes looked out of her window to the long lines by the ticket booth. Hours' worth of lines.

"We have to get inside!" Michael blurted out. "He's in there!"

The parking attendant looked at him curiously. "Who's in there?"

Lourdes watched as Michael stammered helplessly. Her beloved Michael never had a head for strategy in tight situations. He either stormed too hard, bringing about disaster, or blew an ineffectual wind in the midst of panic. *That's why he needs me—to get him through the hardest times*, thought Lourdes. *He needs me for that and much, much more. He must realize that by now.* She threw a glance to the backseat, and pulled the blanket over an exposed edge of Drew's body. She didn't know what had set off Michael's lethal tantrum, and although Drew's death was a bitter pill for them to swallow, Lourdes resolved not to dwell on it right now. They couldn't abandon his body, nor could they bring him home. That meant they would have to bury him themselves—a grim prospect Lourdes was not ready to consider.

"Is there a problem here?" the attendant asked, beginning to notice Drew's lack of animation.

"No problem at all," said Lourdes. "Pleasant dreams"—and the guard collapsed to the ground with a thud and the skitter of loose gravel.

Lourdes then turned toward the crowds, concentrated, and pushed forth an airborne nerve impulse. It struck all the tourists in the lot, and they fell to the ground like a collection of rag dolls in Hawaiian shirts.

Michael turned to her, flabbergasted. It was the first time he had seen how her powers had grown. Clearly he was impressed. "Lourdes, what did you do?"

"I put them all to sleep."

"For how long?"

Lourdes shrugged. "It depends on how tired they were."

They locked the gate behind them to deter new tourists, then drove up the winding road to the castle.

FROM THE COASTLINE, Hearst Castle appeared small and insignificant, but the closer one got, the more its audacious majesty came into focus. It had the semblance of a great Spanish cathedral—a four-story Castile, between two bell towers shimmering with blue-and-gold tile.

Tourists flocked the palatial grounds around the castle and guest houses, chattering to one another, and taking snapshots, but the doors to every entrance of La Casa Grande—the great castle itself—were closed to visitors.

A pair of guards were posted on either side of the wrought-iron gates. One of them shifted position, just enough to display the weapon holstered on his waist.

"I'm sorry," he said, eyeing Michael and Lourdes as they approached. "The castle is closed until further notice."

"We're here to see Dillon Cole," said Michael.

"He's expecting us," Lourdes added. "Or at least he should be."

The guards reacted instantly, looking to one another, not sure what to do.

"Are you one of us?"

"No," said Winston. "We're one of *him*."

The guards considered the prospect fearfully. "Yes," they said, swinging the gates open to admit them. "He has been expecting you."

The interior of the castle was spectacularly overdone, from the Louis XIV armoires, to the Ming dynasty vases. The entire castle mocked itself at every turn with self-conscious opulence. Men and women stood at every threshold, like an unofficial security gauntlet, and Lourdes had the distinct feeling they were passing through layer after layer of protection that surrounded Dillon and his inner sanctum. Until finally, a door opened before them, and they stepped from paradise . . . into Hell.

Michael had hoped to see no more carnage today, but here before his eyes, was a room full of people who weren't much better off than Drew. Michael had to cover his ears from the awful sounds of anguish around him.

"Madre de Dios!" gasped Lourdes. "What happened here?" Then Michael caught sight of Dillon tending to a woman whose many wounds had left her a bloody mess. Winston and Tory were there, too—both of them as focused as surgeons, as they moved around the room.

Dillon caught sight of them, but didn't bother to greet them. "Good. You're here!" he said, as someone closed the door behind them, pushing them off the threshold and into the room.

"Michael!" shouted Dillon. "These people here are way too stressed, and it's getting in the way. Can you do something about it?"

But Michael could only stand there with his jaw dropped; his own sense of panic infusing the patients like a lightning storm, adding to the chaos.

"I *said*, can you do something about it?!"

Suddenly, Michael realized he had been here before. It was the "emergency-room dream." Michael would walk through a door, and find himself an surgeon, in the midst of mortal chaos, with absolutely no medical knowledge. His anxiety continued to sky-rocket.

With nothing but dead air from Michael, Dillon turned his

attention to Lourdes. "Lourdes, could you do something about their pain?"

"Wh–what should I do?"

Across the room, Winston left one patient, and moved on to another. "C'mon, Lourdes," Winston said. "If we can do this, so can you!"

The panic in the room continued to build as the patients continued to resonate Michael's emotional distress. Around them, people began to squirm and scramble to their feet, trying to flee.

"Michael, stop it!" shouted Tory. "You're only making it worse!" Michael could feel his own state of terror stab into the hearts of those assembled, creating greater and greater panic. Lately, making bad situations worse had become a specialty of Michael's. He wasn't about to let his own shortcomings ruin the efforts of the others, so he spun on his heels, and pushed his way out of the room, slamming the doors closed behind him.

In the hallway, he leaned against the cold marble balustrade, and sunk to the floor, dropping his head into his hands. Back in Newport Beach, his emotions had been in tight control for so long—but now they flew rabid and reckless.

Those emotions had snuffed the life out of Drew, who even now grew colder in the backseat of the stolen car. And what would Michael do about *that*? Send a body bag to Drew's parents, with his deepest apologies? Somehow, Michael doubted Hallmark had a sentiment for "Sorry I killed your son."

From beyond the closed doors, Michael could hear the cries of pain fade away. What was Lourdes doing? he wondered. Putting them to sleep? Was she regulating strained hearts and administering some sort of psychic anesthesia?

At least she could give them respite from their pain, but for Michael there was no such relief.

"Something wrong?"

Michael looked up to see someone leaning against a column a few yards down the hall. Michael pointed to the closed door of Dillon's little operating room. "Take a look in that madhouse, and ask me again."

"I was asking about you."

"Nothing wrong with me a nice long coma couldn't cure."

The stranger took a step closer, whistling a tune that seemed familiar, but Michael could not quite place it. "Want to talk about it?"

"Not really."

Then the stranger sat down beside him. "No one with that much trouble in their eyes can be quiet for long."

Michael was about to get up and leave, when the stranger began to whistle that tune again. It frustrated Michael that he couldn't quite place it. He turned and for the first time really saw the stranger's face. There was something odd about it. His curiosity kept him from leaving.

"No point in talking," said Michael. "Thanks anyway."

"Poor Michael," mocked the stranger. "The other shards won't let you play."

Michael bristled. "Who the hell are you, and how do you know my name?"

"Tory and Winston speak of you so often, I feel as if I already know you. Although you seem far less shifty than they made you out to be."

"Shifty? They said I'm shifty?"

The stranger sat beside him. "Deeply troubled."

Michael felt a seed of anger, and resentment toward the others begin to take root. And he let it, finding that the resentment felt good. "Yeah, well, they're the ones who are troubled. Bottomless pits, if you ask me."

"Perhaps they're not the friends you think they are."

Michael studied the stranger, trying to divine what he was getting at, but he only grinned, as if he were the one with Michael's best interests at heart.

"Maybe, maybe not."

Michael studied the face a moment longer, until he finally realized what had seemed so strange. "What are you anyway?" Michael asked. "A guy or girl?"

The stranger shrugged. "Which do you prefer?"

Michael had to laugh at that. "Neither," he said.

"Tell me your troubles. Maybe I can bring you some peace."

And although Michael hadn't cared to discuss it, he found himself spilling his guts into the patient ears of this strange new friend.

★   ★   ★

IN THE CROWDED space of the Gothic Study, Dillon, Tory, Lourdes, and Winston worked their curious magic. Dillon set broken bones, and sent the most malignant of tumors into spontaneous remission, while Lourdes doused pain, and steadied the rhythms of failing hearts. Tory set up one sterile field after another, while Winston regenerated organs, limbs, and nerve pathways that had, until now, been irretrievably lost.

The patients began this triage in terror and confusion, but as the numbers of the healed increased, the fear was subjugated by astonishment. Restored patients became an awed audience, watching as the four worked their wonders on the rest.

It was over in less than an hour, and when they were done, the room was a joyous gathering of healthy people.

The doors were swung open wide to let them out.

"But we don't want to go!" they clamored. "We want to stay here. With you . . . with *all* of you!" And so the Happy Campers at the door led them away, to find them all a place in Dillon's perfect order.

Winston, Lourdes, and Tory had expected to find nothing but misery once they found Dillon—and although he did show them misery, he had also shown them misery's end. As the last of the new recruits left the room, Michael stepped in, looking pale and oppressed, with Okoya lingering in the shadows, just beyond the door.

Michael opened his mouth to say something, but Lourdes cut him off.

"Michael, it was incredible," she said, throwing her arms around him. "You missed everything!"

"I knew I affected people, but it was never like that!" said Winston. "The things I was able to do in there . . ."

"It's because we're together," suggested Tory. "Together we're greater than the sum of our parts."

The others took a moment to consider this, dazzled by the magnitude of the thought. How great were they, really? How much greater could they become?

Dillon, however, remained unimpressed. "This was just one day's work. There'll be more tomorrow," he said, as he straightened out chairs and benches.

"But why?" Tory asked. "Why will there be more? Why are we doing this?"

"Because we *can*," offered Lourdes.

"Not because we can," said Dillon. "But because we *have* to . . . There's so much I need to tell you, I don't know where to start."

And then, finally, Michael forced out what he had been trying to say since he had ventured into the room. "I know where to start," he said. There was a lump in his throat, and the words came out muted. "Okoya and I just brought a friend of mine in from the car . . ."

"Oh no . . . Drew!" gasped Lourdes.

"Before we do anything," Michael said, "I want to give him a decent burial."

Dillon regarded Michael curiously. "Burial?"

"Isn't that what you normally do with dead people?" Michael spat out.

"No," said Dillon. "Actually, it's not."

RUNNING! SPRINTING!

A nameless runner charging backward through a blind race.

He could not remember the moment before—all he could do was feel the motion as he moved across an impossible distance. The space around him stretched like a piece of elastic, until it seemed like . . . a tunnel. He was running backward through a tunnel. The journey lasted only a moment longer, and then he awoke with a single thought in his mind, so powerful that he had to speak aloud. It was who he was. It was his name.

"DREW CAMDEN!" The sound of his own voice woke him, his mind charged and fully alert. He opened his eyes to find himself in the soft light of a strange, octagonal room. The ceiling was inlaid gold, the four-poster bed on which he lay was gold, and soft golden light poured in through windows covered with delicately patterned grills.

"Welcome to the Celestial Suite."

The voice was unfamiliar. Drew sat up, but the speaker had left. Drew only caught a flicker of his red hair as he exited, on his way down the stairs.

But Michael was there, standing and staring.

A pang of regret—a pang of sorrow—came to Drew as he recalled the last time they had seen each other, but he chose not to face that. Not now.

"It's like I've died and gone to heaven," said Drew, throwing his gaze around the Celestial Suite.

"You may have," said Michael, "but now you're here."

"What happened?"

"I killed you," Michael said. "And Dillon brought you back."

There was a pause, as Drew tried to process that bit of information. Finally, Michael said, "Dinner's at seven. Come on down if you're hungry." And he left Drew alone in the eight-sided room, with the faces of more than a dozen statues staring at him, as if waiting to see what he was going to do now.

11. LIFE IN THE KEY OF D

"LAST YEAR, AFTER YOU ALL LEFT," DILLON BEGAN, "I found that I could repair as well as I could ruin, and the more I fixed, the better I got."

The Billiard Room, like most of the rooms in the castle, had a stone yawn of a fireplace, and walls covered in medieval tapestries. Dillon didn't have much use for the room, but it was less intimidating than the vaulted expanse of the Assembly Room, which was far too imposing a place to speak of imposing things.

"Death isn't an easy thing to reverse," Dillon explained, "but I've had practice." He didn't tell them how much practice it had taken. How, at first, he would have to hold corpses in his arms for hours, until the decay gave way to living flesh once more, and their spirits were coaxed back into being. Those were memories better left unshared.

Michael tried to play a game of pool, but his hands shook so much that he missed the cue ball. "Do you need a license to raise the dead, or is that just for cars and guns?"

Winston stood at the far end of the room. Although he had gotten taller, he was dwarfed by the statues on either side. "So now you're in the resurrection business?"

Dillon grimaced, his mind running to find a less loaded euphemism. "Let's just say I charge people's batteries."

The thought brought a collective shiver to the room, which made Dillon angry. "Is it so different from what the rest of you have been doing?" He turned to Michael. "I've been hearing about strange weather systems in southern California. Is that where you've been, Michael?"

Michael hesitated before hitting the cue ball. "Yeah . . . so?"

Dillon turned to Tory. "The dropping crime rate in Miami

keeps making national news. Somehow I don't think it's because of good police work."

Tory looked away. "It's just something that happens," she said. "It was never intentional."

Dillon glanced at Winston and Lourdes, who both looked away, making it clear that they were guilty of some power play as well.

"You've all been out there," said Dillon. "So don't act like I'm any different from you."

"What you do is . . . bigger," Tory said.

Then a voice spoke out from the corner. "Yes—but let's not be fearful of it. Isn't that what you're saying, Dillon?"

It was Okoya. Until now, Okoya had remained a distant observer. In fact, Dillon had forgotten he was there. Okoya was the only one unfazed, reclining comfortably in a plush lounge chair, as if he were William Randolph Hearst himself. He seemed to carry himself like someone born to royalty: such smooth, elegant composure. Dillon wanted to ask Okoya to leave, but Okoya seemed too much of an ally right now. Instead Dillon turned to the others.

"Okoya's right. You can't let it scare you. There's enough people acting strangely around here—at least we could treat each other as if we were normal."

Winston strode closer. "Don't you think there's a reason for them to act strangely? You bring back the dead, you take over a national landmark to play house, and you let all your followers think you're God at sixteen—"

"What *they* think is *their* problem!" snapped Dillon.

"No, it's *yours*," Winston said.

"I don't see a problem."

It was Okoya again. They all turned to him, still reclining in the velvet lounge. His voice was quiet, but commanding. Dillon found himself completely upstaged.

"It's human nature to find divinity in anything greater than oneself," Okoya said. "If they see you as gods, what harm does that do? And besides, their devotion can be used."

"I don't like it," muttered Winston.

"Get used to it," said Okoya. "I would say that your time of hiding is over."

Lourdes sauntered closer to Okoya. "You're pretty accepting of all of this. Aren't you the least bit surprised, or shocked by what you've seen here today?"

Okoya pulled himself up from the lounge, to face them eye-to-eye. "Acceptance is the advantage of an open mind."

"I'm not impressed by your fortune-cookie sentiments, Okoya," said Winston.

"All right, then. Maybe I'm so calm about it because I've always suspected I'd find myself in the shadow of greatness. And being here with all of you feels like coming home."

Dillon pushed his way in front of the others. "And exactly where is home?"

"Hualapai Nation," answered Okoya. "But you already know that."

"Somehow," said Dillon, "I suspect you're a much longer way from there than you'd care to let on."

"I've traveled," Okoya said. "And you'd be wise not to grill someone who comes to you in good faith. It's the sign of a weak leader."

The comment stung Dillon far more than he thought it would—and yet there was something refreshing in it: that after the constant acquiescence of the Happy Campers, here was a personality that actually challenged him. Dillon caught himself grinning, and Okoya returned it. It served to make the others uneasy.

"You still haven't told us why you've dragged us into this nasty game," Winston asked him. Dillon broke eye contact with Okoya, and turned back to the others.

"It's got to be more than just trauma care," said Tory.

"You're right," admitted Dillon, "there is more. I called to you . . . I *gathered* you back together, because it's the only way to fix what's gone wrong."

Winston took a breath for a loud rebuttal, but his brain must have hooked around what Dillon had said. Winston hesitated for a moment, then spoke in a worried whisper.

"What do you mean—'gone wrong'?"

The other shards had moved closer now, pressing in around the billiard table. Dillon took a deep breath to calm himself.

"Five days ago, I swam the Columbia River," he told them,

"and from the moment I climbed out, I felt a shift in the patterns around me . . . Patterns of the present . . . and the future. Suddenly I felt everyone and everything begin a long spiral toward a very dark place."

"You never killed your parasite," Tory reminded Dillon. "Maybe that's what you sensed. Maybe that *thing* has found a way back into this world, and it's starting to destroy again."

"No," Dillon said. "No—if it came back, I'd know it. This is something different. Maybe something worse."

"What could be worse than *that*?" asked Lourdes.

"All I know," said Dillon, "is that the first domino is down. Freak events are going to start piling on top of each other, and then one day, people are going to wake up to find that there *is* no order anymore."

"The apocalypse is supposed to have *four* horsemen," grumbled Winston. "Not five."

"We're not ringing it in, Winston," said Tory. "I think Dillon has a plan to prevent it. Is that what you're saying, Dillon?"

"I think there's a chance, if we're all together."

"But we're not all together," Winston reminded them.

Dillon looked away. He didn't need to be reminded of how incomplete they were without Deanna—how incomplete *he* was.

"It's the best we can do," he said.

"So, if I'm seeing this right," said Michael, "you want us all to bust our asses fixing *whatever* we can, and *whoever* we can . . . and that way, we might keep things from tanking?"

"Bail out the *Titanic*?" said Lourdes.

Dillon grinned. "With a big enough bucket."

Tory came over to him. "You've changed, Dillon," she said.

"I like to think so." Then he picked up a cue stick, and stroked the cue ball. It struck the other balls, sending the solid colors ricocheting around the table, until they had all found a pocket. The eight ball was the last one to drop.

"Show-off," mumbled Michael.

Dillon turned to Okoya. If Okoya had an opinion, he wasn't sharing it. Their exotic guest offered little more than an enigmatic smile. *Does he approve, or disapprove?* Dillon wondered. *And why do I care?* That was the question that troubled him more.

IF THE WORLD was winding down, it didn't seem to dampen anyone's spirit over dinner. Michael noted that the mood in the Refectory was more festive than foreboding, and he didn't quite know what to make of it. A legion of Dillon's Happy Campers did everything short of sponge-bathing them to make them feel comfortable, and although the attention felt odd at first, Michael found himself becoming accustomed to it remarkably quickly.

They sat together at a table large enough to seat two dozen, and were served a feast fit for kings. Michael had tried to sandwich himself between Dillon and Tory, but somehow Lourdes still managed to squeeze her seat next to his. Michael watched as she ate conspicuously small portions, and loudly denied seconds. It was all for Michael's sake, of course—to let him know that her obesity, and any hints of gluttony were gone forever. As if her new blossomed beauty could tip the scales, and make him fall madly in love with her—which was about as unlikely as him falling in love with the reanimated Drew.

Michael tried to forget about it and listen to the dinner conversation.

"I hate to admit it," Winston was saying, "but maybe Dillon's started something here that should have happened as soon as we converged the first time. I mean, for the last year, all I've been doing is 'dealing' with things. The tree that uprooted my house, the branches growing through the windows, the neighbors who were afraid to look me in the face; and that's all I did: deal."

The door to the kitchen opened, and five dutiful workers brought in the next course, setting it before them on Hearst's most expensive china.

"After the things we did today," said Tory, "the things we did together—I can't go back to living the way I did before. Okoya's right; our time of hiding is over."

Michael tried to imagine himself as the world's Peace Bringer; a great soul sent to calm the skies and raise the spirits of the downtrodden. Certainly he had done some of that back home, but he was only playing, really. He wondered how far his power over the natures could go, if he allowed it. How many minds and emotions could he bring into harmony, if he set himself to the task?

"You know," said Michael, "I could really get off, spending my life tweaking people into tune."

"And what about you, Dillon?" said Tory. "I mean, look at all the people who died too young, who could change the world if you brought them back: Martin Luther King, JFK, Princess Di . . . Don't you ever think about that?"

"Yes" said Dillon, between bites of his steak. "Remind me to show you my list."

DILLON LEFT BEFORE dessert, and Michael used Dillon's exit as a chance to escape the table as well. He took a plate of food with him.

Drew wasn't in the Celestial Suite, and while the helpful hordes around Michael leapt at the opportunity to be of assistance, none of them knew where to find him.

Michael found Drew sitting on a stone bench in the basement, in a sort of self-imposed exile. It was a mournful place of unrestored artifacts—wounded statues, torn tapestries—and Michael wondered if Dillon's presence in the halls up above would, in time, mend these forlorn relics the way his aura restored most everything else. Still, no amount of restoration would stop the basement from resembling a dungeon.

When Drew saw Michael, he quickly stood up and made himself look busy, studying the objects around him.

"Hearst must have been a maniac," Drew said casually. "Half the art in the world is in this place."

Michael reached the bottom of the steps, and handed Drew the plate of food.

"It's cold," Drew deadpanned, but Michael sensed his gratitude nonetheless. The food's aroma chased away the mossy stench of the basement walls, and added the slightest degree of comfort to the situation. Still Michael kept a few feet of distance between them, lodging his hands firmly in his pockets, while Drew sat down to eat.

"So," said Michael, "how's life?"

Drew ate hungrily. "Better than death."

Michael ventured a step closer. "What was it like?" asked Michael. "Being dead, I mean."

"There was a lot of tofu and new-age music."

Michael grinned. "You must have gone to Hell."

Drew pondered his plate for a moment. "Actually, I don't remember anything at all. It's as if my mind went through an air lock between here and there. You know what they say: 'You can't take it with you.' I suppose you can't bring it back, either."

Michael finally sat beside Drew on the steps, which was about as awkward as anything Michael had ever done. He kept trying to kill the silence with some meaningful words, something truthful that didn't sound trite, but all that came out were false starts.

"You must hate me in a major way," Drew finally said.

Michael tried to run a little mental subroutine to see if he could find hatred in there. But that was a feeling as absent as love.

"No," Michael told him, "I just feel . . . tricked."

"Yeah. I'm good at that," said Drew. "I even trick myself sometimes." Drew took a few moments to compose his thoughts, and became uncharacteristically serious.

"I never meant the mind-screw." Drew said. "And if it means anything—I really am your friend. The other feeling . . . well, it slipped in when I wasn't looking."

"Yeah—well, as long as it doesn't slip in while *I'm* not looking."

Drew grimaced and chalked his finger in the air. "Point for you. I walked into that one with both feet, didn't I?"

Drew picked through the remnants of his meal, then put the plate down. Even the gentle clatter of the plate on the bench echoed hollowly off the stone walls. Michael found himself filled with questions that he didn't want answered, so he just sat there, looking down at the dusty floor.

"Hell, everyone's got some glitch, right?" Drew said with a smile. "So I figure this is mine."

"And I always thought you were glitchless."

Drew chuckled. "Perfection on three legs, right? Big man on campus. The track coach would have a cow if he knew. Shit, he'd have a whole herd!"

"Your parents know?"

"For about a year."

"Is it bad?"

Drew shrugged. "They kind of treat me like I'm the murderer

of their future grandchildren, but most of the time it's okay . . ." Drew looked up, turning his eyes to a faded tapestry, rather than looking at Michael. "Last week was bad, though," he said. "My father, who never usually talks about it, starts telling me about some guy he found who could 'straighten me out.' You know—like all I need is a good chiropractor. Anyway, I went ballistic, he retaliated, and that's how I ended up at your house that night."

Michael swallowed hard, remembering the troubled man who had come to visit him that same day: The man asking Michael to change his son's nature. The man who must have been Drew's father.

Drew shook his head as he thought about it, and laughed. "Now my parents probably think that I ran off to join the queer circus."

"Maybe you should go home."

"No," said Drew quickly. "How could I leave after seeing what you are—what your friends are? How could I ever go back?"

Michael shuddered to think of Drew as one of the Happy Campers.

"What if I kept a journal for you?" suggested Drew. "A record of all the things that happen from here on in. Anything . . . so I can be a part of this."

Michael forced himself to look in Drew's eyes. It wasn't Drew's usual coolness there—instead there was a whole squadron of emotions, and his feelings for Michael were still a potent part of the mix.

I can live with this, Michael told himself. *If I can part the skies, I can deal with Drew being in love with me, can't I?*

Still Michael felt anxious to get away. He collected Drew's plate and turned to go—but before he did, he had to ask Drew the question. The one question he wanted to ask from the moment Dillon had brought him back.

"Drew . . . If you had the choice—would you want to be straight?"

Drew threw Michael an icy look, as if trying to read where the question was coming from. "Yeah, and if I had the choice I'd piss Pepsi, too, but that's not gonna happen, is it?" Drew held his annoyed gaze a moment more, then just let it go. "Some things you don't get to choose." And that was all Drew said about it.

Michael understood Drew's answer, but he doubted Drew understood why Michael had asked. So Michael didn't push it. Instead he left Drew alone, with a single thought to consider.

"Actually," said Michael, "Dillon could make you piss Pepsi."

DILLON HAD THOUGHT the arrival of the others would give him some peace of mind—he had hoped that somehow the suffocating sense of doom would disappear—but the pall had not lifted, and now Dillon wondered if his fixing frenzy was just an exercise in futility.

If Deanna were here, she'd know what to do, and have the strength to do it. If Deanna were here, we might not even be in this mess.

He left dinner early, unable to bear her conspicuous absence. Then he wandered the castle, trying to map it out in his mind, so he wouldn't feel so consumed by its vastness.

Deanna was lost in a place like this.

And that single thought made it impossible for him to explore, for now he could hear her voice in the eerie echos of La Casa Grande. He could hear her screaming, as she had screamed in the days when her spirit of fear suffocated her. Then he would hear the gentleness of her patient, fearless voice, the way she had been at the end.

As he climbed the stairs toward the kingly suite they had claimed for him, the followers he passed lowered their eyes and stepped aside, as if unworthy of being in his company. At the entrance to his suite, sat an armed guard, who proudly protected Dillon's door, and beside him sat Carol Jessup. She must have taken the role of his personal maidservant. They launched to their feet the moment they saw him, offering him the most courteous of greetings.

Am I doing any of this right, Deanna? he asked in his thoughts, as if she were somehow with him, instead of a whole universe away. *Am I anywhere close to getting things under control?*

The answer came in the form of two dozen cardboard boxes, piled everywhere as he entered his room.

"We weren't sure of your size," Carol apologized, "or the style you wanted . . ."

Dillon need only glimpse the face of a single colorful box to know what was inside every one of them.

Rollerblades.

Pair after pair of Rollerblades.

"You did ask for them, didn't you?"

Dillon was suddenly glad he hadn't eaten much, because he could feel dinner on its way back up.

12. THE TOOLS OF A THIEF

THE BRINGER COULD NOT RAISE THE DEAD. NOR COULD HE banish disease, numb pain, or whip winds into weapons of destruction. But he was a formidable spirit with a crushing power of will. The skills he did not possess would be his to wield soon enough, though—and the thought of it brought an irrepressible grin to his face as he moved through the towering halls of the castle.

Those he passed smiled a return greeting, obviously assuming that his was the joyous grin of surrender—the same surrender that painted all of their faces, now that they were in service to the Shards.

Okoya strolled at a calm, deliberate pace through the lavish corridors, running his hands across the tapestries and sculptures—noting the eons of art and civilization born during his three-thousand-year hiatus. But his thoughts were on weightier subjects.

Five Shards!

And each one greater than the Olympian king who had ordered him chained to the mountain! A quintet of diamonds too bright to behold . . .

. . . And too powerful to devour.

These were souls too large to feast upon—and although his hunger was great, he hid it from the five. These were spirits to master and control—not spirits to dine on. These Shards could be useful tools for the harvesting of a world . . .

But as with any tool, there were dangers. Spirits of such power needed to be broken and harnessed like horses before the chariot—and if a horse could not be broken, it had to be destroyed, lest it turn on it master.

But so far, things were going exceptionally well. The Bringer had already begun to watch and listen—seeking out weaknesses into which he could insert his will, like a hand into a puppet. Deep enough so that he could either play them or crush them—whichever ultimately suited his needs.

The Bringer stepped out into a calm night, and there, on the steps of the castle's front gate, sat a man in the uniform of law enforcement. His head was cupped in his hands like a small child. Curious, the Bringer sat beside him.

"My name is Okoya," said the Bringer. "Spiritual advisor to the stars."

The man looked straight ahead at the fountain, and spoke as if carrying on a conversation with himself. "What am I supposed to tell them? How can I tell them anything?"

"Tell who?"

"I'm with the county sheriff," he said. "They got word of something suspicious at the castle, so they sent me here to check it out. Then, when I got here, they brought me to that redheaded kid."

"And he 'fixed' something?"

"He just *said* something," the deputy told Okoya. "I don't even remember what he said, but suddenly . . . suddenly . . ."

"Suddenly all that was wrong with your life fell into place."

The deputy finally looked at Okoya. "Yes! Yes, that's right!" Tears welled up in his eyes. "How can I turn him in?"

"You won't," the Bringer instructed. "You'll return to your office, report that nothing is wrong, then you'll quietly collect your family and join us."

When it was put to him so plainly, like a clear-cut set of orders, it wasn't a hard decision to make.

"Yes, that *is* what I'll do," he said—as if he had any choice in the matter. The fact was, from the moment Dillon received him, the pattern of this man's destiny was set. It was a pattern even the Bringer could read.

The officer stood to return to his squad car, but Okoya grabbed him by the arm.

"Just one more thing."

The man turned his eyes to Okoya, and Okoya silently, secretly, lashed out. Fine tendrils of pink light shot from Okoya's eyes, dancing across the officer's face, penetrating the pores of his skin. The tendrils reached way down, and drained out the very thing that made the man human:

His consciousness.

His essence.

His soul.

The Bringer devoured this man's life force—just as he had done to many residents of Shiprock, New Mexico, and a string of others between there and here. Each one small but satisfying, like a plate of hors d'oeuvres.

When it was done, the living shell of the county deputy stumbled for an instant, unable to know or understand what had been torn from him.

"Whoa—must have gotten up too fast," the man's shell said, regaining its balance. "Now, what was it you wanted to tell me?"

Okoya let go of his arm. "It wasn't important."

The officer nodded a quick farewell, and returned to his squad car, never knowing that, although his body went through the motions, he was as lifeless a vessel as the car he drove.

Okoya watched him go, wondering how many human souls he could devour in a single day without feeling too terribly bloated. Forty? Fifty? He'd have to find out.

His smile broadened as he went back into the castle. Yes, things were going very well indeed!

13. OLD MAN MURDER

THE SHIPROCK CHIEFTAINS KICKED A FIELD GOAL, PUTTING them eight points ahead of Toadlena, deep into the third quarter. If the streets of Shiprock were quiet on this windy Friday night, it was with good reason: Toadlena and Shiprock Highs had been rivals ever since the game of football came to Navajo land. This had been the Chieftains' most winning season in years, and the games brought out most of the town.

Radio Joe had arrived during the first quarter, but had little interest in the game. Instead he wandered the bleachers, and loitered around the concession stand, munching on some frybread, biding his time. He watched the evening's spectators, making brief eye contact with everyone he passed. He made his way through the stands, squeezing through the crowds, taking a seat, then moving, then moving again. By the time the third quarter rolled around, he had worked the crowd well. He knew the faces and the eyes of the spectators—or at least the ones he needed to remember.

He went out to his truck, a rusted old Ford that had seen him through the latter part of his life, then systematically he began to fill the many pockets and compartments of a hunting jacket he had picked up in Flagstaff. The various weapons all fit handily into the jacket—all except the Winchester 1300 he had taken from Mary Wahomigie. That he hid in a trash can closer to the stadium. The band played a familiar fight song, only the drums and brass instruments making it through the baffling of the crowded bleachers. He whistled the tune, trying to clear and purify his mind for the task at hand.

Across the parking lot, a middle-aged man checked unhappily under the hood of his Corolla.

"Engine trouble?" Radio Joe asked as he drew near.

"Fuel pump, I think. Just had the damn thing fixed last month."

"Mind if I have a look?"

"You a mechanic?" The man asked.

"Electrician," Radio Joe answered truthfully, "but I've fixed an engine or two." He turned to the engine, but only so he could withdraw the hunting knife from his sleeve pouch.

"What do you think?" the man asked, leaning over Joe's shoulder.

Radio Joe turned quickly and buried the knife to its hilt between the man's upper ribs. It slid in silently. Then he twisted it ninety degrees, shredding his aorta and ventricle walls.

The man gasped, and Radio Joe clasped his free hand over his mouth, pushing him back against the side of the car. "Out of respect for your devoured soul, I put this body to rest." Thick blood, almost black in the dim light, pumped out between Radio Joe's fingers, but he did not remove the knife. The man groaned, too weak to scream. Radio Joe took his hand from the man's mouth, then cradled his head, gently helping him to the ground.

"Shh," he said. "Let it come peacefully."

The man gurgled out something that sounded like a question, and then went limp. Only then did Radio Joe pull the knife from his heart. He slipped the body into the back seat of the Corolla, then wiped his hands on the parking lot gravel.

At the south end of the stadium, he followed a large woman into the ladies room, and strong-armed his way into her stall. She screamed instantly, alerting any occupants of the stalls around them.

Sloppy, he thought, chiding himself. He had to be quick about this now, but the hunting knife would not do, for she had already begun to fight him, and her arms were longer than his. Instead he slid out the machete he had always used to slash overgrown weeds from his yard. A single hack to the woman's neck silenced her, but set off a geyser of arterial blood that flooded the floor.

"What's going on in there?" demanded a woman in the next stall.

Again Radio Joe cursed himself, for the element of stealth was the only advantage he had, and now it was gone.

"Oh my *God!*" The woman beside them screamed as the floor tiles beneath her slowly grouted red.

Radio Joe ran from the restroom, knowing he could not afford to give the body the respect it deserved. Things had exponentiated much too quickly, and he knew his next stop would have to be the trash can where he had stowed the Winchester.

The concession stand was at the north end of the stadium, and was understaffed for the crowd the game had drawn. The line, fifteen deep, was filled with the type of diehard snack addicts who couldn't have their game without hot dogs, popcorn, and beer. Radio Joe approached with the rifle by his side—but it was so odd and incongruous a thing, no one took serious notice of it until it was too late. He barged his way to the front of the line.

"Hey, what's up, Grandpa? Wait your turn!" said the teen behind him.

There was a woman behind the counter with oversized earrings and bleached hair. "Can I help you?" she asked.

"Please stand still," said Radio Joe. He was so close that when he swung up the barrel of the rifle, it struck her on the chin. He pulled the trigger, and the woman's expression of shock exploded into a spray of brain and blood that seasoned the popcorn, and splattered into the cotton-candy drum, turning the wispy strands of whipped sugar a deep crimson.

The first scream was his own, his mind recoiling from the grisly act just as powerfully as the rifle kicked. Radio Joe turned and fired into the chest of a brawny man beside him, as the screams began to erupt around him. Then he swung the gun around to a couple who had stopped short their approach to the concession, taking them out in two consecutive shots. In the stands, the band blared the school victory march, as the Chieftains scored another touchdown. The cheers from the crowd blended in with the screams.

People close enough to see what had happened scattered from the concession area in a panic, dropping to the ground, crawling into any crevice available. But the panic only erupted in pockets, and those who were out of the concession's sight line were slow to discover the danger. Joe slipped beneath the stands, where he had noticed a trio of teens drinking beer and listening to music. With his own breath coming out in wheezy cries of grief, Joe pulled out a pistol, and selected two of the three to take out, for those were the two that needed dispatching. The third one stood gawking for a moment at the holes in his dead comrades' heads, then he ran for cover.

The concession area was clear now, and word was beginning to make it to the stands that something was going on back there. Radio Joe came upon two young lovers hiding behind a Dumpster, terrified.

"Please," begged the girl. "Please don't hurt us!" She wore her boyfriend's class ring on a gold chain around her neck.

"Take that off," Radio Joe insisted.

Quickly the girl took off the chain, and held it out to him.

"Give it to *him*," said Joe, "not me."

Not understanding why, the girl handed the ring on a chain to her boyfriend.

"Save your ring for a girl who's alive," Radio Joe told the boy, "I mourn with you." Then he raised his shotgun, and fired into the dark bull's-eye of the girl's right pupil.

Radio Joe next headed toward the field, where panic had begun to take over. Under the bright lights of the field, his chosen targets were easy to spot as they raced from the stands—he had memorized their faces, and their clothes. His own sobs of anguish now ululated like war cries as he raised the rifle, and picked them off one by one.

In the end, Radio Joe was harder to take down than the Toadlena quarterback.

PARKER CHEE, THIRD deputy in the quiet, uneventful town of Shiprock, knew he was sitting nostril-deep in shit as thick as quicksand. This was a big deal. The kind of small-town nightmare that drags in the media vultures. When it comes to carnage of this magnitude, they descend with such ferocity, the whole town would be picked apart by morning. Thirty-two dead in a rampage that appeared to be neither planned, nor random. There was some method behind the old man's madness that no one could yet guess.

"Damn shamans," griped Sheriff Keedah. "They're psychotic, every last one of them." There was nothing worse in Chee's book than a self-loathing Navajo. Keedah never missed an opportunity to berate his own people. Chee longed for the day Keedah was ousted, but in the meantime, Chee did his job, and kept a low profile. While most every other law enforcement officer in the Navajo nation dealt with the crime scene, Chee was charged with minding the prisoner until he was taken away for the type of big-time arraignment reserved for the truly notorious offenders.

Chee found himself drawn to the old man in a sort of morbid curiosity he thought he'd gotten over in his five years on the force. He had seen his share of lunatics, but this old man didn't fit the mold. He had a clarity about him that was almost as disturbing as his bloodbath.

This massacre wasn't the only disturbing thing that had happened this week. There had been a prelude. Chee had sensed a discomfort throughout the week with the citizens he came in contact with. It wasn't everyone—just certain ones. Danny Yazzie, who he pulled over for speeding again; Addie Nahkai, who had a break-in; and more than a dozen others. Bad vibes—or more accurately, no vibes at all. Talking to them had been like talking to a wall. It's not that they weren't listening—it's that they weren't there. Chee would have let it go—attribute it to stress, or too little or too much caffeine—except for the fact that many of those people were now dead.

When the names of the dead began to come in, at first it seemed like coincidence, and then just plain creepy, that at least half of the people this crazy old man had singled out for execution had already made Chee's "absentee" list. And so Chee knew he was in shit up to his high nostril hairs even before he went to visit the old man in his cell.

As Chee approached the holding cell, the old man, who identified himself only as "Radio Joe," had calmly made the space his own. He had collected a host of dead flies and cockroaches from the corners of the cell and was now crushing them down into a fine black powder between his fingers.

"Congratulations," said Chee. "You've just guaranteed yourself the cover of this week's *Time*."

No response from the crag-faced old man. He crumbled a beetle between his thumb and forefinger. Only now, as Chee came closer, did he see what the old man was doing. He was adding the pulverized exoskeleton to a fine-lined sand painting that was slowly expanding from the center of the cell.

"You think that's gonna save you from the gas chamber?"

"Biye Gak misa dtaoopyū," the old man said. "I do not fear death."

In spite of his advanced age, Keedah had roughed up the old man in the interrogation room. Now his face was bruised, lips bloated, yet still he offered no words, no explanation as to why he had brutally massacred more than thirty people.

"If you have something to say, best to say it now," Chee advised. "Before the feds come to take you away."

"Let them come," said the old man, without looking up from his sand painting.

Chee felt his fury rising, and approached the bars. "You killed innocent people, old man. Parents—children. Don't you feel anything, you bastard?"

The old man was unperturbed. "I killed no one."

"There were hundreds of witnesses—your prints are all over half a dozen weapons!"

"You cannot kill what is already dead."

Chee swallowed hard. The shit was lodging deeper in his nostrils but he couldn't pull himself away. "Exactly what's that supposed to mean?"

"A shotgun leaves behind its spent shell. Worthless. Useless," said the old man. "So does this Quíkadi. The ghost-devourer. The spirit *chupacabra.*"

In any other circumstance Chee would have laughed at the suggestion. *Chupacabra* tales had been all the rage lately: red-eyed creatures that drained the blood of livestock. But what the old man was describing was not that same new-age vampire yarn. It was something completely different.

"You're telling me you follow this . . . creature?"

"I clean the waste it leaves behind. I lay the dead to rest."

"You're crazy, old man."

And for the first time, the man called Radio Joe looked up at him. He stood, coming forward, and suddenly Chee realized the bars held no protection for him.

"Am I crazy?" asked Radio Joe. "You would not be here if you did not already know the truth."

Chee wouldn't answer to that. Wouldn't dare think about it. "This thing—what does it look like?"

"It wears the body of a Hualapai," Radio Joe said. "Twenty years old."

"Man or woman?"

"Both."

Chee took a step away, not even realizing he had done it. There had been such a specter in town the week before. They had picked him up on vagrancy, as Sheriff Keedah had zero tolerance for itinerants. When they found no reason to keep him, they let him go, but Chee kept an eye on him until he left town.

"You've seen it, then," said Radio Joe.

"I saw something," Chee admitted.

"Your sheriff's soul was taken by it."

Suddenly the cell key became a weight in Chee's pocket. He could feel the heavy keychain pressing into the flesh of his leg.

"You killed thirty-two people!" screamed Chee. If he could have killed Radio Joe right there he would have, to spare himself from having to consider what he was about to do.

"Then let them take me away," said Radio Joe calmly. "But the job will remain undone."

Chee turned his back, trying to force his legs to take him out to the front office. The phones were ringing off the hook out there. Townsfolk tying up the lines; pressing them for information they simply didn't have, or couldn't give out until the next of kin were officially notified.

But the old man was right. Keedah was another "absentee." He was there in body, but not in spirit—and had been that way ever since his run-in with that genderless transient. Chee knew this to be true, and while Chee's head told him his job was to confine this murderer, his gut told him something else entirely.

"Damn you," whispered Chee. "Damn you to Hell."

Then he turned to the cell, and slowly pulled his keychain from his pocket, inserting the cell key into the lock. The old man watched impassively. Chee turned the key in the lock until he heard the mechanism spring open. Then he removed the key, and returned to the front office, without giving the old man another look.

When Chee reached the front office, Keedah was standing there, in the midst of madly ringing phones.

"What the hell, Chee? What, are you on vacation?"

"Had to take a leak."

"Worst goddamn night on earth, you'd think you could hold it until someone got back." Then Keedah took a glance over Chee's shoulder, and the worst night on earth hit a brand-new low.

Radio Joe lunged out of the shadowy doorway, a steak-knife blade flashing in his hand. Keedah reached for his gun, but it was as if he had no reflexes anymore. *As if his body were just going through the motions of reaching for his gun,* thought Chee. The old Hualapai brought the knife down in a cutting backhand slash, and ripped open Keedah's neck in a single stroke.

The spray of blood caught Chee in the eyes, blinding him momentarily. "Oh shit!" He heard Keedah collapse to the ground, and when Chee cleared the blood from his eyes, the sheriff was dead, his blood no longer pumping out, but oozing slowly onto the green linoleum.

Chee wanted to feel revulsion, shock, horror—anything, but he could not. Because Keedah had been dead for days. The old man was right.

Radio Joe put the steak knife back down on Chee's half-eaten dinner, where he had found it, then knelt down and took Keedah's gun. Chee didn't stop him.

"The one you're looking for—he headed west," Chee told him. "Hopped a train with two others."

"Others?"

"That's all I know."

Radio Joe nodded. "This town is still lousy with the dead," he said.

Chee let loose a sigh of surrender. "Leave them to me," he said. "You find that thing. Stop it any way you can."

The old Indian slipped out quietly into the cold night.

Then Parker Chee, trying to keep Keedah's body in his blind spot, unlocked the ammo locker, pulling out two boxes of .22-caliber bullets. He made sure his clip was loaded, then loaded a second. As he headed out to fulfill his new assignment, Chee regretted that the devourer of souls hadn't taken his soul as well . . . because by dawn it would surely be damned.

14. SIMPLE PLEASURES

THE DEPARTMENT OF PARKS AND RECREATION DID NOT come to evict the Shards from Hearst Castle. The National Guard never showed up to drive them out. Any official who came knocking, quickly pledged themselves into the service of the five—and in that new allegiance, those same officials made sure no word of what was really going on ever made it to the outside world. By the sixth day at the castle, it became clear that they could remain there, anonymous and invisible, as long as they wanted. And their numbers continued to build.

"This place is like a black hole," Winston had commented; "things fall in, and they don't come out." Which, noted Michael, was also an accurate description of a Roach Motel.

At first Drew kept a notebook of all the wondrous things that occurred within the castle grounds, as well as a record of who had joined their numbers—but after the second day, he gave up the pad and paper in favor of a video camera, to journalize the days.

But if anyone truly rose to the occasion, it was Okoya. With a quick mind and powerful spirit, he instantly became akin to a chief of staff. It was Okoya who kept track of the Happy Campers—organizing what they did, and when they did it—and when new recruits walked bleary-eyed out of the Gothic Study, with new leases on life, it was Okoya who led them away to be assimilated into the Great Repair that Dillon had begun.

"They need to be debriefed," Okoya had said. "I'd be happy to see to it personally."

And yet in spite of all of those responsibilities, Okoya made sure he had time to spend with each of the Shards. Plenty of time. As their personal confidant and advisor, Okoya was always there to ease their minds.

★　★　★

"I ADMIRE YOU, Winston," Okoya said. "You know so many things."

It was their fourth evening in the castle. Winston sat on his private balcony watching the sunset, and reading yet another of Mr. Hearst's leather-bound volumes. Okoya had slipped in beside him without Winston noticing.

"Yeah, I'm a regular encyclopedia," he said, shrugging off the compliment.

"What are you reading?"

"Machiavelli," answered Winston. "Personally, I think he's full of himself."

Okoya ran a hand through his shiny hair; the wind lifted it, and cast it about his shoulders. "I'll bet you could write things that would put them all to shame," Okoya told Winston. "I'll bet you could inspire millions. You could convince them to do anything—cultivate their minds in any direction you wanted them to grow."

"Flattery or truth?" Winston quipped.

"I think you know."

The crimsons and cobalts of the sky were quickly fading to a rich violet, as the sun slipped below the horizon. Too dark to read by. Winston closed his book, and rubbed his eyes. It had been an exhausting day. They were getting better at their little medical triage sessions, but the Happy Campers had brought in almost forty people to repair today, most of them so badly injured it sapped all the Shards' strength to do the job. Winston knew this was good work he was doing, but like so much of the information crammed into his brain, he failed to see how it fit into the larger picture. Even if they fixed the ills of ten thousand, in a world so large, it would make little difference. How could it stop this "great unraveling" Dillon was so fond of prophesizing? Dillon claimed to have it all worked out, but Winston suspected that, with all his skills of foresight and pattern recognition, Dillon was flying this one blind.

"Don't you think you could change the world with your gift of growth?" asked Okoya, whose face seemed more exotic than usual in the purple hues of the sky.

"Maybe I could, and maybe I couldn't. Anyway, I can't see the point." Winston folded his arms against the chilling night. He thought he'd have to explain himself further, but Okoya nodded knowingly, and spoke in an intensely hushed voice.

"All the world's philosophy leaves you with more questions than answers, doesn't it? And the more history you read, the more you realize that no one truly learns from the past. You see math and science as proof of the many things we'll never understand; and literature as just a mirror of our own imperfections. You've broadened your vision . . . but lost your faith."

Winston stared at Okoya, not knowing if he should be stunned, frightened, or amused. Okoya had firmly gripped Winston's frustrations, in a way he couldn't grip them himself. It occurred to Winston that Okoya had never really talked like a rural twenty-year-old. He was an enigma, and somehow that made Okoya thrilling to talk to. He wasn't sure whether there was actual wisdom, or just showmanship in Okoya's words, but they were comforting nonetheless.

"Peace of mind is closer than you think, Winston." It was then that Winston noticed the book clutched in Okoya's hand by his side. The same book he had been reading since they had first joined company.

"Haven't you finished that yet?"

"Each reading brings something new." Okoya set the book on the edge of the iron railing before Winston, balancing it perfectly on the tip of a fleur-de-lis. It teetered in the breeze, swiveling slightly. *Like a compass needle,* Winston thought.

"You should give it to Dillon," Winston suggested. "If there's anyone who needs a spiritual compass, it's him."

"It's beyond his comprehension," said Okoya dismissively. "In fact, none of the others would grasp its subtle truths. None of them have the breadth of your perspective. Tell me honestly, Winston; do you really trust any of their decisions?"

Winston found himself uncomfortable with the question. He always challenged Dillon, but that was his nature. Since their arrival, he had always presumed Dillon's competence; that his perspective, as Okoya had put it, was broader than his own. But was there really any evidence of that?

"Dillon sees things . . ." said Winston.

"Dillon is unstable—and the others are not much better. Keep a close eye on them—never turn your back—and remember that trust is best left with your own wits, no one else's." Then Okoya leaned over, and whispered into Winston's ear. "You are a great being. Don't let the others take that away from you."

Okoya left as quickly and quietly as he had arrived, but the book remained, balanced on the spear tip of the iron rail. It seemed almost to float there, as if it had no substance, and the wind could lift it off the ledge, sending it spiraling into the sky. Winston sensed the book was not the only thing perched on the edge of a precipice. He, too, was there, and if he leapt, would he fall or fly?

"You are a great being," Okoya had said. Winston had always been afraid to admit it—but why such fear? If the Almighty saw fit to make him closer to his own image than most anyone else on earth, why should he not accept that? And wasn't false humility in the face of all he knew himself to be, a kind of arrogance in itself?

If this book indeed contained wisdom that set him a plane apart from the other Shards, why not seize that as well?

If I am great, then let me be great. With a powerful lunge of will, Winston reached forward and took Okoya's book into his hands. The volume felt warm and far heavier than it appeared. Winston cracked it open. Its pages were easy to read in the dim red light of dusk, as if it had its own crimson glow.

The book was true to Okoya's promise, and from the very first page, he was gripped. The words fell together like the pieces of a jigsaw puzzle; the ideas put forth were filled with great insight and understanding. Answers to questions Winston never thought to ask—answers so perfect that they were beyond Winston's ability to process . . . and so the words passed through his mind, and he forgot them instantly. Not a single thought could he remember. All he knew was that, whatever he had read, it had fed him— satisfied his hunger for meaning in a way nothing else could.

He went to bed that night remembering nothing of what he had read, but *feeling* his own wisdom; his profound growth and enlightenment from his great feast of words. It swelled inside him, bloating his thoughts, and he began to wonder why someone as important as himself had wasted so much time hiding what he was.

TORY STOLE SOME time for herself, swimming laps in the chilly Neptune Pool. When she was done, the young woman assigned to her service—a former tour guide for the castle—wrapped her in a velvet robe, even before she had fully stepped out of the water. Tory imagined this nameless girl, a cheerleader type, no older than twenty, had followed her back and forth by the side of the pool waiting for Tory to be done, as if Tory was now the central figure in this girl's life. The girl fumbled with the robe, and its hem sopped in the pool as Tory tried to step out.

"It's all right," Tory told her. "I can put on my own robe." Tory slogged over to a lounge chair, removing the wet robe that was now keeping her more chilly than the air, and laid back to receive the sun. The girl, with nothing to do, stood there, conspicuously inactive, which was even more infuriating.

"Why don't you take the rest of the morning off?" prompted Tory. The girl quickly left, as if her freedom was an assignment. When she was gone, Tory closed her eyes, and cleared her mind, feeling the warmth of the sun. Tory hoped the sun would bring the hint of a tan to her skin, which sometimes seemed as smooth and pale as the Greco-Roman statues that stood around the Neptune Pool. Sitting there among the marble pillars and statuary, Tory could, for a moment, feel herself part of another place and time, somewhere, anywhere, far from Dillon and his mission.

When she opened her eyes again, Okoya was sitting on the lounge beside her. "Mind if I join you in worshiping the sun?"

"I'm sure the sun will be kinder to you than it is to me. Skin like mine burns to a crisp in minutes." But then Tory added, "Of course, what do I have to worry about? With us around, melanomas don't stand a chance."

"Perhaps the sun should be worshiping you," suggested Okoya.

There was a clattering of metal, and Tory turned to see the servant girl returning with a silver tea caddy stacked with enough lotions, potions, and oils to fill a small boutique.

"I thought you'd like some skin creams," she said.

Tory turned to Okoya. "I'm sorry about this," she said. "I once asked for some body lotion, and they raided the mall."

"No need to apologize."

The girl made an awkward gesture, something between a bow and a curtsy, and scampered away.

Tory turned her attention to her cuticles, pulling away the fraying skin. "I'm just not used to being served. It feels . . . unnatural." And then Tory laughed. "Listen to me—who am I to talk about things being unnatural?"

Okoya grabbed her hands, looking at her fingernails. "You have such beautiful hands. Why do you pick at them so?"

Tory pulled her hands away. "Bad habit. There's worse, I suppose." Tory grabbed one of the various lotions on the tray, sniffed it, and began to spread it across her arms.

"It smells nice," commented Okoya. "In fact, you always smell nice. The others might not notice it, but I do."

"I could say the same about you. That cologne you always wear—what is it called?"

Okoya shrugged. "The name escapes me."

"Maybe I could try it some time."

"If you like."

Tory smiled. For Tory, Okoya had become closer than any member of her family had ever been. Closer than her boyfriend in Miami, who had gone from putrid to pure before her eyes. Closer even than Winston, with whom she had come so far. Like the others, Tory had given up trying to figure out on which side of the gender line Okoya fell. Even now Tory couldn't tell what was hiding under the loose shorts and colorful T-shirt Okoya wore. But that was all right, because it meant Okoya could be anything and everything. He could be a brother, when that was what Tory needed, or she could be a sister. Today Tory decided she needed a sister.

"Do you bathe a lot?" Okoya asked, in a way that made it clear she already knew the answer.

"You know what they say about cleanliness . . ."

"Yes, but why would *you* need to?"

Tory sighed. "I don't know." Tory figured it was all those years living under a layer of festering flesh, that made it impossible for her to feel entirely clean. The troll might be gone from beneath her bridge, but its memory lived on.

Okoya reached into her pocket, pulling out the small crystalline bottle of cologne that rested there. She pulled the stopper and dabbed a tiny bit of the pale pink fluid on her neck. It vanished as it touched Okoya's skin. Tory thought Okoya might offer some to her, but she didn't.

"Strange," said Okoya, "that the Goddess of Purity can't feel clean."

Tory had a good laugh at that one. Goddess of Purity? Well

sure, why not! The Neptune Pool seemed a place lofty enough for such a fantasy. She didn't mind entertaining it for a moment or two.

The wind shifted slightly, and Tory caught the scent of Okoya's cologne. She breathed it in, feeling it deeply in her lungs and spirit, like a pungent aromatherapy.

"I know in time, you'll be able to feel . . . *purged*" Okoya said. "But then again, perhaps it's the world that needs purging—perhaps that's what you're feeling; the need to burn away the chaff, like a smelting furnace, leaving behind only that which is pure. After all, the world could do with some *human* purification."

Tory pushed herself up on her elbows, and turned toward Okoya, but the sun made her squint, and Okoya's face was painted in dark silhouette. "I'm not sure I know what you mean."

"I mean that you've spent so much time turning your gift of purification inward—but there's nothing left inside you to cleanse. . . . Still you keep searching—sensing impurity that's no longer there; subjecting yourself to boxcars and ragged clothes, as if you had to."

Tory knew there was truth in Okoya's words, but also knew that it was a dangerous truth.

"If you want to ease your compulsion," Okoya advised, "then set your cleansing power free. Use it, the way it was meant to be used."

"I am using it."

Okoya waved her hand in disgust. "Dillon is squandering your talent. Using your insights and taking the credit. Didn't you tell me that you were the one who made that leap of understanding, and figured out the truth about yourselves? That you were the Shards of the Scorpion Star?" Okoya stood and stretched, her stint at sun worship over. "You have a purity of insight," she told Tory. "Protect it. Don't let the others taint it."

And then Okoya left. It was only after she was gone, that Tory noticed the vial of cologne had been left behind on the lounge chair.

When Tory turned, she saw the servant girl standing there once again, but this time Tory didn't send her away with a self-conscious dismissal. Okoya was right. There was no need to be a Cinderella, dressed in rags, cowering in shame. The ball had begun, and it was high time she began dancing. Tory reached out and grabbed the vial of perfume, making it her own.

"I'm tired of swimming in a cold pool," she told the girl. "I'd like it heated."

"But . . . the Neptune Pool hasn't been heated for fifty years," the girl explained. "We'd have to build a whole new heating system."

"Then do it," ordered Tory, as she dabbed the nape of her neck with the stopper. "You have until noon."

And when Tory swam again later that day, the water temperature of the pool was already rising.

IN THE FIRST days at the castle, Michael found himself avoiding Lourdes and her smothering affection. He felt like a hapless puppy caught in the grip of an overeager child, and would do anything to squirm away. And then there was Drew, who did not fawn the way Lourdes did, but still, Michael caught those secret glances that were an ever-present reminder of Drew's attraction lingering just beneath the surface.

There is something you can do about it, Michael kept telling himself—for there was more than one way to mend Drew's broken heart, and end that attraction forever. But it gave Michael a shiver just thinking about it.

It was Okoya who helped Michael gain a bead on the situation.

During those first few days at the castle, Okoya shared with Michael ancient Hualapai tales, and Michael shared with Okoya his music. He had even lent Okoya his Walkman, and it seemed Okoya had taken to the powerful rock tunes and jazz fusion with a passion. In a way, it made Michael jealous—as if his music had suddenly abandoned him for another. But for Michael it seemed a fair exchange—for, since the moment Michael arrived, Okoya had been there with a sensitive ear, always willing to listen; always ready to advise.

Today, they sat together in the Assembly Room, Michael sprawled out on one of the many sofas, while Okoya sat at the piano, playing uninspired scales up and down the keyboard.

"You feel things very deeply," Okoya told Michael; "so deeply that the world around you becomes an echo of what you feel."

Okoya changed keys. "With feelings that powerful, why should it matter that you don't feel love?"

"Because what I feel more deeply than anything else is the hole where it ought to be."

"There's other ways to fill yourself," said Okoya.

Michael closed his eyes as he leaned back in his chair, trying to wrestle down all those unresolved emotions. And then, in a few moments, he realized that Okoya's music had changed. The monotonous scales had mutated into a grand rhapsody spilling forth from the piano. The music seemed charged with red-hot emotion. It wasn't classical, it wasn't Jazz or rock, but a synthesis of all three, and more. The music entered Michael, resonating within him to fill the gaping hollow.

"Why worry about love?" he heard Okoya say, but his voice sounded faint behind the swell of the music. "Why worry about something so unimportant, when you have the power to level mountains and subdue the spirit of millions? A power like yours could bring everyone in the world into line. That's what Dillon wants, isn't it? The world in order? Everything in control? You're the one to do it. Not Dillon."

The second Michael opened his eyes, the music stopped—and he was startled to find that Okoya was not at the piano. Michael could feel his heartbeat in the rims of his ears, as if the music had warmed them, and he had the strange, uncanny feeling that Okoya was standing right behind him, cupping his hands around Michael's ears, as if his hands were a pair of headphones, feeding him that wonderful music.

Michael turned, to see that Okoya *was* behind him—but was peering out of the window.

"The weather's changed for the better," Okoya said. "Music must truly have charms to soothe the savage breast."

Michael wouldn't confirm that it was Okoya's music that had shifted his mood, because he felt strange saying it aloud—as if the music was something he had to keep secret.

But with the music gone, his old frustrations and worries spilled into fill the vacuum. Okoya seemed to know. "Your troubles will go away, you just need to take some action."

"What do *you* think I should do?"

Okoya seemed to know the answer without thinking. "The thing you've been afraid to do," he said.

The thing he was afraid to do . . . Michael knew what that was, but was he willful enough to take such a bold and brash action? "If I'm afraid to do it, then maybe I have a good reason."

"Close your eyes," Okoya said gently. "Think about the music I just played for you." Michael closed his eyes, trying to recall the tune. He couldn't remember the notes, but he did remember their effect on him.

"How did the music make you feel?"

"Powerful," answered Michael. "Invincible."

"But you already are those things. The music can't make you feel what's not already there. It can only remind you of what you already know." Then Okoya leaned close to Michael's ear. So close that Michael could feel the moistness of his breath on the fine hairs deep in his ear canal. It was sensual, but in a very different way— as if Okoya was calling to something in Michael that was levels above eroticism. It touched not his libido, but his soul.

"You can have the music always, Michael." Okoya whispered. "You may take it from me whenever you wish."

Take it? thought Michael. He had always thought of music as something that was given, not taken. But Michael now sensed that Okoya's music was not a passive thing—and that to listen to it took a supreme force of will. To seize it, to envelope it, and to drag it in through his ears. Yes, Okoya might play it, but its power was not in its playing, but in its taking.

Okoya left, but the power of the music remained with Michael. *My music,* thought Michael. *It's mine now, because I have taken it.* And knowing that gave him the fortitude to seize more than just the music, but the moment, and to take that singular decisive action which he had so feared.

AND SO THAT night, while the rest of the Shards slept, Michael climbed the narrow winding steps to the Celestial Suite in the dark, counting each step as he went, like a countdown to ignition.

Drew was asleep. A mosaic of moonlight shining through the patterned window grille painted his face as he lay beneath a down quilt.

"Drew?" Michael ventured forward, and spoke in barely a whisper. "Drew!"

Drew shifted in bed, and opened his eyes. "Who's there?"

"It's me, Michael."

Drew didn't say anything for a moment; he just stared at Michael, not sure what this visit was all about. Michael sat down on the edge of the bed.

"I came to give you something you want."

Drew took a moment to think about it, then pulled his knees up beneath the covers. "Don't play games with me, man. It's cruel."

Michael smirked, knowing what Drew must have been thinking. He should have realized how this secret visit might appear to Drew—but that sort of liaison was not what Michael had in mind. There was a wicked power in knowing his own intentions but keeping them secret from Drew for just a moment longer.

"I didn't come here to be with you, Drew. I came to give you a gift."

"What kind of gift?"

"It's a surprise," said Michael. "Close your eyes."

"I don't know if I should trust you. . . . You killed me once before." But the fact was, Drew did trust Michael. In the end, Drew closed his eyes, and leaned back on the pillow, waiting for this mysterious gift.

Michael had no idea how to accomplish this, for he had never done it before. So he took a deep breath, and pressed his fingers to Drew's face, in something that resembled the Vulcan Mind Meld.

Perhaps, thought Michael, *this won't be so difficult after all.* He summoned up a depth of confidence he had only recently found in himself. Then, with hands pressed firmly against Drew's forehead, he focused on the deep core of Drew's nature, forced his way into Drew's mind—an intrusion far more intimate than anything physical—and then Michael began to reroute the many feelings held within.

Somewhere outside, a single cloud began to turn itself inside out.

★ ★ ★

THAT SAME AFTERNOON, Okoya had advised Lourdes as well. Not with words of comfort, but with a single, unhappy suggestion.

While Michael stole song from Okoya, Lourdes brooded around the Rose Garden. After the day's grueling session of fixing, Lourdes tried to spend some time with Michael, but found herself performing another painful skate down Michael's endless cold shoulder. Since the moment she had kissed him in Newport Beach and received nothing in return, she knew capturing his affections would be an uphill battle, but it had always been a battle she was certain she would win. Now she wasn't so sure.

Okoya eventually joined her in the Rose Garden, and told Lourdes point-blank that Michael's interests lay elsewhere.

"Watch him," said Okoya. "Watch him tonight, and you'll understand what I mean."

So Lourdes did as she was told. She watched Michael through dinner, she shadowed him throughout the evening—and late at night, when she heard the door of his room creak open, she followed in darkness through the winding corridors, and up the stairs to the Celestial Suite.

She knew very well whose room that was.

Standing at the closed doors, she couldn't quite make out their whispers, but her imagination painted for her a picture as complete as could be—and never once did it occur to her that she might be wrong, because it made so much sense. In fact, it all made sense now: the strange way Michael and Drew had avoided each other's looks in the light of day; the quarrel they had on the boat that led to Michael's tornado; the reason Michael returned none of Lourdes's affection.

Because his interests lay elsewhere.

For Lourdes, it felt as if a dislocated joint had suddenly, painfully, slipped into place. She stumbled through the cold hallways, and down stone stairwells, until she finally found herself in the kitchen . . . where Okoya sat, having a midnight snack.

Lourdes sat beside Okoya, and told her exactly where Michael was. She began to sob freely as Okoya put an arm around her to comfort her. No matter how bad things had gotten in the past, she had never cried like this.

"Poor Lourdes," Okoya said. "Poor, poor Lourdes. A will so strong, you could control the movements of armies, but you can't have Michael . . . and now you know you never will." Okoya cut a huge wedge of cherry pie, its filling glistening in the kitchen lights, and piled it high with ice cream. Then Okoya pushed the plate in front of Lourdes.

Lourdes wiped her eyes. "I—I can't," she said. "I have to watch what I eat. If I don't . . ."

Okoya handed her a fork. "If you don't, then what?"

Lourdes thought about it. *Then what?* Gluttony had nourished the beast that once lived inside Lourdes, packing her flesh with fat. But that beast was gone now, and she could control her own metabolism, indulging herself as much as she wanted. She could eat like there was no tomorrow, and endow the fat onto someone else—*anyone else* she chose. And why not indulge? She deserved it. She had earned it—and God help anyone who tried to stop her.

Lourdes took a small scoop of pie on her fork, and ate it. Then she took another, and another, and another, shoveling its luscious sweetness into her mouth, just as fast as she could swallow.

"Eat, Lourdes!" said Okoya, with deep understanding and sympathy. "Eat. . . . Not because you *have to*, but because you *want to*."

And Lourdes did.

MORNING SAW A bright day filled with muscular tufts of confident clouds that knew their place in the sky. Drew Camden, however, did not concern himself with the weather. He did not look out of the window. In fact, lifting his head out of the Celestial Suite's toilet would have been a great victory. His body fought itself, like a patient in the throes of chemotherapy.

Michael's night visit had been a strange and inexplicable event. He had done nothing more than press his hands to Drew's face— yet somehow he had done more than that. Michael had somehow entered Drew's thoughts and feelings as easily as opening a cupboard . . . and then proceeded to rearrange the shelves.

Suddenly Drew's whole world had changed. Drew had felt his mind and spirit stretched and folded like taffy, leaving him dizzy and confused.

He felt many new things now. He thought of the girls in school whose affections he always pretended to return—and suddenly he longed to be back there, finding he now had a lusty passion for them. He thought of the swimsuit issue of *Sports Illustrated*, and regretted that he had read the articles instead of ogling the pictures. He thought of his cousin Monica's tits, and wished he could have a nice long talk with them.

But the more these images filled his mind, the more his head began to spin, and his stomach to churn. Perhaps it was because of the other thoughts still with him. Memories of the feelings he used to have. All those secret, unrealized desires he had shared with no one. They were dead now, but their memories remained—and he now found them so repulsive, that he wanted to reach in through his eyes, and pull his brain out so he couldn't think of them anymore.

But this is a good thing, thought Drew. *A great thing. Michael has done for me what no one else could do. He monkeyed around in my head, and when he left, he left me straight.* Drew clung on to that thought, as he heaved into the toilet again.

15. DOCTOR DOOM AND NURSE HATCHET

SHIPROCK WAS THE KEY.

Two weeks into the siege of San Simeon, Dillon zeroed in on the tragic news reports, and they became the key to deciphering the pattern of destruction. Since he had arrived, he had scoured the media and Internet, but until now his searches had yielded nothing but white noise. And then came the Shiprock Massacre, pulling his attention, narrowing his focus. It was a primer that helped him decode everything else. From that moment on, things began to fall into place, like a puzzle constructing itself. In almost everything he saw and read, the pattern of destruction had finally begun to emerge.

"What pattern?" Winston asked when Dillon tried to tell the others. "I don't see any pattern."

Dillon had called the others to his suite the moment he was certain he could now read the language of the unraveling. So certain was he that he was blindsided by Winston's skepticism.

"If there were anything to see," challenged Winston, "then I would see it, too." Winston stood there, his arms crossed. Michael, Tory, and Lourdes were there as well, and none of them was jumping to Dillon's aid.

"You *won't* see it," Dillon told them. "Only I can see—you just have to trust me . . ."

Silence from the others—but more than mere silence. It was . . . a lack of connection. Not only with him, but with each other. The angle of their stances—the distance they stood from one another—it all spoke of isolation. Disunity. For the life of him, Dillon couldn't understand why.

Dillon dragged his fingers through his hair in frustration, and for a moment he felt his hair stand at wild angles like a mad scientist, but a single shake of his head brought it back into place. "It's not like I'm guessing about these patterns—I don't guess!"

Still nothing. Winston stood with folded arms, Michael's shifting slouch radiated indifference, and Lourdes seemed more interested in the ceiling architecture than in Dillon's warning, as if this meeting were an unwanted obligation.

Tory seemed to be the only one who was even slightly with him on this. "Maybe if you explain it to us . . ."

Dillon took a deep breath to balance his thoughts. "Explain it . . ." He looked around the clutter of his suite, searching for clues that could translate to their understanding—but how could he verbalize a cognitive sense that they didn't possess? He began by handing Tory an article—a small one about a candidate in an upcoming election.

"What is it?" asked Lourdes.

Tory skimmed it, and wrinkled her brow. "Some old fart is running for Congress."

Winston glanced at it over her shoulder. "So?"

"That old fart," Dillon explained, "just happens to be the president of the Flat Earth Society. Two weeks ago, he didn't have a chance. Now, all of a sudden it seems like half of Nebraska is voting for him."

"Have you ever been to Nebraska?" said Winston. "Pretty easy to think the world is flat if Nebraska's all you see of it."

Seeing he was getting nowhere, Dillon switched gears, moving to the computer in the corner. He clicked a button, and brief messages scrolled up the screen.

"I downloaded these this morning from an on-line chat room."

He let them scan the notes for a few moments, then asked. "Do you see?"

"See what?" asked Lourdes.

"The notes! These people aren't talking *to* each other, they're talking *at* each other.

Michael laughed. "That's nothing new!"

Dillon tried one more time. He flipped open a magazine, and presented it to the others. "Nielsen ratings," he told them. They all took in the lists of shows and numbers, but it might as well have been written in Arabic for all it mattered.

"See, look," Dillon said, pointing it out as best he could. "Ratings on the most popular shows have dropped off—and the shows no one ever watches are beginning to get followers."

They kept looking at the ratings, then back to Dillon as if there should be more.

"And that's the end of the world?" Tory asked dubiously.

"No, but *this* is." And Dillon presented them with a picture from the morning sports pages. Crowds at a Nascar race. "This says it all. I mean, look at them. Look at the way this woman is slouching—look at the angle those people are standing—and the directions they're all looking. It's as if they're not there to watch the race—they're just passing time. *It's like they're waiting for something else*—something bigger—but they don't even know it yet."

"I'm sorry, you lost me," said Tory.

"Okay," said Dillon, pacing across the rug, and flexing his fingers to keep from pulling his hair out. "It's like a tidal wave. You know—just before there's a tidal wave, all the water pulls away from the beach, and it gets quiet—as if the shore is waiting for the wave to hit: Well, that's what's happening now."

He picked up the article about the flat-world politician. "People everywhere are slowly losing their sense of reason." Then he went to the computer screen. "People are forgetting how to communicate." Then he held up the magazine of Nielsen ratings—"Everyone's changing their alliances at an abnormal rate"—and finally the picture. "And everyone's waiting for something to happen." He took a moment, realizing he had hyperventilated and was feeling faint, then continued, trying to lock on their eyes one at a time.

"These things that would mean nothing to you, mean everything to *me*. They show me the pattern that no one else can see." He took a deep breath, and spoke slowly. "Within one month," he said, "some crucial event is going to occur—something that no one can explain. That event is going to get stuck in people's minds, and when they can't reason it away, miscommunication will start to spread. Half-truths, and flat-out lies will spread around the world until no one knows what truth is anymore . . .

". . . and alliances will shift."

He turned and grabbed a globe off of Hearst's private desk. "After that, there's going to be a great gathering. I've been studying changes in airline schedules and travel statistics—they all point to it." He showed them the globe. He had already penned in a thousand flight patterns, leaving nothing but blue pen covering most of the world, darkest over Europe and the Mediterranean.

"It'll be somewhere on the other side of the world," he told them. "Millions will go there . . . and die. But it won't stop there. Death will spread out from that spot, until there's nothing left. Human, animal, or vegetable. *Unless we can change the pattern*."

"Is it nuclear?" asked Tory.

Dillon shook his head. "No, that's not part of the pattern. It's something else. Something worse. And so far, all the good we've done hasn't changed a thing!"

Then he clicked on the TV, giving them a final dose to drive his point home. Yet another interview with a Shiprock survivor. There were so many witnesses, the media was having a field day, and would have weeks' worth of interviews to horrify and tantalize the viewing public.

"Take a look at what happened in Shiprock, and tell me if you need any further proof. A man begins a killing rampage that's continued by one of the deputies who arrested him."

"Big deal," said Michael. "So a couple of lunatics decide to start blowing people away. It happens all the time—how are these psychos different from all the others?"

Dillon clenched his fists. "I don't know yet—but this *is* different. It's *important*—I'm just not sure how. You have to trust me!" He waited in silence for their response—hoping their thoughts, and their strength, would bolster his own. He knew they could rise to this challenge. These four had risen to defeat their beasts, they had risen to defeat Dillon in his own dark days. United, they had the power to—

"This is a waste of my time," said Lourdes. "Where's lunch? I'm starved."

"Are we through here?" said Winston, looking at his watch. "I have things to do."

"I'm going swimming," announced Tory.

Michael smirked at Dillon, laughing—mocking. "The secrets of the universe in TV ratings and chat rooms? C'mon, do you really expect us to take you seriously?"

But Dillon suspected nothing he could have said would have provoked anything but indifference from them. Dillon's frustration was a palpable thing now—he could feel it in the air around him, and he had a sudden urge to lash out in anger. He turned away from them, like someone turning to sneeze, hoping to deflect his sudden burst of fury. Then he released it from his mind, full force upon a water glass that sat on his dressing table. The glass shattered, into a thousand pieces. The others turned to look at it with only mild interest.

"Cool trick," said Michael, nodding to the place where the glass had been. "Bet that'll be a real crowd-pleaser with the Happy Campers."

When Dillon glanced at the spot where the glass had been, he had to double-take. Yes, he had shattered the glass, *but the water was still there*, suspended in its cylindrical shape. It was his own power of cohesion that held the water together, refusing to let it spill across the tabletop.

But if he could effortlessly bind these molecules of water, why couldn't he bind the five of them together toward a single goal?

"Later," said Winston, and the four of them drifted out.

Dillon stood there in the vacuum of their exit, completely bewildered. What had happened? Why weren't they listening? Although his encounters with them had been brief before they arrived at the castle, he had thought he *knew* them. He thought he knew their hearts, their minds, their convictions . . .

And their alliances.

The thought made him shiver. It played in his mind for the rest of the day. It still tinted his thoughts later that afternoon, when he met the Shards again for their daily repair work.

There were more than fifty today. It was a bloody business, as there were more injured than sick. The other Shards did not bring up their little summit meeting from earlier that day, and so neither did Dillon. He merely watched them, and listened.

"You're all so damned slow," Winston commented to the other Shards as he moved from one amputee to another, as if he were on an assembly line.

"Can't you hold still?" Tory snapped without a shred of patience, at a woman whose infection she was trying to purge.

Lourdes grumbled about all the places she would rather be, and Michael just sat there, peering out of the window, aloof and apart, letting his sedate mood settle on the wounded behind him.

It wasn't just that they had gotten good at the work—they had also developed an immeasurable distance from the patients over whom they loomed, as if their lives were now on some exalted plane. If the people lying before them were to die in their arms, and Dillon weren't there to revive them, Dillon doubted that the four of them would care in the least.

When one quadriplegic had been relieved of a broken neck, he turned to them. "Who in God's name are you?" he asked, with tears in his eyes.

No answer was given, but Dillon caught Lourdes grinning at the question.

Do they think of themselves as gods now? Dillon wondered. *Are we?*

The fact that he had to ask was not a good sign.

When the last of the wounded had been led off by Okoya for their "debriefing," Dillon watched the other Shards dissolve away from one another, each surrounded by a clutch of followers that clung to them like lint. They made no attempt to push those followers away. Instead, the Shards seemed to take greater and greater delight as those around them jockeyed for position in their attempts to curry favor.

THAT NIGHT DILLON lurked in dark corners, secretly watching the others. He observed Lourdes in the Refectory. She sat with a host of followers who were more than happy to provide her with company as she gorged herself. She was clearly the center of her followers' attention, in what appeared to Dillon like a distorted burlesque of the Last Supper. But by the look of things, this was by no means a final repast. In fact, it seemed like the first of many in Lourdes's future.

Dillon found Winston in the Gothic Study, absorbed in a thin volume with no title. He wore a hand-woven robe so ornate he seemed part of the scenery. The door creaked as Dillon entered, earning him only a fraction of Winston's attention.

"Quiet evening," commented Dillon.

"Is there something you need?" asked Winston.

"Just making the rounds."

Winston turned a page. "Close the door on your way out."

Dillon spied Michael in the Billiard Room, playing pool against a string of followers who made sure that Michael always won.

Then, when he tired of the game, he sent someone to fetch his Walkman and went out for a jog. He passed Dillon on his way out of the castle. "Life is good," Michael said with a wink as he passed, then turned to the Happy Campers in attendance. "Who wants to run with me?" There was no shortage of jogging companions. He put on his Walkman, and ran off. Whatever music he listened to, Dillon noted, it must have affected him deeply, because the entire night sky shimmered with waves of color, like his own personal aurora borealis.

As for Tory, she retired early, and Dillon found himself peering through her keyhole, for a glimpse of what she was up to—and Dillon played the voyeur, as she slipped into a full bathtub, and began to pour a luminous pink bath oil from a crystalline decanter into the waters.

Have I become so suspicious—so distrustful of them—that I have to watch them in secret? He knew the answer was yes. What had brought him to this?

It was here, as Dillon pressed his eye to Tory's keyhole, that someone stepped out of the shadows. Someone with a video camera.

"Shame, shame, Dillon—looks like I caught Big Brother spying."

It was Drew. His voice seemed to quiver as he spoke, and his camera hand trembled, as he peered through the eyepiece.

Dillon tried to hide his own embarrassment at being exposed. "You can't get a good picture if you don't hold it steady, Drew."

Drew shrugged. "Won't matter—it has a built-in image stabilizer," and then he giggled unexpectedly. It wasn't so much a nervous giggle as it was . . . inappropriate—as if Drew wasn't quite fixed in the situation.

Dillon had seen little of Michael's friend since his life had been restored. For several days he had withdrawn into the Celestial Suite, as if cocooning himself. Then, when he emerged, there seemed to be something markedly different about him—but since Dillon hadn't known Drew before, he had no real basis for comparison. All he knew was that Drew in recent days appeared to be a slippery character, never lingering long in anyone's line of sight.

Dillon took a step closer, but Drew took a step back. "What'll you give me?" Drew asked. "What'll you give me if I keep this video to myself, and don't tell the others you were spying on them?"

Dillon stopped short. His rapport with the others had frayed to a tether. If they knew he was secretly watching them, it wouldn't help matters. He hadn't been expecting to be blackmailed by Drew, though. "I gave you back your life," he told Drew. "Isn't that enough."

"Yeah, but what have you done for me lately?"

Dillon took another step toward Drew, and once again Drew backed up—this time into a shaft of light, where Dillon could get a good look at him.

Drew uncomfortably shifted from one foot to another, and back again, as if the ground were constantly sliding beneath his feet like the floor of a funhouse.

Dillon quickly sized Drew up. No, this was not the same person he had fished back from death two weeks before.

"I got an idea," suggested Drew. "Why don't I do the spying *for* you? Sure—the others'll never suspect me. I'll catch them all on tape, and in return, you could give me a shitload of 'servants.' Yeah! Just like the rest of you have. How does that sound?"

"You're kidding me, right?" But there was no hint of jest in Drew's shaky voice.

Drew lowered his voice to a whisper. "I could *tell* you things," said Drew. "Things I've seen, that I'll bet you haven't. Like the way Winston reads—his eyes don't even move, as if it's not words he's getting from the page, but something else. Or how about Michael—those CDs he keeps feeding into his Walkman—I tried to play one, but there was nothing on it . . . at least nothing I could hear. And how about Tory's oils and perfumes? They have no scent! I could find out more for you . . . for the right price." He offered a twitching, feculent grin. "Come on—you can trust me . . ."

Trust? Dillon didn't think so. Of the many unusual things Dillon sensed in Drew's current life-pattern, integrity didn't figure highly. In fact, a lack of integrity—in every sense of the word— was what Dillon felt more than anything else. Drew was . . . "out of focus." Each twitch of his eyes, every tremor of his hands, spoke of incohesion—he seemed to be falling apart from the inside out, and it wasn't the type of thing Dillon could fix any more than he could fix the focus of a blurry snapshot.

No, "trustworthiness" was not currently on Drew's list of attributes. Still, the way Drew buzzed in and out of everyone's business made him the perfect fly on the wall. The things he claimed to have seen—could they be true, or were they just figments of a mind out of balance? The latter was much easier for Dillon to swallow.

"Tell you what: you keep a good videologue of everything you see, and maybe I'll assign you an assistant."

Drew became more shifty, more fidgety. "How about two?"

"Don't push your luck."

Drew took another step back, stumbling over his own feet, and when Dillon reached out to steady him, Drew pulled out of his grasp with a violent jolt.

"Don't touch me, man!" Drew backed away, his posture a gangly knot of misdirected energies. "Just don't touch me, okay?" And then he turned and ran, vanishing into the darkness.

As far as Dillon was concerned, Drew's behavior was just further proof that the world was falling apart.

EIGHTY-FOUR PEOPLE TO fix the next day.

The busy-bee faction of the Happy Campers didn't bother bringing the wounded into the castle. The vans and trucks that carried them, simply dropped them off in the huge courtyard between the castle and the guest houses. They were all laid out before him, beneath the unshielded sun, like a scene from a brutal war.

Dillon knew he was still sidestroking.

But it was more like treading water, wasn't it?

He wasn't getting any closer to shore—he wasn't anywhere near getting things under control. And all their good work wasn't mending the fracturing world. Why was that? Each day there were more followers—not just the numbers of the healed, but others who had heard the stories and made the pilgrimage up the road from the Coast Highway. There were always people coming up the road now, all hours of the day and night, longing to be a part of the Big Fix, longing to be part of something larger than themselves.

"It's human nature to see divinity in anything larger than oneself,"

Okoya had said. Did these pilgrims making the trek to the castle think they were entering a new Jerusalem?

Dillon found himself wondering what his followers did all day while he threw his energies into repair work. Today he found out.

"We've tried to organize them for you," said a woman with a clipboard as she stepped obliviously over the bodies beneath her. She had been there every day. Dillon had come to call her Nurse Hatchet, although she tended to speak more like a Realtor showing a house—which was probably her profession before she wound up here. "Broken bones and internal injuries are to the left, lost limbs and such to the right, and those that died during transport are by the fountain. Would you like something to drink?"

"No thank you." Dillon looked around, hoping Lourdes would show up, to ease the pain all around him. But the others, he was told, were taking their time in coming.

"What about the sick?" asked Dillon. "Tory's going to need to know where they are."

"None today," said Nurse Hatchet. "Only wounded." She offered him a clean white smile, with teeth straighter than they had been yesterday.

Dillon didn't return the smile. He wouldn't force what wasn't there. "What, have we cured all the sick in local hospitals?"

Nurse Hatchet hesitated. "Well . . . yes," she said. "That, too."

Dillon turned to her, feeling a fresh pit open in his stomach. "What do you mean 'too'?" He tried to read a pattern in her face, so he could divine what she meant—but found her strangely void of patterns. Strangely empty.

"To tell you the truth," she said, "we gave up on hospitals days ago. Too much trouble. Besides—you never know what kind of people you're going to get."

Dillon stared at her, still not understanding. And so she pointed to a battered man by an overgrown bush. "That particular client is an architect," she said cheerily. "He'll help us build dormitories when there's no room left in the castle and guest houses." Then she pointed to a woman in a makeshift neck brace, who gasped every breath of air. "And she's a well-known attorney. With *her* on our side, we can keep the authorities away for as long as we want."

"What are you telling me?" demanded Dillon.

"Don't you see?" said Nurse Hatchet. *"We made them for you to fix!"*

Dillon felt the realization begin to surround his spirit, suffocating him with a truth he couldn't yet face. What this woman was saying was unthinkable.

The woman grinned as if she had just sold a house. "And that's just for starters. We've sent people out to bring you back some special orders. They'll be showing up with some very important clients for you!"

Dillon felt his balance slipping and fell back against the fountain, almost falling in.

Eighty-four "clients" before him. People who had been in the best of health until the Happy Campers broke them, so that the Shards would have people to heal. Here was the reason why nothing they did made a difference! And what was even worse than the ruined people spread out before him, were the hundreds of followers who saw nothing wrong with it.

Dillon could imagine them stealing away in the night, selecting their victims, and brutalizing them in his name: breaking bones, tearing limbs, even killing them—for to the followers of the Shards, pain and death meant nothing anymore. To them, pain was a rite of passage, and death was merely a prelude to a miracle. How could he, of all people, not have seen this coming? That the consequences of healing was to create a bloody cult of sacrifice and resurrection. A surge was building in him now, rising like bile in his throat.

"Well, look at that!" said Nurse Hatchet, grinning at the fountain as if it were a well-trimmed Christmas tree. Dillon's hand had inadvertently touched the water, undoing its random, chaotic spray. Reversing its entropy. Now the fountain flowed backward.

The woman showed her dimples, "My, you're just one big barrel of miracles, aren't you!"

The doors of the castle swung open and the other Shards stepped out, with Okoya close behind.

"Crowded today," said Okoya, as he looked out over the dead and dying.

"Not a problem," said Michael, "I'm ready to rock-and-roll."

Dillon pulled himself together, knowing that he had no choice but to restore the hoards that had been battered for their benefit.

And he told the others nothing, for fear that they wouldn't care.

OKOYA FOUND DILLON to be a maddeningly hard egg to crack—and was already considering all the ways he might destroy this willful, uncompromising star-shard should it become necessary. It would not be hard to turn the other four against Dillon now, for they had chosen their paths. They were already set against one another, and were growing enamored of their new lifestyles, feeding off their exalted positions, and off their followers. If they perceived Dillon as a threat to that, they could, and would, destroy him. Or perhaps Dillon could be killed by his own followers. Okoya could find a way to reshape the situation, spinning the hoards of followers into a web that would ensnare Dillon, and tear him limb from limb.

But these were only last resorts. He would only need to be destroyed if he turned on Okoya and tried to unite the others against him. Dillon was a most powerful tool, and could be used in a great many inventive ways. With Dillon beneath his thumb, this well-fattened world could easily pass into Okoya's hands, for him to dine on, or do with as he pleased.

And so Okoya waited, keeping his eye open for opportunities . . . until the day the fountain flowed backward, and Dillon discovered the deeds of his own minions.

Later that day, while the other four Shards lounged around the castle, occupied with their own concerns, Okoya climbed the steps to Dillon's chambers, and talked the guard into letting him in, which was fairly easy, as the guard had no soul. Okoya held in his hand a small statuette of a robed figure, carved in pink onyx. Conveniently sized at eight inches, and warm to the touch, the figurine was a perfect gift for the Shard who had everything.

Okoya found Dillon in the bathroom—the shower to be exact—sitting fully clothed beneath the running water, like a drunk trying to shock himself sober.

Okoya turned off the stream of water that sprayed into Dillon's face. "If you're trying to drown yourself, you should try one of the pools. They're deeper."

Dillon didn't move an inch from the corner of the black marble shower. "Thanks for the advice. You can go now."

"I'm impressed by your melodrama," Okoya said, "but I have something here that might cheer you up." Okoya placed the figurine on the narrow edge of the tub, right in front of Dillon. "I found it deep in the basement," Okoya lied. "Look at the craftsmanship! It might be thousands of years old, and its edges are still smooth."

Dillon eyed it, studied it, but this statue wasn't meant for his eyes.

"What an incredible story this piece must have to tell," Okoya teased. "What delicious patterns of history you'll be able to uncover just by touching it." Okoya sat on the edge of the tub, sliding closer.

"Touch it, Dillon," he intoned. "Feel every pattern, every texture in your fingertips. Your hands have given so much to others. . . . Now it's time to take something back . . ."

Okoya could tell Dillon was drawn to it, and for a moment thought he might seize it and lose himself in sensory overload, savoring the banquet of texture and pattern Okoya had so carefully layered into the figurine's design.

"Take something for yourself, Dillon. You deserve it. You've earned it."

But instead, Dillon stood, never touching the statue. "If I need to get off," he said, "I don't need that thing to do it."

Then he grabbed a towel and left the bathroom.

Even in his frustration, Okoya had to smile. No, Dillon would not be snared by an object of desire—he was far too clever for that. Dillon's ability to size up and sidestep a situation made him dangerously elusive, and all the more desirable a trophy. Okoya took the statuette and it disappeared into his pocket.

In the bedroom, Dillon peeled off his sopping clothes, then dressed himself, keeping his back to Okoya. It was more a gesture of disdain than modesty. *That's all right,* thought Okoya. *This can be done without friendship. It will just take a bit more effort.*

"Do you know what our Happy Campers are doing?" Dillon asked. "Do you know what they've done?"

"I think your followers have been doing you a great service. They're doing everything necessary to make sure the ones you heal will have the greatest possible impact on the world." Okoya positioned himself between Dillon and the door. "Didn't someone once say, 'The end justifies the means'?"

"No, it doesn't." Dillon towel-dried his hair, and stood at the vanity mirror, looking at himself. Looking *through* himself.

"You have a strange way of thinking, Dillon," said Okoya. "You say you want to repair a shattering world, but you're not willing to take hard action. You might as well be treading water."

Dillon's eyes suddenly locked on Okoya's, and Okoya suppressed a smile, realizing he had finally pressed a button.

"What would you do if you were me?" asked Dillon.

Okoya paused for a moment, and took a step closer. "If I were you, I'd stop feeling sorry for myself . . . and I would take control."

"Control of *what*?" snapped Dillon.

"Of *everything*. Control is what you want, isn't it? Control is what you need. Because the only way you'll ever be able to protect the world is if it's entirely under your personal control."

Dillon sat down, no longer angry, but scared. "That's crazy," Dillon said. "I can't do that."

"Oh really?" Okoya began to raise his voice ever so slightly. "How many people were following you three weeks ago? None! But now that it's started, it's moving faster than you can imagine. There's more than five hundred of them now—and every one of them is waiting for you to use them, but all you do is brush them off."

"I won't *use* people."

"It's about time you started."

Okoya had Dillon's attention now, for the first time since they had arrived at the castle . . . but Dillon's eyes had settled on something in the corner.

It was a glass of water . . . only there was no glass. Just water.

Okoya moved over to the dressing table where the water stood, and leaned against the edge of it, making sure he was in Dillon's line of sight. As he touched the table, it shook slightly. The water vibrated like a column of Jell-O, but still it stayed together, an indivisible whole.

"See how wonder surrounds you," Okoya poked a finger into the side of the water column, and pulled it out, licking his finger.

"*You* are the glue that holds this water together, and your power is growing every day."

Then Okoya lunged forward, driving his logic deep into Dillon's uncertainty. "If you know patterns so well, look at the pattern around you," challenged Okoya. "If you took things into your own hands, how long until every person in the world knows your name, and knows what you can do? How long until you become the glue that holds the *entire world* together?"

Dillon was silent as he considered the glassless glass of water. Okoya asked again. "How long?"

"Forty-eight days," whispered Dillon. "Forty-eight days, twelve hours, and nineteen minutes."

16. WATER WORKS

DREW CAMDEN LIKENED HIS CONDITION TO THE AFTER-
math of the flu. A weakness in the knees; a lightheaded, uneasy
feeling; a sense of nonspecific malaise that accompanied everything
he did. It was amazing to him how much there was to adjust to. It
seemed almost every aspect of his life was affected. The way he
thought, the way he acted, the way he coped with any and every
situation, had been carefully woven to accommodate that off-color
strand of his sexuality—but now that that thread had been pulled
out, the fabric of his life made no sense. Tasks as simple as turning
a doorknob took every last ounce of his concentration, and when
he was out among people, the world took on a strange dreamlike
tilt. Everything seemed violently new, and potentially dangerous,
and his interactions with others were . . . well . . . unsettled.

There was a girl, for instance. He didn't know her name, only
that he was deeply attracted to her. He struck up a conversation in
the hallway with her—small talk, really, just to get her attention.
He was even more surprised than she when he looked down to
find his hand deep in his pants, nursing an erection. He felt shock,
mortification, and yet found himself laughing uncontrollably, not
knowing why. It was just one in a string of unexpected events that
had plagued him since Michael had rewired him.

He had asked Michael about all this, and Michael was unconcerned. "It's just a transition, it'll take some time for you to adjust."

Michael was, of course, right. Drew would eventually decipher
his new neural pathways and discover the person he now was. He
just had to weather through this period of discovery.

Thank goodness for the video camera.

As official video-biographer, and Dillon's self-appointed spy,
Drew could rely on his job to distract him—a job that put a mer-
ciful distance between him and the world that he viewed through

the lens. He had recorded quite a few unusual events—definitely videoworthy—and the events only grew stranger day by day.

Today he was busy cataloguing the new backward flow of the fountain, when he caught sight of Okoya following Dillon back to his suite. Drew might have followed, as well, to eavesdrop, and see what conversations went on between these two most unusual of people, but it was the activities of the others that afternoon that pulled his focus—as it had pulled the focus of so many of the followers.

Lourdes was in the ballroom putting on what amounted to a puppet show . . . but her puppets were human. She had taken a whole group of devout followers, and turned them into a kick-line, shoulders linked and throwing their legs high up into the air, like the Rockettes themselves. They laughed and laughed, as Lourdes manipulated the muscles of their bodies like a row of marionettes. Lourdes laughed, too, and Drew hadn't been sure whether this show was for the followers' amusement, or for hers. Either way, it looked wonderful on videotape.

"Is it difficult to control the actions of so many people at one time?" Drew asked her.

"Not as long as they're all doing the same thing," Lourdes answered, indicating the kick-line. "And it's easier when they willingly give their bodies over for me to control. Are you getting all this?"

Drew zoomed in and panned the kick-line of followers, whose laughter was fading as exhaustion began to set in.

"How long do you think they can go?" Lourdes asked.

Drew shrugged. "You tell me—you're the puppet master."

Lourdes frowned, unamused by the title. "The interview's over." Drew then found his own feet taking Lourdes's marching orders, carrying him out of the room against his will.

Drew's camera next caught Winston in the Rose Garden, a place Winston had initially avoided; but now he seemed to relish the sight of the rosebushes weaving themselves like snakes through the trellises as he sat there, the roses blooming around him in yawn-like bursts. In this festival of roses, Winston held court. It was a cross between a game show and an audience with King Solomon. Some tested his knowledge of minutia, others had specific problems to solve.

"We're worried about feeding all these people," said one of Winston's flock. "What should we do?"

"Dig up the lawn beneath my balcony, and seed it with vegetables," he told them. "You'll have a full harvest by morning."

Drew used his zoom lens on Winston, because Winston had no patience for Drew, and couldn't be bothered with something as menial as their videologue. And besides, whenever Drew moved too deeply into Winston's sphere of influence, he could feel his own hair growing, and it wasn't a pleasant sensation.

Drew followed Winston's gaze to the sky, where, to Winston's irritation, Michael was upstaging him with a host of cloud creations. "That's all he's good for," Winston grumbled to his followers.

Drew trekked to a clearing on the far side of the castle, where close to one hundred followers lay on their backs like a Peanuts cartoon, staring up at the clouds. In the center of them, Michael emoted in short, directed bursts. Drew could feel the pulses move through him like Morse code. In this way Michael carved and molded the clouds. He had whipped the high cirrus into a wispy spiderweb. Now he drew together the puff in its center until a spider could be seen lurking there. Then Michael released his breath as if he had been lifting a heavy weight, and the web above began to dissolve into random vapor once more. His crowd applauded and cheered.

It was then that Dillon burst out of the castle with Okoya close behind. Drew quickly spun the video-cam to him, zooming in on Dillon's intensely determined face. Dillon was searching for someone or something, and his mind seemed to race ahead of him like an engine pulling him forward. He stormed past the anti-fountain, which had become a little shrine all its own, and continued on toward the Neptune Pool. There were, no doubt, great wheels of creation turning in his head, as he devised complex, unknowable schemes.

DREW'S OBSERVATION WAS, in fact, correct. Dillon's mind had kicked into overdrive, and was practically burning a path before him. The thoughts Okoya had planted in his mind just a few moments earlier were germinating at the speed of Winston's Rose Garden.

You can be the glue that holds together this failing world, Okoya had said, and Dillon knew he was right. He also knew that what he was about to attempt, if it succeeded, would change everything. It would alter the ineffective course of his actions. If he was able to do this, he would no longer be merely treading water.

In the Neptune Pool, however, there were dozens of people treading water, under Tory's direction, of course. Tory had finally deigned to satisfy all the followers who kept asking for "cleansing," which seemed to mean something different for each of them. No matter; she had concocted an impressive little ritual that was a cross between baptism and synchronized swimming, with her as high priestess and Esther Williams all rolled into one.

As the joyous mobs bobbed blissfully in the water, Dillon strode across the pool deck, and began to run his hands determinedly across the marble railing, and over the statues that surrounded the pool. His strange actions took everyone's attention away from Tory, and it annoyed her. The pool was *her* place, and these were *her* followers. What was Dillon up to?

Drew shuffled across the wet deck, putting the video camera in Dillon's face. "Welcome to 'Lifestyles of the Rich and Godlike,' " he said. "Here we have Dillon Cole, performing some mystic ritual. Tell us, Dillon, just what are you doing?"

Dillon put his hand to a column, rubbing his fingers across it. "Trying to get a feeling," he said.

"A feeling for what?"

"The pressure point," was his enigmatic response.

Word had begun shooting through the ranks that Dillon was being weird by the pool. In the ad hoc shrines where Michael, Lourdes, and Winston performed their sideshow tricks, people ran past. "Dillon's *doing* something," they shouted breathlessly. "He's doing something *new!*"

Soon the audiences had abandoned the other Shards, hurrying down to the pool to see what was up.

Dillon hopped the railing on the western edge of the pool deck. The pool's west side jutted over the edge of the hilltop, so that guests could have an unobstructed view of the Pacific. Dillon fell eight feet as he jumped over the railing, but kept his balance. He turned, and facing the granite block wall that enclosed the pool, he ran his fingers along the weathered stone, and between the cracks.

Up above, Drew leaned over the railing, looking down on

him, camera still rolling. Dillon's fingers swept back and forth, until he centered in on a single block, and then he dragged his index finger across it in serpentine motions, until stopping on a single spot. He reached down, picked up a stone from the ground, and pounded the spot three times. *Clack-clack-clack.*

The sound echoed deep within the structure of the pool.

"Pressure point?" asked Drew.

Dillon looked up and called to him. "Get off the pool deck. Tell everyone to get off the pool deck!"

But by now there were so many people crowding the ledge, and the hillside around him, it seemed impossible to get the mobs moving without some sort of structured retreat. Dillon searched the crowd until finding the other Shards, standing impassively twenty yards away, observing him.

"Lourdes," he said. "You have to move these people."

"I don't take orders," she grunted. "Ask nicely."

"Please, Lourdes—and do it quick."

Lourdes flicked her head, and focused on the crowd. She took a deep breath, bore down, and everyone—*everyone*—turned and marched away, leaving the area around and above Dillon clear.

"There," she said. "You owe me."

When the marching had stopped, the ground still trembled like the pounding of a hundred feet . . . Stones half buried in the hillside began to tumble, and from deep within the structure of the pool came a triplet of sounds growing louder as they repeated. Sounds only barely recognizable as the magnified, mutated *clack-clack-clack* of Dillon's stone against the granite block.

Dillon stumbled backward, focusing all of his attention forward as the pool echoed its resonant frequency through its dense structure, and back to its pressure point, until the granite blocks began to quiver; until the heavy railing began to crumble; until the entire west face of the pool fractured and collapsed in an avalanche of broken granite and marble dust.

Dillon was engulfed by that thick cloud of dust, and Michael, for one, didn't have the patience to wait for the dust to settle, so he blew it away.

What remained brought the crowd to a stunned silence. Drew had to take his eye from his video-cam to make sure he was indeed seeing what he thought he saw.

Dillon stood there, amid the rubble. The statues and colonnade above him were gone. So was the deep end of the pool.

But the water had not moved.

Like the column of water in his room, the pool water held its shape, as if the face of the pool were still there. People still treaded water—from where Dillon stood, he could see the soles of their feet through the wall of water that stayed in place, touched by Dillon's ever-growing power of cohesion.

It had worked!

And it hadn't been any more difficult for Dillon than putting his finger in a dike.

The other Shards came down to get a better view of the feat, but each brought along their own sprig of sour grapes.

"Show-off."

"That's called vandalism."

"Have you lost your *entire* mind?"

"What's the matter, Dillon—playing Jesus wasn't good enough for you? Now you have to play Moses, too?"

Dillon didn't even hear them. "Pack your things," he said. "We're leaving." He turned to the first Happy Camper he saw. "You! Tell all the others there are to be no more sick or injured brought to us. There are more important things to do now."

"Yes, Dillon," the man said, and hurried off.

"You!" he said, pointing to another. "I want everyone ready to go by dawn. I'm making it your personal responsibility."

"Yes, sir," she said, and sped off.

"You!" he said to another. "We'll need buses, cars, vans—"

"Buses have already been chartered, and are on the way," said a calm, familiar voice. "Enough for everyone." Dillon turned to see Okoya stepping out from behind a tree.

The other Shards were fit to be tied.

"Will someone tell us what the hell is going on?" demanded Winston. "Why are we leaving, and why wasn't I consulted?"

"Yeah," added Tory. "Maybe we like it here."

"SHUT UP!" shouted Okoya, putting a brutal end to the questioning. *"You'll do as Dillon says."* And then he softened. "Dillon has your best interests at heart . . . Don't you, Dillon?"

Dillon took in the sight of the other Shards. Just as before, they were standing in isolation; together yet divided. Well, Dillon didn't know how to change that, but he could still make them work together.

"You want to be followed? You want to be worshiped? You want to be loved and adored?" Dillon looked at each of them one by one. "Well, you will be. Not by hundreds, but by *millions*. I'll make sure of it. All you have to do is work with me, and do *what* I tell you, *when* I tell you to do it."

"Where are we going?" asked Michael.

"Somewhere we can put on a show," was all Dillon said for now. He waited to see their response. They all looked to each other, distrustful, none of them wanting to be the first to acquiesce. It was Okoya who coaxed them into submission. "If an alliance serves everyone's interest," Okoya said, "why not take advantage of it?"

"I thought," Lourdes said to Dillon, "that you wanted to save the world."

"We will," Dillon answered. "Once we take control of it."

Then Winston, for the first time in quite a few confrontations, uncrossed his arms. "I think I can live with that."

It was as they headed back for the castle to prepare the exodus, that Okoya leaned over and whispered into Dillon's ear. "Well done," he said. "Everything's exactly where we want it."

Dillon couldn't help but wonder what Okoya meant by "we."

PART IV · A PLUMMET OF ANGELS

17. GAMBLERS AND OTHER SHARKS

A BLACK GLASS PYRAMID ROASTED IN THE DESERT SUN.

From a clear sky, clouds began to fold out from a point in space directly above the pyramid. The many people wandering this end of the Las Vegas Strip took quick notice, wondering where the clouds had come from, and how they had grown so quickly. Then a single bolt of lightning exploded from the sky, striking the very peak of the pyramid, knocking out its electricity.

Inside Luxor's casino, the brightly lit gambling tables were plunged into darkness, and although the backup generator should have come on, it didn't. At the card tables, the dealers stopped their hands in mid-deal. At the roulette tables, the croupiers covered the house chips to make sure none were stolen during the blackout.

One particular croupier stood behind his roulette table in the darkness, yelling, "Nobody panic"—although he was more panicked than the gamblers surrounding him.

Then suddenly, the lights came back on . . . and standing directly before him, staring in his eyes, was a young man with red hair.

The kid was either underage to be in a casino, or a young eighteen, and around him stood four others. Like the redheaded kid, they were all dressed in shimmering gold silk shirts, and spotless white jeans—and had appeared out of nowhere while the casino was dark. They all wore the faintest hint of a smile, as they looked directly into the roulette croupier's eyes, as if they knew something he didn't. It was unnerving, and he had to look away.

In a moment, the gambling resumed.

"Place your bets!" the croupier called out. He pushed the wheel, giving it a faster spin, and took the small, white ball in his hand. Various gamblers around the table stacked their chips around the velvet betting board. The redheaded teen and his friends only watched, as he released the ball. The ball hugged the rim, fell toward the wheel, skipped a bit, and landed in a green pocket.

Double zero.

Moans were heard around the table. No one had bet it. Few people ever did. The croupier raked in the chips, clearing the board for the next wager.

Still the redheaded kid and his friends only watched, but now the croupier thought he felt a strange aura, like heat at the edge of a fire. And then, there was the breeze—not just the hotel air-conditioning, but a breeze that seemed to pull down cigarette smoke from the high atrium above, and send it swirling in an eddy around the table.

"Place your bets!" he said again. He was sure it was just his imagination.

Bets were placed randomly around the table. Square bets, street bets, columns and lines. The redheaded boy and his friends did not wager. The croupier released the ball, it spun around then bounced in and out of numbers, and found its pocket.

Single zero.

Moans from around the table. No one had bet it. Few people ever did.

Now that strange aura began to pulsate, as it grew stronger—and it wasn't just him. He could see some gamblers around the table, as well, beginning to loosen their collars. The croupier raked in the chips, and took a deep breath to try to chase away the strange feeling. "Place your bets!" he said.

And this time, the redheaded boy pulled a five-dollar chip from his pocket. He placed it on number one. When all bets had been placed, the croupier released the ball, it spun around the lip of the roulette wheel, and fell out of orbit, landing in number one. The kid had won.

The croupier raised his eyebrows. "You must be lucky. First time playing?"

"Yes," said the redheaded kid. The croupier gave him his winnings, and the boy said, "Let it all ride—this time on number two."

The swirling breeze around the table was getting denser. The croupier could feel it on the hairs on his forearm. It was more than just that, though, for as he looked on his forearm, he could see the curly hairs there begin to grow thicker, denser, as if they were growing at an unnatural speed. And there was that bald man in the corner. Was it just his imagination, or was that man not quite as bald as he had been just a few minutes ago? What was all this about?

The croupier gave the ball a spin. It orbited four times, and dropped squarely into a pocket.

Number two.

Exclamations of surprise echoed around the table, but not from the boy and his friends. It seemed as though they were expecting to win. The croupier felt the pulsating feeling grow as he gave the boy his winnings, like a presence that was pushing on him, pressing on his heart and lungs, until he could feel his heart and breath match the steady rhythm of that strange pulse . . . And yet, he realized, it wasn't a bad feeling at all. It felt good in some odd way. *He* felt good, although he couldn't say why. This time he returned the young man's smile when the young man said, "Let it ride on number three."

By now a small crowd had begun to gather around the table— the kind that always gathers around a winning streak. But more people than usual were gravitating toward this unusual sequence of events. The croupier let the ball go, it orbited four times, and dropped.

Number three.

The exclamations of surprise exploded from the onlookers. In less than five minutes, this boy had raised his pot from five, to five thousand dollars. The pit boss had taken notice, and the hidden camera above their heads had taken notice as well, for security was zeroing in on the table from across the casino floor.

"Let it ride on number four," the boy said. Five of the other gamblers around the table moved their chips over next to his. The croupier was sweating now, breathing quickly, accepting the rhythm of the pulsating beat. His own excitement was souring, because he knew he wasn't just witnessing this, whatever it was, he was a part of it. Before security could arrive, he spun the ball and the wheel. Watching intently until it fell . . .

. . . into pocket number four.

A cheer erupted around the table. The black kid turned to the redheaded boy and said, "Very good, Dillon. You could buy a house with that." And the croupier laughed, because it felt so good to know his name. Dillon. Security guards pushed their way through the throng, getting between Dillon and the table.

"Sir," said one of the four guards, "may we see some identification for you and your friends?"

"We don't have any," said the blonde girl.

"Then I'm afraid you'll have to come with us."

At that, their smiles only grew wider. Dillon looked the man over from head to toe. He sniffed the air around the man as if smelling his cologne, and then he reached up to an old scar that cut diagonally across the guard's forehead. As soon as Dillon touched the scar, it began to bubble and fold, until it was gone.

"What the . . . ?" But before the guard could say anything further, Dillon caught him in his gaze.

"Vietnam?" asked Dillon.

The man nodded dumbly.

"Helicopter or plane?" asked Dillon

"Helicopter."

"I can hear the weight of their deaths in your voice," Dillon said. And then he whispered, *"But there was nothing you could do. From now on, you'll stop blaming yourself."*

Then the man—who was the toughest guard in the hotel—released his breath with a gust, almost as strong as the swirling cigarette smoke, as if the world had gone from night to day. Then he smiled like a baby. Neither he nor the other guards made a move to eject Dillon and his friends. Instead, they joined the spectators.

"Tory," Dillon said, loudly enough for everyone to hear, "this place reeks of cigarette smoke. Could you clean it up?"

"My pleasure." She raised her hand in an overtly dramatic gesture toward the swirling wind that now spun with cocktail napkins and cigarette butts, and in an instant the thick, smoky air was crystal-clear. Dillon turned back to the table, and when the croupier looked down, almost everyone had already placed their bets on number five. Dillon looked at his own immense pile of chips.

"Let it ride on five," he said simply.

"But . . . there's a five-thousand limit to this table," said the croupier, apologizing as best he could.

"That's all right," said Dillon. "Five thousand on five, then." He spun the wheel and let the ball go. When the ball went down, he paid Dillon and everyone else their winnings, without even looking to see where the ball had landed.

THE TABLE WAS shut down less than five minutes later, and so Dillon and his four friends left, the swirling wind, suddenly blowing straight through the doors at the end of the casino, like a carpet of wind to carry them out. They marched out of the hotel with dozens of people following them diagonally across the street, toward the green towers of the MGM Grand, and straight for the blackjack tables.

FOUR HOURS LATER, with a parade of two hundred people behind them, they marched into the lobby of the Mirage. They had made their way down the strip, having broken the bank in half a dozen hotels. They had taken everything from the Bellagio's craps tables. They had tapped out the slots at Bally's. They had emptied the vaults of Caesar's Palace, by way of baccarat. And finally they pirated Treasure Island in a game called pai-gau, which none of them had ever heard of before.

Now, Dillon and his co-conspirators stood in the hotel's lobby, where a giant tank filled with sharks and Caribbean exotics graced the reception area.

Dillon tapped the glass of the giant shark tank three times with a gambling chip.

A few minutes later, as a strange vibration built in the walls around them, they met a representative of the March of Dimes. With the cameras of three local news stations in his face, Dillon held out an extremely heavy sack to the woman's shaky hands.

"I would like to present the March of Dimes with a three-million-dollar donation, as a personal gift."

"Who shall I say it's from?" the woman asked timidly.

"You can say it's from Dillon Cole," he instructed. "Dillon Cole, and the surviving Shards of the Scorpion Star."

And then he turned to the cameras. "Tomorrow," he said, "there's going to be a disaster. But don't worry." And he smiled. "I've got everything under control."

The vibration in the walls then became a high-pitched whine that ended with the crash of glass as the shark tank shattered. Hotel staff dove over the reception desk to escape the falling glass, and when they looked again, the shark tank seemed entirely unharmed. Except for the fact that its glass face was lying in ruins on the floor.

All eyes turned to Dillon for an explanation for this marvel, but he and his friends had disappeared in the confusion.

In a hotel where white tigers disappeared daily onstage, smoke and mirrors and sleight of hand were nothing new. The manager was ready to laugh at this interesting trick . . . until a small nurse shark poked its nose out of the water-wall, tore the pen from his breast pocket, then swam off with it to the back of the tank.

18. ROLL UP FOR THE MYSTERY TOUR

"**IF THE IDEA WAS TO DRAW ATTENTION TO OURSELVES,**" said Lourdes, pleased with the outcome of the day, "I think we did a good job."

They were twenty miles out of Las Vegas; eleven buses with no posted destination driving southeast on Boulder Highway. The lead bus was a well-appointed coach—a traveling hotel suite, really, done up in oak and leather and filled with all the creature comforts that one could cram into a bus. It was reserved for the five shards.

"Shouldn't we each have our own buses?" said Tory. "After all this is Las Vegas—it's not like less is more."

"If we could arrange for buses, why not planes?" suggested Michael. "Really jazz up the show!"

"When we need planes, we'll get planes," said Dillon. "Right now buses are more than enough."

Tory swiveled in her leather chair. "Cleopatra did not ride around in a bus."

"Oh," said Winston with a smirk, "is that who you are now?"

"Don't get snotty—I was only using her for comparison."

"And besides, if anyone's Cleopatra, it's me," said Lourdes.

"History says she was as ugly as sin," said Winston. "Maybe you're right."

"Drop dead."

Just past Boulder City, Dillon instructed the driver to pull off the road, into the desert. There the eleven buses formed a circle, like an old-fashioned wagon train, around a campsite that Okoya, who had gone on ahead, was already in the process of setting up. Dillon was the only Shard who felt the need to go out there. Truth was, the others were famished from their day at the casinos. More than famished—they felt vacant. It was a feeling that gave Tory the urge to rub her arms compulsively, as if trying to shed some invis-

179

ible layer of grime. The hunger made Winston feel a sense of futility in all he did. It made Michael acutely aware of the absence of love in his heart, and for Lourdes, that hunger reawakened her hopeless longing for Michael. Surely a nice all-you-can-eat buffet could have been fit into their Las Vegas schedule—but the very thought sickened them, for their hunger was not for that sort of food.

Tory peered out of the window, where the busloads of followers poured forth, pitching tents, and setting up camp, in preparation for tomorrow's main event. "What we do now is crucial," Dillon had said. "We can't afford to make mistakes." Of course, no one but the Shards and Okoya knew what the event would be, and as for the Big Show itself, Dillon was in charge of that. They would all be handed their parts when the time came, but for now, they didn't feel a burning need for dress rehearsals.

As the bus driver left, Okoya stepped in carrying a sack of goodies.

"While you were all working," said Okoya, "I found some things I thought you might appreciate."

As he reached into the bag, Tory snuck a peek. "Ooh! Is that a new skin lotion?" She asked, practically growing fangs at the thought. "I'd kill for a good lotion!"

"Would you?" Okoya said. He pulled out the container of lotion, but put it down, out of Tory's reach. Tory leaned over to get it, but Okoya held her back. "Patience," was all he said.

He reached into the bag again, and produced a cake, with a deceptive white creme frosting, that gave way to dark chocolate and a glistening cherry filling when he cut it. "For you, Lourdes."

"Black Forest!" she exclaimed, holding her hands forward like an anxious Oliver Twist. "I love Black Forest."

Okoya handed her the slice of cake, and she dug her hand into it, without waiting for a fork. Then he reached in and came up with a magazine. "They were selling some . . . uh . . . *interesting* magazines on the strip," he said to Winston. "There are some pictures in here that are not to be believed. Have a look, Winston. You might learn something." He gave Winston a wink and tossed him the magazine.

"Me next," insisted Tory.

Okoya ignored her, and pulled out a new Walkman for Michael. "Top of the line, and I've tuned the radio to a fantastic station I've found here—you're going to love it!"

He handed the device to Michael, and although Michael felt his own Pavlovian urge to slip into a comfortable beat, he didn't put the headphones on just yet. Instead he watched. By now Tory was rubbing her hands in front of her like a fly as Okoya reached for the bottle of lotion. Okoya took his time, spilling a drop of the lotion onto his index finger. "It's fragranced with the essence of ten different kinds of rose, and guaranteed to make you feel as fresh as the day you were born," He held it toward Tory, but not close enough for her to smell it.

"You said you would kill for it," said Okoya. "Did you mean what you said?"

She kept her eyes glued on the viscous pink liquid dripping down his finger. "Definitely."

Then Okoya reached to a compartment in the bus's kitchenette, peered inside, and retrieved a crystalline ice bucket. Inside was a silver ice pick. Instead of giving Tory a dollop of lotion, he gave her the ice pick.

"Kill Winston," he said. "And you can have the whole bottle."

Tory stood immobile with the pick in her hand, giggling at the thought.

"Go on," prompted Okoya. "You want your lotion, don't you?"

Tory looked at the sharp end of the ice pick, and found herself turning it toward Winston's chest. Lourdes filled her mouth with cake and eyed Tory, but made no move to intervene. Winston spread his arms pushing his chest forward.

"C'mon," he said with a grin. "Right here—right through the heart!"

Perhaps it was because Michael had not yet plugged into his music, or just that he had dredged up a moment of clarity, but whatever the reason, in the midst of everyone else's laughter, Michael realized that Tory was pulling her hand back, like a gun hammer cocking itself. She was actually going to do it!

Michael dropped his Walkman and lurched forward as Tory began her downward arc. He firmly grasped her wrist, and the pick stopped an inch from Winston's chest.

"Tory—what are you doing?!"

Tory turned to Michael as if he had done something wholly inappropriate.

"The lotion," she said simply. "I want the lotion. For my skin."

"You almost stabbed Winston!"

Unconcerned, Winston vanished behind his magazine. "Big deal," he said. "Dillon would have brought me back."

"That's not the point!" Michael turned, hoping to find support from Lourdes, but she was digging her hands into the rest of the cake.

"It would have been interesting to see if he could actually die," she said matter-of-factly. "For all we know, we've become immortal."

"Immortal?" said Michael incredulously. "What about Deanna? She was one of us, and she died."

"That was then," said Lourdes; "this is now."

"How could you be so flippant about it?" yelled Michael. "How could you be . . ." But even as he thought it, he knew it wasn't just them. He wasn't much different. How self-absorbed had he been lately? How malignant had his own arrogance become; the thrill of being worshiped, the self-satisfaction his own power now brought him?

"What's happened to us?" he dared to ask.

"We've risen above where we used to be," said Winston. "Our perspective has changed, that's all."

Michael had to admit that he was right. Their outlook, their desires and needs, were markedly different than they had been three weeks ago. Their place in the world was so much grander than they ever imagined it to be.

"We used to be limited by fear, and small-mindedness," Winston said, puffed up by his own sense of wisdom. "Not anymore."

But as Michael stood there, a splinter of that old limited perspective came back . . . and for a moment, he was not a god—he was just a kid. A kid with more power than he knew how to wield.

Michael knew that in some way, Okoya's music had bolstered his pride—his hubris. It added to his sense of comfort and confidence. He didn't need the music—he *wanted* it. Okoya hadn't forced him to listen—it was Michael who had seized upon it, keeping himself emotionally sated.

But there was an advantage to hunger.

He dropped the Walkman in his hand, knowing that if he didn't, he'd be swayed by those rich melodies that he, too, might kill for.

"I don't like what's happening here," he said.

Okoya had a radar fix on his eyes. "It was only a game, Michael," he said, with such control in his voice, Michael felt the urge to nod in agreement in spite of himself. "You get way too emotional," continued Okoya. "You should be more like Lourdes. She'll go far." By now, Lourdes had finished her cake, and was licking the whipped cream from her fingers. She glowed with Okoya's compliment.

Michael felt the air around him become oppressive and cold. Dewdrops began to form on the ceiling of the bus.

"Hey!" Winston said. "If you have to rain on someone's parade, take it the hell away from me, will you?"

"Yes, Michael," said Okoya. "Perhaps it's time you left."

Michael didn't need another invitation to leave. In spite of his hunger, he stepped over the Walkman, and hurried out the door without further word.

Tory saw him go through the corner of her eye, but her attention was on the ice pick still in her hand.

Is that my hand? she thought. *Was that me bringing the pick toward Winston's chest?*

There was a sentence playing over and over and over in her head now; the words Winston had muttered when Michael saved his life. *"Big deal. Dillon would have brought me back."* Was she so great a soul that she was beyond the need for conscience? And was her lust for Okoya's aromatic potions so powerful that it made even death seem unworthy of her attention?

"Dillon would have brought me back."

Was life so cheap now that murder meant nothing?

She wanted to let these thoughts slap her—perhaps enough to slap her off the alabaster pedestal she had so willingly climbed on—but Okoya approached with a palmful of pink lotion.

"You've earned this," Okoya told her, "for helping me find the weak link."

The ice pick dropped from her fingers, she leaned forward, and Okoya stroked the smooth fluid across her cheeks like war paint. The scent hit her, and instantly any thoughts of what was right, what was wrong, what was clean and what was foul, were snuffed in the sweet flood of a million rose petals.

MICHAEL FOUGHT OFF the dewpoint, determined not to telegraph his emotions to the world. His emptiness had returned in full force, growing unbearable by sunset. A hunger, deep in the channels of his ears. *Is it possible,* Michael began to wonder, *to be nourished through one's senses, rather than through one's stomach?*

Michael took sustenance that evening from the campsites of the followers. It was the first time in days he had eaten real food, but even so, it was unsatisfying—vapid, and flavorless in some fundamental way. It was as Michael wandered from campsite to campsite that Drew came to him with a request.

"See, there's this girl," Drew said. Michael immediately knew where this was headed, and he had no desire to go there.

"Drew, I'm tired. Talk to me tomorrow."

"Can't wait. No, no—can't wait," he said, his words coming out in anxious staccato beats.

Michael picked up the pace, and Drew followed, pushing people out of his way to keep up.

"The thing is, she doesn't like me," said Drew. This was no surprise to Michael. Drew had not quite mastered the finer points of conversing with girls he was attracted to. In fact, many of those ill-fated conversations ended abruptly with Drew executing one of several bodily functions, none of which were too pretty.

Lately Michael's ears had been so occupied with his Walkman, and the adulation of his followers, he really hadn't cared to hear about Drew's misadventures. But now, with his mind clearer, Michael found it all terribly uncomfortable—even more uncomfortable than Drew's former crush on him.

"All I want you to do," pleaded Drew, "is make her fall in love with me."

Michael tried to shut this down now. "No," he said. "Period. The end." Michael wove faster through the campsites, thinking he could board one of the buses and lock himself in the lavatory—anything for some time alone.

But Drew continued to pester him like a mosquito. It wasn't like him; Drew Camden had never been a pest or a nuisance. It made Michael even more determined not to give in.

"Come on, Michael, you'd do it for any of the other followers—why won't you do it for me?"

"Because," said Michael, "you're my friend—you're not one of *them.*"

And then Drew pulled out his trump card.

"You made me like this! Shit, the least you could do is help me out here!"

Finally Michael stopped and turned to him. The light of several campsites played on Drew's face, creating strange, unfamiliar shadows—but it wasn't just the light. It was the way Drew looked—the way he acted. His character had dropped several octaves, and it occurred to Michael that he did not know this reinvented person before him. He wasn't sure he even wanted to.

"What if I give you my running suit? The one you like," Drew offered, probably not even considering the fact that it was back home, hundreds of miles and one lifetime away. "Will you do it then? Huh?"

Reconstituted beef. Perhaps it was just his hunger, but that was the thought that came to Michael's mind. It was at some fast-food dive. They called it a steak sandwich—and although it looked like steak, and smelled like steak, the thing was mushy and flavorless. The small print said it was "reconstituted beef"; apparently ground up and, through some mystical process, pressed back into little steaklike rectangles, losing everything worth keeping in the process. Michael couldn't help but feel that Drew was now a living loaf of reconstituted beef.

The thought was too much for him, and suddenly Michael wanted to do anything to get the new and improved Drew out of sight and out of mind. "Fine, I'll do it. Where is she?"

Drew grinned like a kid in a candy shop. "This way," and he trotted off, leading Michael toward his current love interest.

Drew barged into the girl's tent and pulled her out, against her protests. "Angela, I'd like you to meet Michael Lipranski. See, Angela, didn't I promise you a personal introduction?"

Angela, at the sight of Michael, began to wring her fingers self-consciously. "Hi," said Angela timidly. "I volunteered to be one of your personal helpers, but there was a waiting list."

Drew hovered a few feet away, shifting his weight from one leg to another. "Come on, Michael, do it. Do it quick!"

It would be easy enough; all he had to do was plant the feeling so intensely in her the moment she looked at Drew, that it would shade everything she ever felt. She would love Drew unconditionally for the rest of her life, or until Michael decided to change it. But as he looked into this girl's eyes, Michael had a sudden sense of foreboding—a dark flashback to something he had once seen, once felt, but couldn't place. He had seen those eyes before, but on a different girl. Suddenly a chill wind blew a rain of sand across them, stinging their faces, as Michael realized where he had seen that look before.

It was the same expression, the same blank eyes he had seen on a girl a year ago, when he had witnessed his parasite seize the girl with his violating blue flames and devour her. Maybe no one else could see it—but Michael knew exactly what was wrong.

This girl had no soul.

"Aw, come on, Michael," said Drew. "What's taking so long?"

Michael grabbed Drew and pulled him away.

"Hey! Don't touch me," whined Drew, trying to wriggle free from Michael's grip.

"This isn't the girl you want, Drew. Trust me, it's not."

"Huh?"

Michael turned from Drew, and randomly began grabbing followers around him, looking for signs of life inside—and in half the people he encountered, he found the same soulless void.

How was this possible? At first, he thought it might be Dillon—that his spirit of destruction had returned, and had now developed a taste for something more than devastation. . . . But no. That was a spirit impossible to miss. If that *thing* were back in this world, bells and whistles would be ringing in all the Shards' ears. It was not Dillon . . . but if not him, then who?

Michael had a feeling he knew.

"You promised, Michael!" complained Drew, stomping up a dust cloud. "You said you'd do it! You lied!"

"Drew—there's something I want you to do."

Drew looked at him warily. "What?"

"Tonight—I want you to stay up. I want you to keep an eye on Okoya. Follow him and tell me everything he does."

"And then you'll fix me up with a girl?"

"Whatever you want, Drew. I promise. But first, Okoya."

Drew thought about it and accepted. "Deal. Hell, I don't sleep much anyway."

IN A FEW brief hours, the miracle of the waters had become the number one attraction in a town known for its spectacle. There was no keeping the crowds out of the Mirage lobby, and as for management, their hands were filled with other problems. The casino, which consistently raked in a healthy percent of all cash wagered, suddenly wasn't the cash cow it used to be. In fact, the house was losing.

The lounge atop the Stratosphere tower offered Radio Joe a bird's-eye view of the Strip, and the mobs pressing in around the Mirage a mile away.

"My wife says she wants to have his baby," slurred the slovenly man sitting on the barstool next to Joe. "I told her if the kid really is God, he sure as hell wouldn't want to screw *her.* That tore it. She ran off and joined them out there in the desert, saying Hail Marys, or Hare Krishnas, or whatever the hell they do." He downed his scotch, and demanded another.

Radio Joe kept his cap pulled down low on his face so as not to be recognized, for his face was still on every magazine. He didn't think it mattered much here, however. The liquor was flowing in rivers today, and few in his line of vision could see straight. "You say this boy had red hair and fair skin?" Joe asked.

"Yeah. Couldn't be any older than eighteen. Name was Daryl, or Dalton—something like that."

In the corner a slot machine hit, noisily spitting out coins into a tray that was already overflowing. The cowboy sitting in front of it let out a victory cry. "This baby's looser than my first wife."

The bartender poured the slovenly man another scotch. "I hear the MGM just shut its casino down," he said.

"No kidding! Them too?"

That makes three, thought Joe. How many more would go? How many casinos had this boy visited? Radio Joe had been searching for days for a sign of the Quíkadi, but instead had found this redheaded teen. He knew there had to be a connection, but didn't know what it was yet.

"I've lived here all my life," the bartender told them, "and I ain't ever seen nothing like this. It's like the kid put a fix in every casino he passed."

The cowboy's slot machine hit again in the corner. "Yahoooo!" he bellowed. "I'm poppin' more cherries than a highschool senior!" Then the machine next to his came up a winner as well.

It wasn't just the slot machines, Radio Joe had noted. The odds on the table games had somehow changed as well; the random order of dice thrown and cards turned was now less random than before. These events had divided Las Vegas into three factions: those who swarmed the Mirage; those who swarmed the casinos; and those who watched from a numb, plastered distance.

"Have one with me," said the slovenly gambler, then he called out to the bartender. "One for the chief, here."

Radio Joe graciously accepted, but didn't drink it. He needed his wits about him.

"When I was a kid," said the drunk, "I once thought I saw the Virgin Mary in a pancake—but my damn brother ate it." He took a swig of his scotch. "My dad died of a heart attack the next week. Totally unrelated, of course, but you never stop wondering."

The cowboy came up with three oranges, and security arrived to shut down all the machines on the lounge level—and probably the entire hotel.

"Some people think it's the Second Coming," the bartender said, breaking the cardinal law of barkeeping, and pouring a drink for himself. "Other folks say it's the end of the world."

The slovenly man clinked glasses with him. "Yeah. Too bad nobody's taking bets."

IT WAS SUNSET when Radio Joe pushed his way through the anxious crowds around the Mirage, determined to see for himself the sight that had arrested the attention of the city. The rumor was that federal agents were about to close the whole place down, until they could either discover or fabricate a rational explanation for the wall of water. But Radio Joe suspected that no amount of government intervention could close this Pandora's box.

He shouldered his way through, creating his own right-of-way, against the disapproval of those around him, until he was finally in the lobby. Police in riot gear fought a losing battle to peacefully disperse the crowd, but they were outnumbered, and their strategies were all geared toward angry mobs, not joyous ones. With so many children present in the arms of their parents, no one dared authorized the use of tear gas or lethal force, and so Radio Joe watched as the line of police gave way. The eager hundreds funneled forward, leaping over the reception desk, toward the shark tank. Radio Joe became just one among many pressing their palms forward into the wall of water, wanting not just to see the miracle, but to *feel* it as well.

As he reached his hand forward, Joe's fingers went from air into cool salt water, without any hint of a barrier between. A bright yellow fish swam between his fingers. Tiny bubbles dislodged from the hair on his wrists and floated up, out of sight.

Around him the wide-eyed throng was being dragged away one at a time by police officers, but still more kept coming. Radio Joe wondered if these people understood what they were witnessing. That this place, this moment in time, marked the end of the Age of Reason. A new time was coming, and Joe feared what this new age might be. He now knew that the devouring spirit he had pursued was just one of many players in a dark and bewildering pageant. There would be hundreds of souls by now that the Quíkadi had devoured, and there was no hope of Radio Joe ever cleansing the world of its waste, much less fighting it. Who knew what other mystic acts had taken root in the world as well?

He pulled his hand out of the water-wall, knowing there was only one thing for him to do now. He would leave here, go to the place where life began, and wait there for it to end.

It was as he turned that a woman in the crowd made eye contact. He read her quizzical look, and although he shielded his face, he wasn't quick enough.

"Shiprock!" she said under her breath.

He turned and ran, but was met by the crowd pressing in, pushing their way toward the water-wall.

"The Shiprock Slayer!" screamed the woman. "It's the Shiprock Slayer!"

More eyes turned to Radio Joe. He heard more voices now, seconding the accusation. One of the riot policemen turned his way.

He knew if he was to escape, he would have to use the crowd to his advantage, and so he dropped down on all fours, serpentining an unpredictable path through the forest of legs.

"That way!" he heard a voice shout. "He's over there!"

But the farther away he got, the less interested the crowd was in his identity. The only thought in their mind was getting to the water-wall before the whole lobby was shut down. He battered his way through them, and out of the lobby. Once outside, the crowd wasn't quite as dense, and he could move more quickly, but so could the ones pursuing him. To his left and right were more crowds, more police, and up ahead was a railing that guarded an oasis of palms and ferns. In the center of the Oasis stood a mock volcano that erupted with precise regularity on the hour, twenty-four hours a day. Once a highlight of the Strip, it was now just part of the scenery. The five o'clock eruption had already begun, gas jets spreading fire over waterfalls and into the dark lagoon. Tongues of flame licked out, covering the surface of the water.

"Stop him!"

He felt a hand grab for his collar, and miss. There was only one route for him now, and no time to linger on the decision. He climbed the railing and leapt into the flaming lagoon, leaving his destiny to the fires of the volcano.

DILLON NEEDED SOME time alone that afternoon—some time to prepare.

The other Shards had spent much of their hour-long ride from Las Vegas riding the high of the glorious day. Dillon had to admit, he got caught up in it, too.

He had watched the news on the bus's TV screen and had enjoyed the sight of his own face. Locally, their little show had supplanted the Shiprock Massacres as the leading news stories. If the bloodbath in Shiprock was a sign of the coming chaos, then Dillon was already stealing focus and seizing control. He relished the expert attempts to explain his windowless wall of water, which, like the pool at Hearst Castle, would remain until someone chose to drain the water out. It made Dillon feel big—so much larger than life, he felt he might burst out of his own skin and swell until he stood taller than the mountains.

"Keep your eye on the big picture," he had told the others. *"We're not doing this for ourselves"*—but it was something he had to keep reminding himself. Elevating himself into broader public view was just a means to an end. Still, he couldn't deny the glorious feeling it gave him.

Once their campsite was established, Dillon wasted no further time in idle talk. He had left the circle of buses, and headed toward a craggy ridge a mile away.

He made his way up the rocks that reddened in the late-afternoon sun. Winston had said he was playing Jesus and Moses wrapped together, and it did feel as if he were climbing the face of Sinai as he scaled the jagged rocks.

Dillon was slowly becoming used to such comparisons, feeling more at home in the company of prophets and saviors—and he dared to wonder, when this was all over, where his name would fall in the records of the divinely touched.

These were heady thoughts. Thoughts he had caged, ever since he had found his powers—but now, on the eve of his ascension into the limelight, he needed to ponder them, for his confidence needed to grow large enough to blanket the world.

He reached the top of the bluff, and stared down at the magnificent man-made wonder that lay on the other side, still swarmed by tourists. Even from a distance, its concrete expanse was breathtaking.

Okoya arrived some time later. Dillon didn't hear him until he spoke.

"To think it was built by mere human hands," Okoya said, when he saw the view. "It rivals the Pyramids, and the Colossus of Rhodes."

"Take a good look," said Dillon. "It's your last chance."

Just a few short days ago, Dillon had felt threatened by Okoya's presence; mistrustful and suspicious. But such feelings felt small and distant as he stood on the hilltop. Nothing could threaten him now.

"What will it be like after tomorrow?" Dillon wondered aloud.

Okoya sat beside him. "Once, the world was flat and sat at the

center of the universe," Okoya said. "But people learned otherwise, and they adjusted. We are on that precipice of change again.
Tomorrow the world will be a very different place."

"People will have no choice but to accept us."

Okoya agreed. "You are too powerful to deny, and too dangerous to challenge."

Dillon tried to imagine the days ahead. Would they usher in
an era of peace? Would they find themselves in the company of
kings and world leaders? He could barely imagine himself meeting
world leaders, much less instructing them on global affairs. And yet
that would be the task set before him.

The thought was too immense to grasp, so he laughed at it. "I
wonder how they'll feel to have the world in the hands of a pack
of sixteen-year-olds."

"You won't always be sixteen," said Okoya. "And it doesn't
surprise me that you'll be rising to the throne of humanity. What
surprises me is that it's taken you so long."

"Did you know," said Dillon, "that I can find no pattern when
I look in the eyes of some of the followers?"

"Really? That's odd."

"No," said Dillon, thinking he understood why. "It makes
sense if you think about it. . . . Now that they've dedicated their
lives to the cause, they have no pattern but the one I give them."

"Blank slates," suggested Okoya.

"Yes—waiting for me to write on."

"What could be better?"

Okoya stood and kicked a rock down the hillside. It tumbled,
kicking up dust on the way down. "I'm worried about Michael,"
Okoya said.

"He's a loose cannon," Dillon admitted.

"We may need to take care of him," said Okoya.

Dillon waved it off. "Yeah, yeah—I'll take care of everybody."

"No," said Okoya. "That's *not* what I mean."

Dillon stood, finding an unexpected seriousness in Okoya's
face that he couldn't decipher. Then Dillon burst out laughing.
"Very good! You had me going there. And I thought you didn't
have a sense of humor!"

Okoya laughed too, dismissing his own grave expression.

"Ruling the world is easy," said Okoya. "Comedy's hard."

They chuckled a few moments more, then Okoya became pensive. Reflective.

"You remind me of someone I once knew in the Greek Isles. He was a lot like you at your age—although not nearly as gifted."

"The Greek Isles?"

"Just because I come from a reservation, it doesn't mean I haven't traveled."

Dillon took a pointedly invasive look at Okoya, to once again divine the source of his worldliness—but all he found were the simple patterns of a rural life. But that was somehow untrue. It was merely a facade, someone else he was hiding behind.

"Who are you, Okoya?"

The expression on Okoya's face changed then, becoming open and unambiguous. "I'm someone who wants to put the world in the palm of your hand."

Okoya left, and as night fell, Dillon found himself still transfixed by the view, eerily lit by a rising blood moon.

He resolved to remain there till dawn, preparing his mind for the task at hand. Meditating on himself, Dillon thought of the network of connections already spreading forth, linking Dillon and the Shards with signs and wonders in millions of people's minds, as they turned on their evening news. Tomorrow those numbers would flare, as they became witnesses to the impossible—a miraculous wake-up call to the world, too huge to deny.

Forty-five days from now, there would be no doubters. That day would see an end to war, disease, and despair. There would never be another Shiprock Massacre—he would see to that. His binding strength would be a protective sheath around the world.

He looked again to the view before him. Lake Mead stretched to a rocky shore, and before it, the concrete expanse of Hoover Dam arced across a deep ravine, holding in the lake.

Dillon smiled.

Tomorrow this troubled, crumbling world would believe in miracles.

19. BLIND RUN

DREW CAMDEN WAS NO SLEUTH. CONSTANTLY DISTRACTED and uncharacteristically clumsy, he was poorly suited to spy on Okoya. However, the carrot Michael had hung in front of him was powerful motivation.

He positioned his bedroll in view of Okoya's tent, into which the mysterious Indian had retreated after dinner. For hours he listened to irritating songs around the campfires, and heard stories. Storytellers were emerging in this new order, weaving lofty dramas about the Shards that had no basis in fact whatsoever: how the Shards were ancient and ageless; how their semblance of youth was only a guise. Drew didn't bother to contradict them.

Other followers had been assigned the task of receiving new arrivals, who drifted in from the Boulder Highway in a steady osmotic flow. By two in the morning, most everyone but the posted watch had settled down.

The night was much colder than it should have been, and the sky up above was punctuated by a brilliant spray of stars. If Michael and the others were illuminated with the fragmented soul of a star, Drew wondered as he lay there, what did that make him? What did that make everyone else? Tiny, insignificant smithereens? He wondered how long until the Shards would find people too small for their attention.

Well, thought Drew, *better take my share of favors now, before Michael's pedestal gets too high.*

There was a flap of fabric, and Drew rolled over to see Okoya step from his tent. Drew slipped out of his sleeping bag and followed, taking his video-cam with him. He kept his distance as Okoya strolled among the sleeping campers. There seemed to be no destination; he merely meandered, glancing from face to face of the ones who slept beneath the open air—as if looking for some-one.

Finally, Okoya stopped by a clutch of sleeping bags behind a larger tent, out of view from everyone else.

Drew watched as Okoya knelt, then put a hand behind a sleeping woman's neck, and tilted her head slightly back, as if he were about to resuscitate her. Then, the space between Okoya and the woman arced with a wave of soft, crimson light that lit their faces for a few moments, then faded.

The woman rolled over, and pulled her sleeping bag up to her shoulders, never waking up. Okoya moved to the man beside her, repeating the same procedure.

Drew wasn't sure what he was witnessing—but he did know that he must have hit the jackpot. Whatever this was, it was infor-mation for Michael—and that meant Michael had to make good on his promise.

Okoya moved on to a third camper.

All it would take to clinch this would be a video! The light created by Okoya's strange encounters would create enough of an image to see. Drew quietly raised the video-cam to his eyes, slid his thumb over the red button and pressed it.

The machine beeped twice as it went from STANDBY to RE-CORD . . . And in the silence, those two tones might as well have been the chimes of Big Ben. The glow died suddenly, and Okoya's head turned as smoothly as an owl's, directly to Drew.

Drew suddenly felt like a small rodent caught in Okoya's owl-ish gaze, and he bolted. Tripping over campers, barreling into tents, he tried to make it to where the Shards slept.

"Michael," he called. "Michael, help me!" But he realized that he had lost his sense of direction in the large circle of buses, and didn't know where he was. Whichever way he turned, Okoya was behind him. There was a narrow space between two buses, and Drew raced for it. Regardless of what had changed in his heart, head, and character, he still had the body of a runner, and flight was now the only defense he had.

He burst through the circle of buses, escaping into the open desert beyond—his legs churning as he fixed on glowing lights just over the jagged hills . . .

★   ★   ★

MICHAEL, TORY, LOURDES, AND WINSTON slept beneath a large canopy set against their bus. The ground was covered with tapestries torn from the walls of San Simeon, and they slept on beds taken from the castle as well.

As the night scraped along, Tory lay awake, plagued by Winston's words.

"Big deal. Dillon would have brought me back."

Did that make it acceptable, then, to take his life? Did murder suddenly have no meaning? No consequence?

"Big deal."

She thought back to that first moment she and Winston had found Okoya sitting beside them in the coffee shop. That wasn't a chance meeting, was it? Somehow Okoya had known who they were—and now she realized that Okoya was using them . . . but toward what end? She sat up in bed, throwing off the covers, and let the frosty night chill her bones, because comfort was now an enemy. It had kept her complacent for far too long.

Michael slept in another bed a few feet away, wrapped in several dense quilts, yet she could hear his teeth chattering. Tory realized that it was his own cold that filled the night air.

"Michael?"

She went over to him and peeled the covers away from his face. He was awake, and looked awful, as if the life had been drained out of him.

"Michael, what's wrong? Are you sick?" And then it occurred to her that he couldn't be sick. None of them could.

"Hungry," Michael rasped out.

"I'll get you something to eat."

But he grabbed her arm before she could leave. "No," he said. "Not that kind of hunger."

She met his eyes, and she knew what he meant. Although there was a loud part of her mind that was screaming denial, she forced herself to listen to a quieter voice within herself, that told her what she had been afraid to hear. "This is about Okoya, isn't it?"

Michael gritted his teeth to keep them from chattering. "Listen to me Tory: A year ago, when we killed our parasites, we thought we came away unhurt—but we were wrong. Those things left holes in us that we didn't know how to fill. So we invited Okoya into our lives to fill them for us, plugging up those holes."

"With what?"

"I don't know . . . but it's in the music and perfumes. It's in the words Winston reads, and the food Lourdes eats."

He's delirious, Tory thought. *He has to be. . . .* But her voice of denial was losing its bite in the face of what Michael said. How many mornings had she woken up to luxuriate in a hot bath scented with oils Okoya had supplied? It would whet her appetite for every indulgence the day had to offer. And when she was hungry, it was no longer food she desired, but the charged aroma of purity Okoya was more than happy to provide. Tory had heard of holy men who never ate, and who were said to draw their sustenance from the air itself. Was this transcendental appetite part of the Shards' curious physiology? And if so, what had they been dining on?

"You did the right thing when you left the bus this afternoon," Tory told Michael. "Okoya is . . . I don't know what Okoya is—but she's not our friend. *It's* not our friend."

Michael rolled over in bed then, and Tory caught sight of his face—pale and wan—just as it was a year before when his soul had harbored the blue-flamed beast.

Okoya is like that beast, thought Tory, *but different.* Not a parasite, but a predator—which was far more dangerous.

She took his hands into hers and tried to warm them but it did no good. "Are you going to be all right?"

"Sing to me, Tory," he whispered. "Something bright. Something warm."

And so she slipped beneath the covers with him, holding him to share her warmth, and with her lips to his ear she began to gently sing an old Genesis tune she remembered. " 'I will follow you, will you follow me . . .' " Michael laughed at her choice of song, for there had been way too much following lately. " '. . . all the days and nights that we know will be . . .' " She sang to him until she could feel the slightest warmth begin to return to his fingers, and the sting of chill begin to leave the night air. Perhaps it lacked the feeding emotional flood of Okoya's music, but it was something.

"We have to find Dillon and warn him about Okoya," Tory told him.

Just then came the clattering sound of tent stakes flying and the tearing of nylon.

"Michael! Michael, help me!" yelled a far-off voice.

There was a commotion way across the campsite—the shouts of people suddenly woken as someone crashed over them.

"Oh no!" said Michael. "It's Drew!"

He heaved himself out of bed, finding the strength to walk. Tory led the way, pulling Michael along with her.

"I told him to watch Okoya—to find out what he was up to."

They crashed over the debris of overturned tents, until they came out of the circle of buses. About twenty yards out, was a red blinking light. They ran toward it, to find Drew's video camera lying in the sand.

In the distance, two figures sprinted across the desert, one in pursuit of the other.

"We'll never catch them," said Michael, but even so, he threw his legs out before him, running as best he could.

"Let me help you," Tory put her arm around his waist and threw her weight into his stride. Together they forged toward the lights of Hoover Dam.

OKOYA'S WILL WAS more powerful than anyone's on Earth—but there were limitations to his stolen human body. Although he drove that body to pursue Drew Camden, Drew was a fast runner, and Okoya could not overtake him—but he did not lose sight of him, either. He pursued Drew past the jagged hills—where Dillon slept alone that night, dreaming of greatness—until he reached the two-lane highway that rode along the ridge of Hoover Dam. Drew was already at the dam, in a panic. Under the bright spotlights, he tried to flag down help, but traffic was sparse this time of night—and what few cars came his way, had no intention of stopping for a lunatic waving his arms in the middle of the road.

Okoya ran onto the dam's paved rim at full speed, as Drew hurried to a metal doorway and pounded on it—but it would not give. However, a guard farther away had seen him, and crossed the road toward Drew. Okoya picked up his speed to intercept.

"What's all this about?" said the guard, obviously thinking he could get this situation under control.

"He's trying to kill me!" screamed Drew.

"Hold on, son," said the guard. "No one's going to—"

Okoya reached them, and wasted no time. He took the guard out with a single punch to his Adam's apple. The guard crumpled, and Drew took off again, climbing the waist-high stone guardrail on the canyon side of the dam. Drew balanced himself precariously, as Okoya grabbed for his feet. Then Drew leapt—disappearing over the edge.

It was almost eight hundred feet to the bottom of Black Canyon, and Okoya was sure that Drew had taken his own life, saving Okoya the trouble . . . until Okoya climbed the guardrail, and saw Drew heading down a narrow flight of metal stairs leading to a catwalk that hugged the dam's curved face. Okoya resumed his pursuit. Down below, Drew reached a rusted metal door in the middle of the massive face of the dam—it was where the catwalk ended. Okoya practically glided down the steps toward him as Drew kicked the door again, and again, until its rusted lock gave way, and the door burst inward into darkness.

Okoya frowned. Luck had no business being with this boy tonight, and Okoya resolved to make Drew's end doubly cruel because of it. Okoya followed him into the narrow concrete-lined access corridor. Its walls were wet with seepage and there were no lights in the tight, claustrophobic space. The distant vibrations of the power plant down below made it impossible for Okoya to hear Drew's footsteps. He knew Drew would head toward the power plant, where there would be night workers to hide behind.

Fine, thought Okoya. *See how he does in the dark.*

Okoya strode forward, confident within the blindness. . . . For darkness was not a stumbling block to the Bringer, but a comfort, and a reminder of home.

MICHAEL AND TORY arrived at the dam five minutes behind them, and as they reached the road, they saw Drew and Okoya immediately. Their moving figures on the catwalk stood out across the halogen-lit face of the dam. Tory was about to race toward them, but Michael grabbed her hand.

"No," he said. "This way." And he thanked God for the fact that his father was a heavy gambler, for he had dragged Michael to Las Vegas countless times as a child, and had visited Hoover Dam more than once. He remembered enough to know that the best way into the dam wasn't through the dam itself, but through an elevator shaft in the adjacent Visitors Center, that descended 520 feet into the bedrock of the canyon.

They broke out a window of the Visitors Center, climbed through, quickly found an elevator, and began a long drop into the bowels of the Earth.

DREW RACED BLINDLY though the black corridors, smashing into walls, his hands out in front of him. He tumbled down a staircase, slipped down some sort of spillway, then plummeted through a shaft that deposited him in an unseen, foul-smelling muck. With hands stretched before him, he groped forward until finding a hint of light, which led him to yet another stairway heading down.

Finally, Drew came flying out through an open gate and landed with a metallic clang against a platform that hung above the massive, moaning turbines of the great power plant. He could hear the rush of water, as Lake Mead once again became the Colorado River, surging through the powerful turbines, generating electricity. As he had hoped, there were workers down there—enough to protect him. Even if they didn't believe a word of his story, at least he would be safe.

He made a move to head down the ladder, when he was grabbed from behind. He turned, and Okoya, not even winded from the chase, gripped Drew by his shirt, lifted him up, and held him out over the platform railing. Drew screamed, trying to draw attention of anyone down below, but the drone of the generators was just too loud for him to be heard. Now the only thing keeping Drew from falling to his death was Okoya's angry grip.

"Please!" begged Drew. "I'll do anything, *anything*! I won't tell anyone what I saw. I'll spy on Michael and the others for you— would you like that? Just please, *please* don't hurt me!"

"Your cowardice disgusts me."

Drew was certain that Okoya would release his grip and let him die a painful, coward's death. But instead, something else happened.

Red tendrils lashed out from Okoya's eyes, gripping something deep within Drew . . . tearing it from him . . . and in that moment, Drew Camden ceased to exist.

★   ★   ★

MICHAEL AND TORY arrived just in time to see it happen, and there was nothing they could do.

"Put him down!" screamed Michael. The soulless Drew still squirmed in panic in Okoya's grip, his legs dangling out over the generator floor fifty feet below.

"Thank goodness you're here!" said Okoya. "He's a traitor! He tried to sabotage Dillon's plan." He lifted Drew back over the railing, and dropped him on the platform. Drew scrambled away to a safe corner behind Michael and Tory.

"Stop the lies," Tory said. "We know what you are."

Okoya then flashed them his superior grin. "Do you?"

"I've seen the soulless shells you leave behind," Michael said, taking a step closer. His legs shook, and his muscles felt as if they'd been flayed, but he forced himself to stand firm against Okoya.

Okoya dropped all pretenses then. "Your kind dines on flesh," he said; "mine dines on *spirit*. Are we all that different?"

"We're nothing like you," growled Michael.

"Are you so sure?" Okoya got a radar fix on Michael's eyes, as he had done so many times before. "You, Tory, and the others have now risen to the top of the food chain . . . just like me." He looked at Tory. "Feeling hungry, Tory? Feeling *dirty*? You've grown beyond the need for normal food—you know that, don't you?"

Tory took a shuddering step back.

"And what about you, Michael? There's no strength left in you at all. I can give you what you hunger for—the food of the gods—if you're willing to admit to yourself how much you desire it."

Then Okoya cupped his hands before him, and Michael watched as the pores in Okoya's arm opened up, spilling forth a red, glowing perspiration that rolled in rivulets down his wrists, and into his cupped hands, becoming a thick, viscous pool of liquid light. Okoya's high-energy diet.

"It can be anything you want it to be, Michael. A musical feast for your ears, a perfect texture you can feel against your flesh, an aromatic salve, or a banquet fit for a king. Whatever sense you choose to feed." The pool of light in Okoya's hand then changed, becoming silver and reflective. "Or perhaps you'd like to feast your eyes on a vision of your own future."

And as Michael gazed into the silver pool, it became a window, and Michael could not look away. Cupped in Okoya's hands, he saw a shimmering city. Glorious spires beneath crystal-clear skies. A place that did not yet exist . . . but would.

"They will build entire cities to you, Michael. Thousands of gleaming towers lovingly erected to your name."

There was a magnificent dwelling, open to the sky, because the elements of nature had no hold over this place. In the center of all this, surrounded by an opulence that made Hearst Castle seem like costume jewelry, Michael saw himself, clothed in light, surrounded by thousands—*millions*—who lived only to satisfy his pleasure, whose greatest joy was to be in his presence, deep within the inner core of his powerful sphere of influence.

"Why not satisfy all your senses at once?" Okoya brought his hands forward, and Michael found himself cupping his own hands to receive the liquid vision.

"Michael, don't!"

But he could barely hear Tory's voice anymore. The vision poured from Okoya's hands into Michael's, not a bit of it spilling. The image in the surface shimmered, but the vision stayed in focus. He could hear it now: the sounds of worship. Singing voices— Okoya's music multiplied a thousandfold. He could smell the future—a luscious aroma of all his favorite foods swirled into one. He longed to take this vision inside him. To drink it in, to taste it. To feel it flow through him, infusing him with the strength of his own future. It was everything Michael had ever craved. All he had to do was take it in . . .

But as he gazed at it, as he *listened*, there was something else he heard there, too. It had been there all along in the sights, sounds, smells, and flavors Okoya had put before them—but Michael had not been attuned to its frequency until now.

This pool of light was alive.

And it was screaming.

Michael pulled his gaze away from it, forcing himself to see Drew who still cowered in the corner. Even from here, Michael could tell that Drew's soul had been taken from him by Okoya. And suddenly Michael knew exactly who he was about to dine upon.

Still, he brought this liquid manna closer to his face. To smell it. To feel it. To taste it.

"I knew I could count on you, Michael," said Okoya triumphantly.

Although Michael's mind and body wanted to drink it in, he fought the crushing urge and instead hurled it away.

In the direction of Drew.

"No!" cried Okoya.

The shimmering globule of life-energy struck Drew in the chest, and exploded like mercury into a thousand droplets that coursed around Drew's body. Drew arched his back and gasped, as his soul returned to him through the pores of his skin, and back to that intangible place inside.

Okoya's surprise only lasted for an instant, then his face became blizzard-cold.

"You've squandered your last chance for greatness, Michael," he said. "You and Tory have both outlived your usefulness."

Suddenly Drew bolted from the corner, heading toward the doorway that led back into the inner structure of the dam.

"Drew, no!" Michael leapt after him. And in that moment of confusion, Okoya grabbed Tory, twisted her arm behind her back, then pushed her into the opening as well, slamming the gate. With one hand Okoya held the gate closed, and with the other, ripped an iron rail-post from the concrete wall—partly with his human strength, and partly with the sheer force of his will. Then he jammed the pole through the handles of the gate, securing it so firmly that it didn't give an inch. Tory and Michael rammed their bodies against the gate, but it was no use—and their screams would never be heard over the turbines—nor would they be seen from this unlit, remote corner of the rafters.

Okoya laughed heartily. "How marvelous!" said Okoya. "I don't have to kill you now; Dillon will do it for me—and he won't even know it!"

Okoya strode away, his laughter dissolving into the awful warbling whine of the turbines.

For more than half an hour, the three of them kicked at the gate. Michael hurled a wind at it, but it only sifted like water through a sieve. Finally they realized the only way out was up, into the cold concrete hell of the dam.

"We'll get out, right?" asked Drew, searching for some hint

of reassurance. "I mean, it might take some time, but we'll get out of here, won't we?"

Michael and Tory both turned to him. Could it be that he didn't know?

"What is it?" said Drew. "It better not be bad news. I'm not ready for bad news."

"We don't *have* any time," Tory said coldly. "In a few hours Dillon's going to shatter the dam."

20. DAMMED

LAKE MEAD, THE LARGEST MAN-MADE LAKE IN THE WORLD, stretched for 115 miles behind the half-million-ton concrete plug called Hoover Dam. Although it had never seen the likes of Dillon Cole, the dam was by no means a stranger to the bizarre; from the psychotic behavior of heat-maddened workers during its construction, to the ninety-four deaths recorded by the time it was complete. Most of those deaths were workers boiled under the heat of the unforgiving sun. But then there was the scaler, who fell into the pit of Black Canyon, only to have his body bickered over by the Nevada and Arizona coroners for hours because, during construction, there was no Colorado River to divide the two states, and no one could agree in which state—besides postmortem—the body lay. There were macabre tales of dying laborers crawling across the unfinished concrete abutments of the dam, just to get to the Arizona side before they died, because death benefits in Arizona were far better than in Nevada. And then, of course, there was the eerie fact that the last person to die while building the dam, was the son of the first person to die while building it. But, to the disappointment of tourists everywhere, the horrific tales of hapless workers slipping into the wet concrete, only to be sealed within the walls, were untrue. No one had been entombed in Hoover Dam. Yet.

DILLON, REFRESHINGLY CHILLED from a night communing with himself, woke up in time to see the sunrise. It spilled over the red mountains, shimmering on Lake Mead to his left, and cutting across the pit of Black Canyon to his right.

By seven A.M., Dillon stood at a view spot on the rim of the dam, near a broken window at the Visitors Center. Before him were two identical bronze statues, massive, with stylized human faces, muscular chests, and sharp, pointed wings held straight up, as if poised to puncture Heaven. He looked down at a star chart beneath his feet. Tiny dots of brass stars were imbedded in blue concrete, each star perfectly placed to be a precise image of the night sky. But it wasn't quite perfect, was it?

Dillon knelt down, and pressed his thumb over a single star, erasing it for a moment from the constellation of Scorpius.

Mentarsus-H—a star which was no longer there, but its living soul was here on earth. *Or at least five-sixths of it,* thought Dillon. And, reflexively, Dillon turned up to the winged statue that looked so much like the Spirit of Destruction that had tricked him into killing Deanna. Her gift had been the conquest of fear, and a transforming power of faith. There was no telling how much smoother today's event would have gone with the strength of Deanna's faith, and her love.

But he couldn't let himself dwell on Deanna, either. Events were turning much too quickly now, and he had come here for a reason.

Although the Visitors Center hadn't officially opened yet, there were already tourists wandering the deck. So far, no one had recognized him, and he hoped no one would.

He strolled around the Visitors Center, and down the road that curved along the rim of the dam. He knelt to the ground, putting his ear to the curb, like someone might put their ear to a railroad track to listen for an approaching train. By now he had gained the attention of a few tourists, who laughed, wondering what might be wrong with him. He didn't bother to look at them; he just moved on, rubbing his hands along the concrete, until finding a spot on the sidewalk where a tiny weed grew through an insignificant hairline crack. He traced his finger along that crack until stopping at a single point, and then, when no one was looking, he pulled a small stone out of his pocket, and tapped the spot three times . . .

. . . *click . . . click . . . click.*

Then he stood, stretched, and casually left, heading back across the desert to his circle of followers three miles away.

Behind him, the two noisy lanes of traffic crossing the dam made it impossible for anyone to hear the tiny triplet of sounds that slowly grew louder as it echoed back and forth through the concrete superstructure.

THE DAM WAS only forty-five feet wide at its rim, but at its base it extended back beneath the waters of the lake to a width of five hundred feet. Five miles of tunnel wove through the concrete dam and the bedrock on either side of it. Some tunnels were built for maintenance, others for drainage, and still more seemed to serve no function at all, beyond being havens for rats. There were even some crawlways that didn't exist on any blueprint—cavities left by unscrupulous foremen hoping to conserve concrete and time when the dam was being built. The result was a lightless, interlocking maze, full of hopeless dead ends and stagnant dead air.

"What time is it?" Michael asked. "I don't even know if it's daylight yet."

Holding hands to keep from losing each other, Michael, Tory, and Drew squeezed forward between the slimy stone walls of the catacomb.

"I don't know," said Tory. "I can't see my watch."

Drew, who fearfully brought up the rear, said nothing. For hours they had poked around in absolute darkness, following the squeals of rats that ran over their feet—only to find them disappearing into holes too small for humans to fit. Michael had begun to leave scratch-marks on the wall with his pocketknife. But as they pressed forward, going this way and that, sliding down spillways, and scratching their way up chimneylike shafts, they began to feel their fingertips coming across those same scratch-marks again. They were going in circles.

"I'll create a storm high above the dam," Michael suggested, "so they'll see it from the campsite, and they'll know we're here."

He concentrated on shaping an angry cumulus into a pointing finger far above their heads. Soon they began to hear the rain, but it didn't quite sound right . . . and then water began to rush past their ankles.

"Michael," asked Tory, "what did you do?"

"I don't like this," complained Drew. "I don't like this at all."

The rats around them were swimming now. They could feel them clawing at their pantlegs for purchase.

"Make them stop," said Drew. "Please make them stop!"

Michael pushed his stormy feelings out one more time. Now the water not only came from below, but from above—raining on them in the narrow corridors, spilling down the walls, and Michael realized exactly what had happened. His power wasn't strong enough to penetrate the hundred yards of concrete above. His storm had nowhere to go but the narrow passageways around them, pulling moisture from the stone and condensing into a drowning flood:

"Stop it, Michael!" shouted Tory. "It's not working!"

Michael shut the storm down, but it was too late. He could hear the rush of water draining from passageways above. "Hold on!" Michael yelled, but there was nothing to hold on to. The flash flood surged past them, heading for lower ground, and the current pulled them off their feet. Coughing and sputtering, they were dragged down, deeper still, into the dam, until finally landing in a chamber where the water spilled from a dozen holes above their heads.

The three tried to find each other in the darkness.

"Where are we? What is this place!" cried Drew, as if someone would be able to answer him.

How stupid, thought Michael, to have all the power they had, and yet be unable to escape from a big block of concrete. Between himself and Tory, they could do little more than drown themselves and create tunnels full of disease-free rats.

"Do something!" screamed Drew.

But Michael was out of ideas. "I don't know what to do!" The water, which only a moment ago was at their knees, was already rising past their waists. In the icy chill, Michael could feel his muscles threatening to cramp.

"I can't drown in here!" wailed Drew. "I can't die in a place like this!"

"Shut up!" screamed Tory impatiently.

They lost each other, each trying to find a spot where water wasn't cascading down over their heads. The water reached their chins, and Michael felt his feet leave the floor. He kicked to stay afloat, but breathed in a mouthful of water, beginning to gag.

That's when he heard the clanging of a machine as it roared to life.

In an instant the water level began to drop.

"It's a pump!" shouted Tory.

Michael felt the floor beneath his feet again. "This room must be some sort of sump," he said. "A place to catch the seepage from the dam! It probably pumps the water right out into the Colorado River . . . If we can find the intake, we could get out that way . . ."

"And be dragged through the paddles of the turbines," added Tory. "Thanks, but no thanks."

They waded toward each other's voices as the water was pumped out. Michael coughed, dislodging more fluid from his lungs. The water fell beneath their knees, then their ankles. A hissing *suck* heralded the last of it being drawn out through a grated hole in the floor, leaving the three of them waterlogged and despondent.

"This is *your* fault, Michael!" accused Drew. "You made me go after Okoya. We're gonna die because of you!"

Michael could swear he heard Tory's teeth grinding in anger. "It's because of Michael that you still have a soul!" she chided, then added, "Dillon should have left you dead. We'd all be better off."

Michael reached out and found her hand in the darkness. "It's okay, Tory—it's not him talking."

"No?" grunted Tory. "Who is it, then?"

Michael considered that. *Someone I don't know. Reconstituted beef.*

Thinking back, there were many mistakes Michael had made since setting off in search of Dillon, but there was one that stuck out in his mind. It was the first thing that had made him truly feel like a god. The one willful act that sold him into Okoya's bondage. The changing of Drew's nature.

How could Michael blame Drew for being less of a person than he had been, when the change was Michael's doing? At the time, Michael had convinced himself it had been for Drew's sake, but that wasn't entirely true. He had done it for himself; to hurl Drew's attentions away from him.

Although Michael couldn't see Drew in the blackness, he could hear his uneven breathing, and he slid across the grime of the sump floor until he bumped against Drew's sopping jeans.

"Who's that? What are you doing?"

"It's just me, Drew." He grabbed Drew's arm.

"No! Stop that! Don't touch me—just get back over there."
Drew struggled, but Michael held him firm.

"There's something I have to give you," said Michael.

"Whatever it is, I don't want it!"

"Maybe not. But you need it." Michael pinned Drew into a
corner.

"What's going on over there?" asked Tory. She had no idea
that Michael had denatured Drew. For Drew's sake, he chose not
to tell her now.

"Get off me!" screamed Drew. His voice echoed around the
chamber. "Leave me alone, you freak!"

Michael put one hand against Drew's face, and pressed the
other heavily against his chest.

"I don't want you to!" cried Drew. "I don't want you to!"

"Shhh," said Michael. The calm in his voice brought a slight
warmth to the air around them. "Shhh. It will all be okay."

In a moment, Drew stopped struggling, and Michael forced a
surge of energy out through his palms until it flowed through Drew
like a circuit.

"I'm afraid," whispered Drew.

"That's okay," answered Michael.

Michael then reached his thoughts down, until he found
Drew's denatured self, and folded it in upon itself, collapsing and
re-forming it back to the way it had started: strong of character . . .
responsible . . . trustworthy . . . and undeniably homosexual.

Suddenly Drew was holding Michael, rather than pushing him
away, and Michael allowed it because he knew that this was not
about sex. It was an embrace between brothers. An embrace between friends. And so he returned it.

Drew let Michael go first, and they both let their minds clear
for a moment.

"Would it be appropriate," asked Michael, "to welcome you
back?"

He heard Drew breathe heavily in the darkness, reorienting
himself to his inner landscape. "It might be."

"Wild ride these past few weeks, huh?"

"Yeah, a regular spin cycle," Drew said. "I wouldn't recom-
mend it for pregnant women, or people with back trouble."

Michael grinned, and then quickly, before he had the chance

to change his mind, he leaned forward and gave Drew a kiss. It didn't feel right, it didn't feel wrong, it just felt strange. But at the moment it also felt necessary. "Hold on to that one," Michael told him quietly, "because it's the only one you're going to get from me."

"I can deal with that."

Then from somewhere across the chamber, they heard Tory. "If you two are done fighting, you may want to check this out. I found a vent we could probably squeeze through, if I can get the grate open."

"Can I help?" asked Drew. He confidently slid past Michael, toward the sound of Tory's voice.

With hands held out before him, Michael crossed the chamber, to work the gate with Drew and Tory, and soon all three of them were way too focused to hear the faint triplet of sounds slowly building as it echoed back and forth in the concrete around them.

WITH THE DAM set on autodestruct, Dillon hurried back to the campsite. As he neared it, he could see rows of police and state troopers lining the road a few hundred yards away. They kept a safe distance, as did the news helicopters circling above—for they had already learned that anyone who went in, came out a devout follower, or did not come out at all. Dillon knew that the best law enforcement could do, was to hold back the influx of curiosity-seekers . . . but that would soon be impossible, because, by the time this day was over, they would be seeking more than just their curiosity—they would be seeking the face of God. But what they would find would be a divinity of five. Dillon could sense the eyes of the nation aligning in a single direction, focusing on this spot in the desert where Dillon's extraordinary event was already beginning to unfold.

When he approached the circle of buses, he heard cheers from within. The followers had gathered around Okoya, who stood atop a boulder. Dillon couldn't hear what Okoya said, but whatever it was, it stirred up the followers. And although their excitement charged the dry desert air, Dillon found himself troubled—not because of their enthusiasm, but because it was focused on Okoya, and not him. Dillon had to fight his way through the dense crowd, until they saw who it was and began to part for him. It seemed to

Dillon that there were twice as many people here today as there were yesterday.

Okoya stepped down from his high spot. "Is it done?"

Dillon nodded. "The road is jammed with cars. We're going to have to walk—and we don't have much time."

"I'll get them going." Okoya turned to leave, but Dillon grabbed him.

"I wanted to make an announcement: to prepare everyone for what's about to happen—what they're going to see."

"I've done that already," said Okoya.

Dillon felt a wave of anger rise in him. "Who gave you permission to do that? It should be me announcing the descent into Black Canyon."

"You were supposed to be back at dawn," Okoya said impatiently. "You've already wasted enough time; don't waste any more." Okoya pulled out of Dillon's grasp, and went to gather the crowd.

As Dillon headed for the canopy where the other Shards had slept, he began to wonder why Okoya was the one to step forward. The way each of the Shards had been jockeying for position, Dillon would have assumed any one of them would leap at the chance to usurp some measure of power.

But Michael and Tory were nowhere to be found, while Winston and Lourdes appeared far too content at the center of their own petty universes to be bothered with actually *doing* anything. He found the two of them sitting beneath the canopy. Lourdes was lost in a deep emotional involvement with breakfast, while Winston faced away from her, practically vanishing behind the morning paper. Sitting on velvet chairs, on sandy tapestries pilfered from Hearst Castle, they were a surreal disconnect, like a Magritte painting; both comically and tragically absurd.

"Where are Michael and Tory?" Dillon asked.

Lourdes squeezed the juice from her grapefruit into her mouth before answering, "I haven't seen them all morning."

"They took off," said Winston. "Okoya seems to think they left with their own little splinter group."

"What?"

"People do get tired of taking orders," Winston said, barely veiling his own threat of desertion.

"You should try some of Okoya's hash browns," said Lourdes. Dillon's head was swimming now, his mind fighting to grasp how things could have slipped so far. How could Tory and Michael abandon them?

The rich aroma of steaming, butter-fried potatoes played in his nostrils, and as he looked at the bowl of hash browns, it hit him that they smelled a bit *too* good, hitting his olfactory with such intensity, Dillon found his own hunger becoming acute. Indeed, it seemed all of their appetites had elevated beyond the commonplace, to things far more enticing. Dillon leaned closer, picking up the bowl in his hands, focusing his thoughts on the potatoes before him. Although they looked like hash browns, its pattern was like something else entirely. In fact, to Dillon, those little shoestrings seemed to be squirming and writhing—weaving in and out of one another. . . . *Like worms,* he thought—but with a life-pattern far more complex. A life-pattern that was . . . that was . . .

The moment he realized what he was looking at, Dillon yelped as if his hands had been seared, and he hurled the bowl away. It shattered on a boulder, splattering red liquid light that dripped to the ground, disappearing into the sand.

Winston put down his newspaper.

Whatever the spell had been, it was now broken, for now Lourdes's fork didn't hold hash browns. Instead the tines dripped with vermillion light. It oozed from the corners of her mouth like blood. She wiped her mouth with the back of her hand, and watched as it soaked into her skin, vanishing. She looked to Winston, and then to Dillon, already beginning to turn a pale shade of green. "If that wasn't hash browns," she asked, "exactly what have I been eating?"

"Not just you," said Dillon, turning to Winston. Winston looked down at the newspaper that had seemed so innocuous a moment ago. There were no words on the page—no pictures, just rows of random letters and symbols that his brain had translated into meaning. Even now he was still drawing something from the page as he gazed at it—a faint stream of red light passing from the page to his eyes, like a long draft of a cold drink. Finally Winston shuddered, breaking free—and the moment he did, the paper itself began to dissolve away, bubbling into that same liquid light.

Okoya arrived a moment too late to preserve his illusions.

"What a waste," he said. "I worked hard to prepare these things for you."

"Okoya," said Winston, with a fearful quiver Dillon had never heard in Winston's voice before, "what have we been . . . *consuming?*"

"The souls of your followers, of course," Okoya answered serenely.

Dillon stared at Okoya, but he wasn't seeing him. Instead Dillon saw patterns of thought and action rearranging themselves in his own head. Everything Dillon had done, from the moment he had been dragged from the Columbia River three weeks before, until now, had been based on the single, unwavering belief that his efforts would hold together a world that was about to fall apart. What he had planned today was founded on that belief. He had been certain that holding back the waters of Lake Mead, would propel him into the spotlight—a position of power that would allow him to seize enough control to keep the world from slipping into chaos.

But this event was not my idea, was it? Dillon realized. *Wasn't it Okoya who suggested that I could be the glue that bonded the world?* But if Okoya's only interest in the human spirit was its nutritional value, why would he support Dillon's efforts? How could preserving humanity serve Okoya's agenda? The answer was that it wouldn't.

"I don't feel so good," said Lourdes, stumbling off her chair to the ground, to join Winston who was already on his knees, clutching at his eyes, as if he would gouge them out.

A group of Happy Campers stumbled up. Seeing Winston and Lourdes in agony on the ground, one of them asked, "Is everything okay?" The man gripped his own stomach in pain. In fact, quite a few of the Happy Campers around them were doubling over.

And then Dillon finally made one more connection. "Shiprock" he said. Winston looked up at him from the ground. "It's where you and Tory met Okoya, isn't it?"

"It was two weeks before anything happened there . . ."

But Dillon now suspected that wasn't true; that a massacre had occurred long before any blood was actually spilled.

"Nothing has changed, Dillon," Okoya said slowly. "You will still have the world at your fingertips, believe me."

But was that what Dillon wanted? he wondered. It was a thrilling thought, to reign with supernatural power . . . but such a thing would mean a complete shift in the fundamental structure of the world. Power would no longer be divided among equals around the globe, because now there was a vast inequality, unlike anything the modern world had known. Five elite beings. They would not just be playing gods—in every way that mattered, they would *be* gods . . .

. . . and because of it, the very structure of civilization would crumble.

"It's too late to do anything but move forward," Okoya demanded. "There's nothing more to think about."

Dillon thought to the globe he had so painstakingly sketched patterns across. *"There will be an event,"* he had told the others, *"something so inexplicable, that the world cannot look away."* In turn, that event would ignite an even larger, more devastating event—like a detonator's charge ignites a warhead.

Until now Dillon could see almost every pattern around him, except his own. But now his own was finally revealed—through Okoya—and the house of cards he had built all his efforts on, collapsed, revealing the bleak pattern it masked.

Holding back the waters was not a way to ward off that igniting event—it *was* the igniting event.

And Dillon was the detonator.

"I don't know what you are," Dillon told Okoya, "but I won't let you use us anymore."

If Okoya was concerned, he didn't show it. "You'll do what needs to be done, Dillon. Because a few miles away, there's a dam that's about to crumble by your hand. It's too late to stop that now. The way I see it, you only have two choices—allow the dam to burst, and kill hundreds of thousands of people downriver . . . or you can hold back the waters and save all those lives." Okoya cracked his superior smile. "I know you'll do the right thing."

Dillon knew he was snared in Okoya's trap, but he was not about to let Okoya claim victory. There were moans all around them now, and Dillon turned around to see almost all the followers doubling over in pain, their bodies reflexively mimicking Lourdes as she lay on the ground, every ounce of her body reviling her cannibalistic feasts.

Dillon knelt to Winston, whose eyes were filled with a grief and revulsion that skewered his spirit more painfully than any blade.

"What do we do, Dillon?" Winston begged. "What do we do now?"

"You have to get Lourdes out of here," he said, glancing back at the crumbling followers.

"I can't," said Winston shaking his head, barely able to move himself. "I can't, I can't, I can't."

"But you will," Dillon demanded. And somehow, the force of his will was enough to get Winston to his feet. He helped Lourdes up, and the two of them stumbled away, into the desert.

In a few moments, the followers' groans began to lessen, and they began to lift themselves off the ground as Lourdes moved out of range.

Dillon looked at Okoya once more, hardening his resolve. Suddenly this spirit-predator didn't seem quite so sure of himself.

Okoya bolted past Dillon. There was a sound in the air like a sonic boom, followed by a rush of wind, and the light around them changed. In an instant the reason for the sound and light was clear, for, ten yards away, a hole had been punctured in space, and beyond it, was a plain of crimson sand.

Okoya had punched a hole out of this universe, into the Unworld—and he was racing toward the hole.

Dillon dove for Okoya, grabbing his legs and bringing him down.

"Help me!" Dillon called, and instantly there were a dozen followers with him, wrestling Okoya to the ground, just a few feet from the gaping hole in the world. Okoya fought to escape, but in spite of his ability to rape souls and manipulate situations, he was a slave to the physical limitations of the body he wore, as easily restrained as any human.

"You have no power beyond what you steal, do you?" Dillon said. "You've turned us against one another, you've used our powers toward your own ends. It stops here."

Okoya struggled against his captors, but it was useless. With Okoya subdued, Dillon's attention turned to that hole in the world. There were followers around him, gaping in wonder, accepting it as yet another mystery of the strange, youthful gods who guided them. But Dillon's awe was of an entirely different nature . . . because through that hole in the world was a distant mountain. And there was a palace carved into the stone of that mountain. Dillon knew that somewhere in that palace, resting on the dusty remains of a dead king, sat Deanna's body—only a few miles away . . . through that hole.

Then Dillon realized that Okoya was watching him from beneath the tackle of assailants . . . and smiling. So Dillon tore his attention away from the mountain palace.

"Make sure he can't get away," said Dillon.

"How?" someone asked.

"I don't know. Chain him to a boulder, for all I care." And then Dillon strode off to gather his band of a thousand followers for the march to Black Canyon.

He looked back only once, to see the hole in the world close with a twinkling of light, locking Deanna a universe away once more.

21. BLACK CANYON

PEOPLE DIDN'T KNOW WHY IT WAS HAPPENING, BUT EVERY-
one certainly knew *what* was happening. As cracks in the face of
the dam divided and multiplied, engineers abandoned the power
plant, terrified as they rode up the violently shaking elevators to
solid ground. Tourists had long since run off, any boats left on Lake
Mead were rapidly powering to shore, and from high above the
dam, a swarm of news helicopters added to the mayhem.

A hundred miles downriver, alarms blared in the casinos of
Laughlin, but all the roads to higher ground were so jammed that
no one was moving, unless they were moving on foot. Even farther
downstream, in Lake Havasu, the new home of the famous London
Bridge, there was no relief from the panic. All around the lake,
people packed what little memories they could, abandoning the
rest, barely able to believe that the world's greatest dam was only
minutes from giving way. It seemed London Bridge would be falling down after all.

DEEP IN THE bowels of the dam, Drew Camden kept his panic
controlled, constantly telling himself that there would be light
around the next bend—that they were one junction away from an
escape. They would make it out of here, and somehow, he would
get back to his new old life.

Boom boom boom . . . Boom boom boom . . .

The triple beat echoed around them like a dark waltz, growing
louder by the minute. Tiny pebbles of concrete fell like sleet in the
dark.

"How much time do we have?" Drew asked.

"I don't know," answered Tory. "This thing isn't exactly the
wall of the Neptune Pool. It could be a minute, it could be an
hour—there's no way to tell."

Michael stopped suddenly. The others bumped into him in the dark.

"What is it, Michael? Did you find something?" Tory asked.

"I think . . ." said Michael. "I just think it's time we got ourselves ready . . ." He took a deep breath and let it out. "Ready to die, I mean."

"Been there, done that!" said Drew, quickly cutting him off. "No burning need to do it again." Then he heard Michael fiddling with something, and reached out to see what it was. Michael was leafing through his wallet.

"Um, I don't think we're gonna buy our way out of here, Michael," said Drew.

"Do you two have any ID?" Michael asked.

The shaking around them grew stronger, and the significance of the question hit home. They would need identification, if they didn't make it out—so that whoever found them would know where to send their bodies.

The percussive waltz grew louder, filling with discord and sibilance.

"Maybe . . ." said Tory, with a quiver in her voice. "Maybe it's best if we don't. I wouldn't want my mother to know I ended up like this."

"No," said Michael. "They *have to* send us home—or else Dillon won't know how to find us."

It was something Drew hadn't considered: Dillon bringing them back. With all that he had seen, Drew didn't even know what death was anymore. Was it an end? Was it a beginning? Or was it just an inconvenience?

"My name's engraved on my bracelet," said Tory.

"Put it in a pocket," suggested Michael. "A zippered one, if you have it."

"I don't have anything," said Drew, and Michael handed him something laminated.

"It's my library card. It'll be good enough to get you home."

Drew slipped the card into his pocket. "Yeah, but I'm not gonna need it, 'cause we're getting out of here. C'mon, let's move out!"

"The Cowardly Lion finds courage," Tory said.

"Things change," Drew answered. "I'll tell you all about it sometime."

DILLON COLE ALWAYS had a plan, but as he marched with his thousand followers, he had nothing—no plan; nor a single idea of what he should do.

Shiprock.

The thought of that massacre still nagged uncomfortably in his mind. The details of it—the missing old man, and the deputy who had continued where he had left off—such a horrible thing . . . and yet Dillon knew there was a message in it for him, like a flare in the desert that was meant for his eyes only. Something so important. Dillon had seen the massacre as the beginning of the end, but if Okoya had thrown his perspective so far askew all this time, perhaps Dillon was seeing it all wrong. In a world turning upside down, perhaps a massacre is not what it seems. He followed the path of that thought to its logical end, and finally saw the light of the flare.

As Dillon reached the rim of Black Canyon, the thousand followers spread out, craning their necks to see the incredible depth of the gorge, and the majesty of Hoover Dam rising almost a mile away.

There was a switchback trail that led down into the canyon—but before leading them down, he turned, shouting to the crowd, "Some of you will come down with me. The rest will stay up here."

Shouts of disappointment surrounded him.

He could feel the ground beneath his feet rumbling with the shaking of the dam, as it tore itself apart from the inside out. There was not much time for choosing the members of this expedition, but he had to take the time to do it. Putting his hand out, he began to touch their heads.

"You will come. And you . . . and you . . . and you."

The followers pressed forward, each one hoping to be chosen. He saw Carol Jessup—the woman who had been one of the first to follow him. "Please, Dillon," she begged. "After all we've done to help you, please take us."

Dillon looked into her eyes, then the eyes of her daughter and husband. "I'm sorry, Carol," he said. Then he touched her husband's head. "You will come down with me, but your wife and daughter have to stay." He could see the sting of betrayal in the woman's eyes. Her husband hesitated. "I said, leave them and come with me. Now!" The man obeyed, kissing his wife and daughter, who cried at the prospect of being called, but not chosen.

He continued through the mob, looking into their eyes, making his choices that, to them, seemed random and capricious. Out of the thousand, he chose almost four hundred to march with him down the switchback trail into the depths of the canyon.

TORY, MICHAEL, AND Drew knew they only had minutes left—if that—for the echoing booms had evolved into the throaty roars of shattering stone, as the dam began to fail.

Dull thuds echoed from above, as the falling pellets of concrete sleet became hail, impacting on their backs.

Tory saw a shadow of a golf ball–sized chunk of concrete drop past her.

Wait a second. . . . A shadow?

"We're getting closer!" Michael shouted. "Keep moving—there's light up ahead!"

They scrambled under the hail of falling debris, pulling themselves into a corridor no more than two feet wide. In a dim gray-on-gray, they could finally see the cratered walls. The ground was littered with heavy chunks and up ahead they saw spears of light.

"I think this is the way I came in!" shouted Drew over the thundering around them. "Come on!"

They moved more quickly now that they could see, ignoring the rusted iron rebar jutting from the walls, tearing at their clothes. Finally they turned a corner, and saw what was perhaps the most wonderful sight of their lives—an open doorway flooded with light. They picked up their pace, their exhaustion quelled by the adrenaline rush of their salvation.

Drew had not intended what happened next.

He was in the lead, just a pace in front of Michael and Tory, and so was the first to emerge onto the catwalk that hugged the face of the dam—and then something struck him from above. He cried out in pain as it clipped his shoulder, breaking his left collarbone. Drew saw it only for an instant: the massive bronze form of an angel, its sharp, pointed wings aimed down instead of up, like the arms of a diver. The falling statue tore the catwalk away from the fractured face of the dam, and then plummeted through the power plant four hundred feet below, at the foot of the dam.

The catwalk swung out wildly, like a crane, with Drew still on it. He felt his body slide off, and reflexively he reached up a hand, grabbing on to the rail. With his collarbone broken, his left arm was useless, so all he could do was cling with his right hand to the railing, while his feet dangled above oblivion.

"Drew, hold on!" he heard Michael shout from the doorway in the dam. "Don't let go!"

Drew's fear swelled, about to overtake him, and he knew the moment it did, he was gone. . . . So he clenched his teeth, strangled his fear, and began to pump his legs back and forth as if he were on a swing, like a human pendulum.

"Go on, Drew, you can do it!"

He swung, he swung again, and once more. He kicked up a foot; it brushed the edge of the catwalk. "Damn."

He gave a final push, swung his leg up, and hooked his ankle around it, pulling himself onto the twisted platform.

Then he saw Michael and Tory. The catwalk had swung a full twenty feet away from the dam, and the corridor where they both stood opened onto empty air. They were trapped.

"I won't leave without you!" Drew shouted.

"Don't be a moron!" Michael screamed back. "Get the hell out of here!"

"But . . ."

"Just shut up and go!"

"I'm sorry," he wailed, wishing there were something he could do. "I'm sorry . . ." He took one last look at them before reluctantly scrambling up the catwalk. With his left arm dangling by his side, he pulled his way along until he reached what was left of the dam's rim. No one was foolish enough to be up there anymore. The guardrail was gone, and the disintegrating road was full of fissures spreading wider and wider.

Drew leapt over one fissure after another until he reached solid ground, and then threw himself against an outcrop of boulders, clinging to the quaking canyon face for dear life, as the entire dam began to give way behind him.

★   ★   ★

IN THOSE LAST few moments, Michael and Tory clung to one another as concrete bolides the size of Cadillacs dropped past them, whistling against an updraft that surged up the face of the dam. The mouth of the tunnel fell away.

"Watch out!" Michael pulled Tory back as the doorway crumbled. Then, from behind, a blast of pulverized concrete dust shot past, like steam through a pipe. It shot into the updraft, and was carried away like smoke.

Updraft? thought Tory.

There were only seconds left now.

That's Michael's *updraft!* Tory realized. *That wind is his will fighting the dam!* But how powerful was it? How powerful could he make it in the seconds they had left? Not strong enough to stop the mountainous concrete chunks, but maybe—

She grabbed him, making him look at her.

"What's the wind, Michael?" she demanded. Michael shook his head, not understanding.

"What does it *feel* like? In your gut—in your head. How does it feel *inside*?"

"Fear," shouted Michael. "Terror. . . ."

"Then be frightened, Michael! Be more frightened than you've ever been in your life. And be it *now!*"

Michael turned to see the dust flowing into the updraft, and finally it clicked.

He grabbed Tory, clutching her with white knuckles, then he screamed a blood-curdling shriek of absolute fear—and instantly the whistling of the updraft raised in pitch as its strength increased.

The floor gave way beneath them as Michael held Tory, screaming his terror into her ear, and she screamed back into his. Neither of them had the gift of flight—but if Michael's updraft could make them fly as well as that boat on Pacific Coast Highway, perhaps that would be enough. They clung to that thought as they leapt from the dying dam into the wind.

A MILE DOWNSTREAM, Dillon and four hundred of his followers watched it happen. Chunk after chunk of concrete exploded away, until the entire upper face slid like a sand castle, into the power-house below. The powerhouse exploded. An instant later, the lower shell of the dam tumbled, leaving nothing but a cloud of dust shooting heavenward. Another explosion from the buried powerhouse, and then silence.

Behind Dillon, the chosen ones grew silent.

Through the dust, they saw what appeared to be a dark, V-shaped wall of still water—but the air was not clear enough to be sure just yet.

But Dillon was sure.

His power had grown beyond all limits, because holding back the waters of Lake Mead took so little effort, it felt like a mere reflex.

A power like that did not belong here.

Behind him, the four hundred squinted to see through the dust cloud, none of them knowing that they were already dead. Dillon had separated his followers precisely. These were the ones who had been visited by Okoya. These were the soulless. The shells of life, with nothing living inside.

They did not belong here, either.

The Shiprock Slayer had begun the task of removing the soulless—Dillon realized that now. And he also realized that he was the only one who could complete it. Now he focused all his effort on the wall of water. He knew what he had to do, but it wasn't easy to fight the order his very presence brought. He hurled his thoughts ahead of him, turning them chaotic and disjointed. He battered the water-wall with his mind, struggling to give entropy a foothold once more, so that this lake would fall out of his control, and spill free.

At last he felt his barrier fall, like the tearing of a membrane. Suddenly, the ground rumbled once more, and through the dust cloud burst a white, churning wave five hundred feet high, surging down the canyon toward them.

As the water approached, Dillon had to remind himself that he was not killing the people around him. Okoya had already done that. But for the thousands that would die downstream, Dillon had to accept responsibility.

For so long Dillon had struggled to find redemption—fixing all those who were broken so that he might forgive himself for the destruction he had once caused. But it had never been for them. He had done it for himself; to finally feel worthy. It was a selfish need, masquerading as selflessness.

No more.

For there was only one way to save the world now, and it meant that Dillon Cole had to die in disgrace and never be redeemed.

Let me be despised by the world, he silently prayed. *Let my name be spoken with nothing but hatred. Let this act be so horrible, that it shatters the pattern of destruction I've helped to create, and sets the world back on its proper track. A world where not a single soul worships me.*

The wedge of churning foam pounded forward, a quarter mile and closing. Behind Dillon, the dead-alive followers waited for Dillon to stop it.

But instead, Dillon raised up his hands to receive it.

LOURDES DID NOT see it, but she knew something had gone wrong. She knew because of the strange pillar of dust shooting toward the sky like a mushroom cloud. She knew because of the roar of rushing water, and she knew because of Okoya's scream of fury from somewhere within the circle of buses, a hundred yards from where she and Winston lay doubled-over in the sand.

Apparently Okoya had not gotten what he wanted, which meant Dillon had chosen to destroy himself, rather than the world. He had chosen not to be Okoya's ruling-puppet.

Lourdes sat up. The revulsion she felt as she had stumbled away from camp had resolved into a pain in her gut, and a sense of unreconciled need—a craving for what only Okoya could supply.

Winston sat in the dust, his hand over his eyes, weeping. All his supposed wisdom, and he couldn't see this coming. Oh, he had grown, all right. He had grown arrogant and self-absorbed—they all had.

"How could this have happened?" cried Winston. "How could we have done this to ourselves?"

Lourdes tried to find some sympathy. She tried to find a feeling to comfort both of them, but all she found inside was the angry pit of her stomach; and so she left Winston, not caring about his tears. Fighting her hunger, she strode back toward the circle of buses.

The place was deserted. All had gone to follow Dillon. Everyone, that is, except Okoya. Okoya was stretched out against the face of a bus—his arms and legs tied in four different directions with heavy nylon tent cords. He'd pulled and tugged at his bonds, but the job had been well done—he was not getting free. It almost amused Lourdes to see this master of minds rendered impotent by mere nylon ropes.

Lourdes approached, keeping her stride steady, counting each step as she drew closer until she stopped, only a few feet away.

"Always a pleasure to see you, Lourdes," Okoya said. "Release me, and—"

"And what?" Lourdes took a step closer. "You'll crown me Queen for a Day?"

Okoya pulled against his bonds one more time. "Everything that was Dillon's will now be yours."

"I don't need you for that," said Lourdes. "I know what I'm capable of. If I want the world on a silver platter, I'll put it there myself."

"Then why are you here?"

"This is why." Lourdes squeezed her hands into tight fists, and pushed forth a single nerve impulse. Instantly Okoya began to gasp for air as his heart seized in his chest.

"How does it feel to have our powers turned against you?"

"If you kill this body," gasped Okoya, "it will free me to jump into another. There are hundreds of people on that road; I could be any one of them, and you'll never know when I'm coming."

Lourdes squeezed her fists tighter, but knew Okoya was telling the truth. She released the hold on his heart, and the color returned to Okoya's face as he pulled in deep, wheezing breaths.

"You don't know how to kill me," Okoya sneered, "and it's a waste of your time to try."

Maybe so, but as long as he was in that body, he could feel every measure of its pain. Lourdes brought her fist back, and smashed it heavily across his jaw, and then again, and then again, making sure every punishing blow had the full force of her anger. But no matter how many times she struck him, it made her feel no better. In the end, Okoya's face was bruised and swollen, but his evil spirit would not break.

"I gave you what you wanted," he said through swollen lips. "You should be grateful."

She turned and strode off. She did not go back to Winston, nor did she go to see the flood. Instead she headed off in the opposite direction. Okoya had put a hunger in her that could never be satisfied again. She hated Okoya for putting it there, she hated Dillon for having brought them here in the first place, and she hated Michael, for the love he had killed in her.

Her knees felt shaky, her legs weak, but her fury gave her strength to walk away from all of this and not look back.

22. TURBULENCE

A BODY-BRUISING SLAP OF COLD, AND A TUMBLING LOSS OF control—Dillon had finally given his will over to the will of the water. He felt himself whipped against boulders in the churning currents and his senses began to leave him. Then, in the midst of the maelstrom, Dillon felt a calm numbness begin to surround him like a bubble of peace within the flood, and all Dillon could hear was the heavy beat of his own heart. *So this is death*, Dillon thought, as he began to feel himself slip out of consciousness.

MEANWHILE, ON THE ridge above, the remaining followers, spectators, and a half dozen airborne news crews watched as Dillon and "the chosen ones" were taken under by the torrent. At first, the followers on the ridge didn't know what to make of it, but as the water continued to pass, wails of anguish began to fill the air as they realized that this was not the glorious event they had been promised; and their minds began the long, arduous task of reconciling what they had just witnessed.

Somewhere in that reconciliation, they would come to accept that Dillon Cole had tricked them all; that he was just another false prophet, and in the end brought nothing but death and destruction. For all those who stood on that rim, for all those who saw Black Canyon fill with white water, there would be many sleepless nights, but in the end, the dead would be buried, and the living would return to the lives they had led before being touched by Dillon . . . and in so doing, set the world back on its balance.

This is what Dillon had wanted—and it all would have come to pass, had Dillon's power not been stronger than even he could comprehend.

The water surged down the canyon at 200 miles per hour. By

the time the canyon widened, the wave was crashing toward the hotels at Laughlin—at 175 miles per hour. In Laughlin, those unlucky enough to be stranded there caught sight of the white foam of the water-wall in the distance as it crashed toward them—at 150 miles per hour. Several news helicopters, barely able to keep up with the surge at first, found themselves easily matching the pace of the flood's leading edge, clocking their speed at 100 miles per hour, just ten miles out of Laughlin.

There was a figure caught in the telephoto crossbars of one cameraman's lens. He was riding the crest of the flood's leading edge, lying on his back. By all rights, he should have been churned down into the water's killing depths—yet somehow, was not. Instead he was surrounded by an island of calm water amid the chaos. His eyes were closed, so there was no way of telling if he was dead, or merely unconscious.

It was five miles out of Laughlin that the rushing water inexplicably slowed to below the highway speed limit.

MICHAEL'S POWERS WERE not hell-bent on self-preservation.

The moment Michael and Tory fell into the powerful updraft, they were dragged skyward, and as Dillon tumbled beneath the waves during the first moments of the flood, Michael and Tory were tumbled up by the wind.

At a height of ten thousand feet, the dust-filled shaft of wind burst apart, spreading out like a mushroom cloud. Michael and Tory continued to cling to one another as they rode the shock wave of wind, no longer knowing up from down. Michael knew his skill was not one of precision, but of broad strokes. Storms and cloud sculptures were a far cry from controlled flight. The air was now too thin to fill their lungs, and unforgivingly cold. Michael tried to move his fingers and found that he couldn't even feel them.

"What happens now?" Tory cried into Michael's ear.

Michael knew he didn't have to say it, because she already knew.

"Whatever happens, I won't let you go."

And in that instant, as he held Tory's shivering body, he knew he had finally found in his soul the faintest glimmer of love.

But it was too late to change the course of the wind.

★   ★   ★

GRIPPING COLD.
  Breaking clouds.
  A long, frozen fall.
  And then nothing.

The sudden sense of Michael and Tory's death snapped Dillon to consciousness. He opened his eyes, and thought the blinding light that shone on his face was the spirit of God, until a helicopter cut across it, and he realized it was only the sun shining through the breaking clouds. He was alert enough to realize that he was alive, and to know that he was floating in strangely serene water. Yet why did he hear it churning all around him?

A moment more, and it all came back to him—everything until the moment he had lost consciousness. Now his body no longer felt the battering it had received from the water. He had already healed himself—although his lungs still felt heavy from the submerged breaths he had drawn.

While still underwater, he must have unknowingly created an oasis of calm around himself like a reflex. That bubble of calm water had lifted him to the surface and carried him along, acting as a buffer between him and the raging torrent.

But there was something more going on here—he could feel it, like a chill that wound up his spine. Only it was longer than his spine—much longer.

The feeling stretched out the length of his body and beyond; shooting hundreds of miles to the south through the soles of his feet, and hundreds of miles to the north through the top of his head. Then he realized that the churning water—still bubbling and brewing, was no longer consuming the landscape before it. The hotel towers of Laughlin stood only a mile or two away, but drew no closer. The entire flood was in fact standing still—treading itself like the waters of a washing machine. Dillon then felt himself moving again, and he once more sensed that cold strand shoot through him like a thousand-mile vein. Then, in a moment, he understood exactly what was happening.

Laughlin would not be washed away today.

Lake Havasu and the London Bridge would be perfectly safe.

This should be a good thing, thought Dillon, but it was not. It was bad news in its rawest form, as terrible as Michael's and Tory's deaths. Dillon released a delirious laugh—a cackle of bitter surrender as the flood began a powerful backwash toward higher ground. No matter how hard Dillon had tried to scuttle his "miracle of the waters," it was going to happen anyway. For his power had grown far beyond his ability to control it—and now, even against his will, Dillon's influence had fallen upon these waters, caressing them into submission, from Mexico to its tiniest mountain tributaries . . .

. . . And the mighty Colorado River was flowing backward.

PART V · THE BACKWASH

23. THE FIRST WAVE

WINDS IN THE UPPER ATMOSPHERE HAD QUICKLY SHRED-
ded Michael's fierce storm into wispy threads of ice vapor. By
noon, thousands more had gathered around the Nevada and Arizona sides of Black Canyon, because, where Hoover Dam once
stood, the Colorado River Backwash was its most impressive. At
that point, the waters gushed back into Lake Mead, at a steep upward slope—a river rapids flowing against the pull of gravity.

The white water running back into the canyon that had been
Lake Mead, was filled with the bodies of those chosen followers—
but the mourning for the dead was overcome by the sight of the
backwash.

It was an image that burned itself into the world's collective
consciousness, because it was so wholly inconceivable, no one
could wrap their mind around it. Rational thought meant nothing
in the face of this wonder, and people knew that from this day
forth, nothing they thought or believed could remain the same.
Like a train hurled from its track, day-to-day life started grinding
to a screeching halt, as alliances began to shift, and people began
believing in the divinity of the martyred Dillon Cole.

They had no way of knowing that he was still alive.

Even when he washed up the rapids where the dam had stood, he appeared to be just another victim lifelessly pulled along with the flow. No one noticed the small lily pad of calm that protected him, as he surged semi-conscious up the Colorado River.

DREW CAMDEN HAD stumbled away from the canyon before the waters reversed. His shoulder was badly swollen, the pain making him hobble like Quasimodo as he crossed the desert back to the campsite. He wasn't sure what he expected to find there, but he didn't know where else to go. Yellow police lines were spread like cobwebs, blocking everything off, and he burst through one like a racer at a finish line. The campsite was deserted except for the police.

"My God, it's another one!" one of the cops shouted. "Don't let this one get away." They were on him in an instant, hurling questions.

"Dam . . . broke," Drew muttered. "Friends died. Two of them." The cops looked at each other.

"It was a lot more than two, kid," one cop said. Drew stared at him blankly.

"Forget it," the cop told him, "it's not your problem." There were paramedics around him now. They secured him to a back-board, and packed his shoulder with ice.

"Don't worry," one of them said. "You'll be fine. The doctors'll patch you up, and have you home in no time."

Home. It was a place Drew hadn't the luxury of considering for quite some time. Between the alternating current of his own personality, and the events he had been a part of, Newport Beach seemed far, far away. In a way, he had been caught up in Michael's tornado all this time, hadn't he? From the moment the sharks leapt up the beach, he was drawn up in a current that left him at the mercy of the winds. He had been destroyed, reborn, shredded, and reconstructed, and now he had been spat back out again.

When he got home, he would have much to tell people: things about the Shards, and about himself as well; things that needed to be said.

As he lay there, he heard voices around him and snippets of conversations talking of even stranger events at the river.

". . . damnedest thing . . ." ". . . it never hit Laughlin . . ."
". . . whole thing flowing backward . . ."

He heard radios reporting on it. Police had crowded onto one of the buses, watching it on TV. "That can't be what it looks like . . ."

It's not over, thought Drew—but whatever happened now, he instinctively sensed that he was not a part of it anymore. He was not one of the Shards—and although he had envied Michael at first, he now realized there was nothing envious about that kind of power in this kind of world. Tears filled his eyes, and one of the paramedics gave him a shot of morphine for the pain.

As they carried him toward a waiting helicopter, he began to struggle against his bonds, trying to force a single thought out before the morphine took effect. "Okoya . . ." he said weakly, his thoughts slurring. "Bad. Dangerous. Must find . . ."

A paramedic looked to his partner. "The kid's ranting."

"Who isn't today?" his partner said.

The paramedics ignored him as they carried him to the helicopter and past a bus, where the frayed ends of nylon cords dangled limply from the mirrors and bumper.

24. THE CONFLUENCE

Life began at the Confluence. At least that was the belief of many Southwest tribes. It was the place where the Colorado and Little Colorado merged into a single river. It was a place of magic. A place of powerful spirits, both good and evil.

Radio Joe—second-degree burns on his hands and part of his face from the real flames of the fake volcano—had taken a car, sold it for a horse, took the six-hour trek down into the Grand Canyon, and waited at the Confluence for the world to end. When the river began its backward flow, he knew the time was near.

He watched as body after body drifted by in the current, and he awaited the coming of a god, or a demon.

At Twilight, as Radio Joe cooked himself a hot meal over an open fire, he saw a raft approaching him on the river. He thought he recognized the raft's single occupant—but wasn't certain until the raft had been beached and the visitor's face, bruised and swollen, was lit by the flames. It almost looked surprised when it saw the old man, but hid it quickly.

"You've abused their body," Radio Joe told the dark Quíkadi; the thief of souls. "I would think a creature of your power would have kept it in better shape. Unless you've met your match."

"Don't anger me, old man."

Radio Joe reached into his pot and offered a helping of stewed rabbit.

"I don't need your food," it said.

"Then what do you need?"

"I'm looking for the one who changed the course of the river," said the thief of souls.

"And you think it was me?"

Then the thief leaned closer into the fire, until beads of sweat appeared on his bruised face—still the perfect synthesis of Lara and Jara. "I think you have eyes that see more than most. Tell me what you've seen on the river."

Radio Joe gnawed his meat. "I've seen bodies carried around the bend, deeper into the canyon. I've seen fish swimming in perfect schools. I've seen the holes in my shoes close as I stood in the water."

The thief waited for more, but Radio Joe offered nothing further.

"I know he's nearby." said the thief. "I think you know more than you say."

"And if I do?"

"If you don't tell me all you know, I'll do what I should have done to begin with. I'll leave you worse than dead."

"And what about Lara and Jara?" demanded the old man. "Are they worse than dead? Did you devour their souls?"

"They sleep," said the thief. "They merged into one, and now they sleep."

Radio Joe nodded. If he hadn't destroyed the twins, then he spared them for a reason. But perhaps he didn't need them anymore. He decided to gamble.

"Free their spirits, and I'll tell you what I know."

The thief of souls was taken aback. His face hardened, and for a moment Radio Joe thought he was done for. But then the thief grinned. He gave his head a shake, flicking his long mane of hair from his eyes—and as he did, Radio Joe felt the soul of the twins pass clear through him.

And behind him, his horse began to whinny and buck.

"There," said the thief. "I've freed them." His gaze intensified. "Now tell me what you saw."

"I saw him float past here, two hours ago," said Radio Joe. "The water bore him like a pillow as he slept, refusing to let him drown."

The thief turned his eyes to the two rivers, tracing the larger one's winding path. But the hour was late, and the outline of the river disappeared into shadows as pitch-dark as the new moon.

"The Colorado travels north a ways, then winds back to the

south," Radio Joe told him. "Camp in the shadow of High Pebble." He indicated a pillar of darkening red stone in the distance. "You'll see him at dawn."

The thief wasted no time with thank yous. He slipped back into the shadows, and disappeared.

When he was gone, Radio Joe left the fire, his kettle of stew in hand. His horse was tied to a rock, but tried desperately to pull itself free, with a spirit the young gelding hadn't shown before. It looked apprehensive and angry as Radio Joe approached, but it calmed as he brushed its mane.

"You're free from it now," he told the spirit of the twins. Then, taking out his knife, he cut the horse loose from its bridle. Instantly it took off into the canyon. Radio Joe listened until the hoofbeats were overwhelmed by crickets, then he turned and headed with his bucket of rabbit stew toward the small cave in the canyon wall behind him.

"I HOPE YOU like rabbit."

Dillon was awakened by a gruff voice, and reached up to peel back the blanket that covered him. His memory was foggy, but he vaguely remembered being pulled from the river by the old man. The muscles in Dillon's arms and legs had been knots of hard rubber, and his jaw had locked from chattering. The old man had carried him to this cave, rubbed warmth into his arms and legs, and covered him with a blanket. It was the last thing Dillon remembered before slipping from consciousness.

Now his muscles felt looser, and his body felt warm. Dillon had never tasted rabbit before, but right now, it smelled awfully good to him. The old man served Dillon the stew in a cracked bowl, but the crack healed quickly enough . . . and hadn't the blanket that covered him once been dilapidated? Even in this desolate cave, he could not escape his aura of mending anymore than he could escape his own shadow.

Dillon ate with his fingers, trying to put those thoughts aside.

"You should know, that I don't have much luck with hermits," Dillon said.

The old man shrugged. "I'm not a hermit, I'm an electrician."

It was as the old man turned, that Dillon had a moment of déjà vu. He had seen this face before. "Do I know you?"

The old man hesitated before answering. Then he said. "People call me Radio Joe."

Dillon's hand began to shake, and he put down the bowl, as he realized the significance of the name. "The Shiprock Slayer."

Radio Joe smiled. "I'd be lying if I said I'd been called worse things." He picked up Dillon's bowl, studying where the crack had healed. "But the task was beyond me. You completed what I began."

He held out the bowl to Dillon, and Dillon took it. "What are you?" Radio Joe asked.

Dillon considered the question. "Damned if I know," he said, finally. Truthfully. For at that moment, he didn't know. He couldn't say if he was good or evil; a hero or destroyer; a gift to this world, or its greatest curse.

"Does the river still run backward?" Dillon asked.

The old man nodded, and Dillon was not surprised; it had only been a matter of time until his powers grew too strong for his will to control.

"I hear talk of a river up north," Radio Joe told him, "that also flows in from the sea. Its waters are healing, and to drink of it means to cheat death."

Dillon closed his eyes. "The Columbia River." Did every place he tread bear the indelible print of his influence now? And would the rivers flow to the sea once more if he were dead? He didn't know. He didn't even know if he *could* die—and that thought added a new level to the misery, because it meant he didn't even have control over his own existence.

How strange, he thought—to seek control over everything, and find himself in control of nothing at all. Powerless, in his own power.

Radio Joe watched Dillon eat, and ladled him a second helping. Only after he finished did he offer Dillon the unpleasant news.

"It came looking for you," Radio Joe told him. Dillon felt his world-weariness settle more heavily on his shoulders. Dillon knew Okoya would not rest as long as Dillon was alive.

"Do you know how to destroy it?" Dillon asked.

Radio Joe only picked through the bones in his own bowl. "This rabbit," he began, "not much left of it now. I suppose if it still lived, it would want to know how to destroy me. To a rabbit, we are the evil ones. But by what means can a rabbit destroy us?" He dropped the bones into the sand. "It must fail, because what we are, and what we know, are far beyond this poor rabbit's ability to ever understand."

Dillon felt his stomach grumble. It was as if he could hear the spirit of the rabbit growling in his gut. He swallowed hard to keep his meal down, and wondered if a vegetarian lifestyle was in his future. "I can't destroy it," Dillon realized.

"If you don't understand its life, how can you bring about its death?" The old Indian took Dillon's bowl, turning it face-down over the bones of the rabbit. "Maybe it's best to let it be. Leave it to do what it does, and stay out of its path, forever. Because without someone like you to do its bidding, it could never have the power it desires. It could never devour the whole world."

Dillon stood. His knees still felt weak, but he knew his strength was coming back. He walked out of the cave and turned up his eyes to the clear night sky. A trillion stars. The living eyes of the universe staring down on him.

Yes, he could run from Okoya, like a frightened rabbit running from the hunter . . . but if he did, those trillion eyes of heaven would be there in accusation, every night of his life. He had often thought about it, but now beneath that Grand Canyon sky, he truly began to wonder whether his life was an accident brought on by the sudden death of a distant star, or was there more to it than that? Did his existence serve some purpose he had yet to learn? If so, it would explain why the world seemed so reluctant to let him die. Or to run.

"I can't run from Okoya," he told Radio Joe. "I can't run from him anymore than I can run from myself."

Radio Joe offered him a knowing nod. "It is said, 'Wherever you may travel, wherever you may roam, the center of the circle will always be your home.' "

"Ancient wisdom?" asked Dillon.

"John Lennon," answered Radio Joe.

The old Hualapai added more wood to the fire, sending sparks streaming into the night. "Ten miles west of here, you'll come to a place called High Pebble. He'll be there at dawn, looking for you." He handed Dillon a flashlight. "Here. The batteries died, but I suppose that won't matter to you."

Radio Joe had called that one right; as Dillon held the flashlight in his hands, the batteries began to charge. In a moment, it glowed a dim orange flicker that kept glowing brighter.

"What about you?" Dillon asked, but Radio Joe seemed unconcerned.

"I've retired to the canyon. Either they find me here, or they don't. If they do, it doesn't matter, because the worst of it is over for me." Radio Joe gave Dillon his jacket. "Cold night," he said.

Dillon took the jacket with a nod of thanks. "I'll bring it back to you when it's all over."

Radio Joe pursed his age-worn lips. "Never make promises you may not live to keep."

25. CANYON OF SPIRITS

HIGH PEBBLE, WHEN VIEWED FROM THE CANYON RIM, DID appear to be a tiny speck of rock, but up close, the boulder was so huge, its shadow could cover a small neighborhood. The spot was one of those magic tricks of nature—the elements having eroded the softer stone beneath it, leaving the boulder perfectly balanced atop a thin spike twenty stories high.

The Bringer, however, had no room in his heart for aesthetics. He cared nothing for the majesty of the place. To him, the Grand Canyon was no more than a ditch, and High Pebble was just another indication of how absurd this world of matter was.

The Bringer smiled. The old man had been true to his word, at least. From the base of High Pebble, Okoya could see the river as it wound mile after mile through the canyon. But when the light of dawn hit the canyon, Dillon was nowhere to be seen.

So intent was Okoya searching for signs of Dillon on the river before him, that he never sensed the presence coming up from behind.

"Looking for me?"

Startled, Okoya spun to see Dillon leaning up against the pillar of rock, as if he had appeared out of thin air. Okoya seethed, furious to be caught off-guard, but he quickly took control of the situation.

"Well," Okoya beamed, his face stretched into a steely smile. "If it isn't the river rat! Quite an impressive show you put on. I'd pay to see it again."

"It won't happen again," said Dillon.

"No?" Okoya swaggered closer. "Obviously you have no clue of what's happening to you, do you?"

Dillon kept silent. He merely stood his ground, impassive, as if none of it fazed him. This was not the state in which Okoya had expected to find Dillon. The boy was far too composed. "Your powers have reached what you might call a 'critical mass.' " Okoya said. "The circle of your influence is exploding beyond your ability to control it. Rivers you touch flow toward higher ground, and the earth beneath your feet drags to life that which was dust. The world you see before you will turn upside down. But there *is* something that you can do . . ."

Okoya sensed Dillon's resolve begin to collapse. "What?"

"Let me harness your power!" demanded Okoya. "The strength of my will is the only thing now that can keep it from raging wild."

"And let you devour every soul on Earth? Let you destroy all there is to destroy?"

Okoya laughed, genuinely amused. "You seem to think there is something here worth preserving. But this world is *nothing*, and the people here are *nothing*. They're fodder for greater beings, like me . . . and you."

Okoya took a moment to let the words sink into Dillon's slow human brain. He knew he was offering Dillon little more than a collar and leash, but he made it sound more like a crown and scepter—for the Bringer knew that slavery was a far more powerful thing when the slave was willing.

"And if I refuse?" asked Dillon.

"Then I'll kill you."

"The flood couldn't kill me; what makes you think you can?"

"Do you think you're immortal? Your power makes you difficult to kill, but not impossible. Anything from a blade through the heart to a well-placed bullet could do the job." Then Okoya grinned wickedly. "And you know all about well-placed bullets, don't you?"

Dillon's fists clenched, probably wondering how the Bringer knew the circumstances of Deanna's death. There were many things the Bringer had learned—and Deanna wasn't Dillon's only weakness.

"I can see you're already willing to throw your life away, so I'll make the stakes worth your while. If you refuse my enlightened leadership, I will kill you . . . and then I will devour the souls of everyone you brought back from the dead. I'll seek out everyone whose life you suffered to mend"—Okoya suppressed his smile as he delivered his coup de grace—"and I'll start with the boy you call Carter."

Dillon's eyes became feverishly angry. "You leave Carter out of this."

Okoya began to enjoy this more and more. "He'd become like a younger brother to you, hadn't he, that feral child rescued from the town you destroyed? He'll be exceptionally easy to find."

"Stay away from him!"

Okoya raised his hand to silence him. "I'm not finished. That's what will happen if you refuse. However, if you accept, that's an entirely different matter." Okoya tossed his hair, becoming coy, almost feminine. "Let's talk about Deanna."

Dillon looked away, and Okoya could feel Dillon slowly wrapping around his finger.

"All your powers," said Okoya, "and you can't bring her back. You could give her life again, if you could reach her; but there are some places you can't travel . . . *But I can!*"

Okoya waved his hand, hurling the power of his mind like a ball from his fingertips. The view before them began to ripple like a heat mirage, there was a blast in the air like a sonic boom, and the air pressure instantly changed. The whistle of the wind changed pitch, the rich smell of the Earth took on a bitter odor, and the red canyon light around them grew even redder than before. Beside them, Okoya had torn a hole to the Unworld, its jagged edges rippling with spatial distortion.

Okoya had chosen his point of entrance well, for there in the distance was the Palace of the Gods—just a few miles through the breach. Dillon stood before it, staring at the mountain palace, transfixed by the possibility.

"Either the death of everything you care about," said Okoya, "or Deanna's life—these are the things that rest in the balance. You choose."

Dillon did not take his eyes away from the hole, and Okoya resisted the urge to kick him, just to get him moving.

"If I agree," said Dillon, "you'll stay away from Carter and anyone else whose life I've restored."

"I will leave alone anyone you wish me to leave alone. Consider their souls a gift from me."

"How do I know I can trust you?"

Okoya chuckled. "Don't you know me by now, Dillon? I serve my own interests—and it's in my best interest to keep you happy." Okoya slapped Dillon on the shoulder with a firm grip. "In fact, it's best for me if you're the happiest man on Earth."

Wind drained from the red sands of the Unworld into the Grand Canyon, trying futilely to equalize the pressure between the two dimensions.

"You have a destiny, Dillon. You tried to fight it by denying your own followers, and still they were drawn to you. You tried to fight it by letting loose the flood, but still the event you tried to undermine only became greater. The pattern of your own future must be clear to you by now, Dillon. Let me help you embrace it." Okoya could feel the moment Dillon surrendered: his shoulder went limp, his posture slackened, his breathing slowed.

And finally Dillon leapt through the hole.

AN INSTANT OF black, numbing cold as he crossed the boundary, then the feel of gritty sand beneath his feet. He didn't turn back to watch Okoya scrutinizing his actions from the other side of the hole. Instead he marched deeper into the Unworld, until the breach was nothing more than a speck of light behind him.

Nothing had changed here. A sea still spilled from a distant tear in the sky. Rusting wrecks of cars, planes, and other, less-identifiable vehicles littered the sands, filled with the bones of the dead occupants, slowly turning to sand themselves. He took inventory of the only landmarks he knew, as if recalling them could give him some sense of comfort in this alien place.

To the left was a great ship, lying crushed on its side, and somewhere beneath it were the remains of Winston's furred beast. Far to the right, was a mound of rotting blubber, its stench weaving in and out of the wind—all that was left of Lourdes's beast. Beyond that, was the shore where Michael's parasite of lust had dissolved into the sea. And just before him was the old propeller plane, which had become the tomb of Tory's hive of disease. The parasites had all been destroyed. All but two—Deanna's, and his own.

Dillon continued toward the mountain palace in the distance for hours, letting the steady cadence of his own footfalls hypnotize and numb him. He knew what he had to do—Okoya had left him little choice. The question was, could he go through with it? With each step toward the mountain palace in the distance, his longing grew, and yet he stopped only halfway there. The hole through which he had come was completely out of sight many miles behind him. The urge to get to Deanna was almost overwhelming, but he fought it, forcing himself to stay put. There was little to hear in the dead air around him, but still he waited, keeping his ears attuned to the slightest rustling of the dry briar-weeds around him.

"I'm here!" he called out to the sky. "I'm waiting for you. Show yourselves!"

The light in the sunless ice-blue sky never changed, so he had no way to measure the passing of time. He waited there for hours . . . until at last he heard them.

It began as a distant *whoosh, whoosh, whoosh* in the air, chased by the sandy hiss of something slithering across the ground. He turned to see his winged creature of destruction approaching in the distant sky, with the Snake of Fear winding the sands beneath it.

So they *were* still here! Still waiting for a great soul to leech upon, for they could not survive outside the Unworld any other way. Dillon knew that these hideous creatures wanted a way out of this place. But he also knew how to keep them from leeching onto him. All he had to do was refuse to invite them in.

The Spirit of Destruction circled above him like a vulture, perhaps wondering why Dillon had chosen to return, then it flapped its huge wings as it settled before him, creating a dust cloud. The Snake of Fear came in from behind, darting from rock to rock, cautiously making its way closer.

Dillon had anticipated this moment, just as he had anticipated that Okoya would punch through to the Unworld and bribe him with Deanna. He knew coming here would lead to this confrontation, and although he feared it, it was also something he was counting on. He only hoped Okoya's arrogance had blinded him to what Dillon was about to do.

Before him, his creature snarled, its gray face a hellish forgery of Dillon's own. Its muscles rippled, and it flexed its sharp talons as if it were about to pounce and gouge its way back into him, burrowing into his soul. It said nothing to him at first—it just watched, waiting for some part of Dillon's soul to open so it could squeeze its way in.

All I have to do is refuse to let them in, he reminded himself.

He turned his gaze to the spirit of fear slinking up behind him. "Out where I can see you," he told it.

It recoiled, then gave him a wide berth as it saddled up beside the creature it partnered with. Dillon tried to forget how much the terror-serpent's face resembled Deanna: a twisted image of her with no eyes.

"He's come to kill us," hissed the serpent.

Dillon showed them his palms. "With what weapons?"

The Spirit of Destruction regarded Dillon a moment more, trying to divine his purpose here, but Dillon chose not to reveal it just yet. As long as his intentions were secret, he had the upper hand. Finally his parasite spoke. *"I've missed living in your flesh,"* it said. *"I've missed being a part of you."*

"You were never a part of me," Dillon told it. Dillon could sense its hunger for destruction, its hatred of him, and its resentment at having been cast out. Did it forget that it had won their last battle?—that it had ultimately destroyed what mattered most to Dillon: Deanna.

It unfolded its wings, taking on a looming, imposing stance. *"Why are you here?"* it demanded.

"I'm here to give you an escape from this place."

His creature did not take its eyes off him, its distrust oozing like a fume in the air.

"It's a trick!" hissed the serpent.

"No trick," said Dillon.

His beast folded its wings once more, and although it did not move any closer, a slight turn of its head told Dillon that he had snagged his deadly doppelgänger's curiosity. *"You would bring us back to your world?"*

Dillon took a moment to look toward the palace one last time. Yes, Deanna was there, and yes, his longing for her had been almost insurmountable. But there were things far more pressing now, and so Deanna would have to wait. He knew Deanna would understand.

"I can offer you a bargain," said Dillon. "Step inside . . . and we'll discuss it." The creatures slowly began to advance, the beast of destruction clicking its talons, the serpent of fear salivating at the prospect of freedom.

All I have to do is refuse to let them in . . . But instead Dillon bared his own spirit, and gave them permission to crawl deep inside.

OKOYA DID NOT see Dillon returning toward the portal, for he had approached from a different direction. There seemed to be something strange about the boy; there was a look in his eyes—a look that spoke of both insatiable hunger and deep-seated fear. Okoya knew what this meant; it was Dillon's hunger to rule the world, and his fear of Okoya—the very two things that gave Okoya complete control over the young star-shard. He only hoped the one called Deanna could be as handily yoked as Dillon.

"Where is she?" asked Okoya. "Didn't you bring her?"

"She'll be here soon." Dillon made no move to step through the breach. He stood just inside the Unworld, as if waiting for an invitation to come in. Which in fact he was.

"May I . . . *come in?*" Dillon asked, slowly and precisely.

"You've taken much too long," Okoya said impatiently. "It's a simple resurrection. I don't like my time wasted."

"Yes," said Dillon, "but may I come in?"

"I hope you don't plan on being this irritating in the future," said Okoya. "Yes!" he said, "By all means, *please* come in!"

"Thank you," Dillon leapt through the breach at Okoya, and his momentum took Okoya to the ground. That's when he saw the truth behind Dillon's strange expression. Okoya tried to resist, but was too late, because he could already feel a new, unfamiliar hunger burrowing into his gut, and a cold sense of terror constricting his mind.

AS FOR DILLON, he couldn't expel these creatures fast enough.

He had trekked across the red sands, back to the breach, feeling those things within him leeching on his soul, filling him with that old familiar hunger for destruction, and fear so intense it made every footstep an ordeal. Not even in his darkest of nightmares had he seen himself wilfully bringing these creatures back to Earth, but he knew they wouldn't remain on Earth for long . . . because just on the other side of the portal, was something that suited them more than a human star-shard. Perhaps Dillon was a great soul, but Okoya was also a great soul . . . And Okoya was a soul who could travel!

As the two parasites gripped on to Okoya, Dillon heaved them out of himself with all the force he could muster, and in his mind's eye, he saw it happen . . .

. . . And he saw, for the first time, Okoya's true form. It was a creature of light and unlight—both luminous and deadly dark at the same time, as if its own living light was forever feeding the living darkness of its shadow. It had no form beyond the pseudopod tentacles it used to devour life—but now those tentacles flung wildly, as the Spirit of Destruction tore it open with its talons and crawled inside, followed by the Spirit of Fear.

"I've decided this world *is* worth preserving!" Dillon shouted at Okoya. "But you're *not!*" Dillon pushed himself away, and his image of the parasites and the tentacled creature of light faded. Now all he saw was Okoya, lying in the dust, convulsing and writhing in agony, tearing at his own tangling hair.

"Help me!" screamed Okoya. "Help me, Dillon, help me!" And the Bringer gouged at his own face, knowing—perhaps for the first time in its life—the feeling of terror. Okoya struggled to get to his feet, then fell again, trying to cast out the creatures he had invited into his soul—but not even his will was great enough to cast them out. They had burrowed too deep. They were home.

He no longer saw Dillon, for Dillon no longer mattered to him. All that mattered was escaping the parasites' choking grip. Okoya turned, and leapt through the hole, but he didn't stop there—for just beyond the portal into the Unworld, Okoya punched a second portal—and for the first time, the Unworld resembled to Dillon, what he already knew it to be—just a space between the walls of worlds—a buffer zone to protect one world from another

Okoya leapt into the Unworld, took a single stride in that space between, then hurled himself through the second breach, into the world he had come from.

Dillon caught sight of that other world for an instant—a universe full of living light and living shadow. But the moment Okoya crossed back into his own world, both portals sliced shut with the speed and finality of guillotine blades.

Once the echo of Okoya's final screams had receded to the far recesses of the canyon, Dillon sat down, and allowed himself several deep breaths of relief. He had unleashed one evil on another, and now the creatures of fear and destruction were the problem of Okoya and his world. Maybe Dillon couldn't destroy Okoya—but at least he could give him what he deserved.

In the quietude of the canyon, Dillon shed a tear for those who had lost their lives to Okoya, for Michael and Tory, whose end could not have been pleasant, and for Deanna.

"I'm sorry, Deanna," he said aloud. But this was not the time or the place for Deanna to live again. He didn't know if that time would ever come; he only knew that he had made the right choice.

Dillon took a moment to glance up at High Pebble, precariously perched on its finger of rock, threatening to plunge at any moment, as it had for thousands of years. But the boulder wasn't falling today. *As for tomorrow,* he thought, *well, who can say?*

Around him, the dust began to gather into sand, and the sand began to gather into pebbles, stroked into cohesion by Dillon's presence. He knew he had to move on.

It would have been a long trek out of the canyon, but on his way he came across a wild horse that seemed more than happy to bear him up the narrow rocky path.

26. ALL THINGS UNKNOWN

PHOENIX, ARIZONA. A GRAVEYARD. BY NO MEANS THE old-fashioned type where stones loomed large and foreboding, but the modern kind. The kind of place with master-planned aisles, and small, shin-high markers on an endless, rolling lawn. Two gravestones side by side marked final resting places of Davis Roland Cole and Judith Martha Cole. Beloved Father and Mother.

Dillon knelt, and put two sprigs of flowers in the small holders on the stones.

"I wish I could tell you all the things that have happened since you've been gone," Dillon told them. "You have every reason to be ashamed of me . . . but maybe now . . . maybe now you can be proud of me, too."

Nearby, Winston kept a respectful distance. Then, once Dillon had stopped talking, he ventured closer.

"I never liked graveyards," Winston said. "They do everything to make 'em user-friendly, but no graveyard's ever gonna be a friend of mine."

Still on his knees, Dillon adjusted the flowers, which he knew was unnecessary, because whatever he did, they were in a perfect, orderly pattern.

"Any feelings about where Lourdes might be?" Dillon asked.

Winston put his hands in his pockets and shook his head. "Only that she's somewhere far away."

It was not good news, because now they needed to be together even more than before. They could not let what Okoya had done to them keep them divided. Dillon stood, but kept his eyes fixed on his parents' gravestones.

"So," said Winston with a shrug, "are you going to do it?"

Dillon looked down at the two gravestones. His own parents had been the first two casualties of the Spirit of Destruction—their brains had been scrambled so badly just by being near Dillon, that they simply couldn't hold on to life. It had been an untimely and unjust way to die—and if anyone deserved to be brought back, they did.

He turned to gaze at the endless fields of the departed. There was a funeral in the distance to his right, and to his left, an old woman shed tears for her husband. But they were good tears. They were natural tears.

"No," said Dillon. "No, I'm not going to." And he didn't just mean his parents; he meant everyone—from the ones whose lives had ended when he had crossed the Pacific Northwest, to the ones whose deaths had had nothing to do with him at all. No, he would not bring any of them back.

"Death has got to *mean* something, Winston." Dillon wiped the tears from his eyes with the heel of his hand. "Even if it's awful, and even if it's unfair, it's got to mean something. I know that's screwed, but somehow it's also right."

He expected Winston to disagree somehow—he never had found approval in anything that Dillon did. But this time Winston surprised him.

"I've done some terrible things, too," said Winston. "I suppose I could make myself feel better by making a hundred people walk again, but then I'd never know if making them walk was the right thing to do, or if I was just doing it for myself. Best to get our own heads on straight first."

So Winston did understand. It was comforting for once, to be on the same wavelength with him.

"One problem, though," Winston added. "You made a promise back at the castle, that we'd never be hurt as long as we followed you. Tory and Michael were part of that promise."

Winston was right. Dillon had made a promise, and it left him in an irreconcilable dilemma. For as much as he wanted to live by his conviction that he would never abuse the power of resurrection again, he also knew that he would break his own rule for Tory and Michael, if he got the chance.

He wished Winston could offer him some pearls of wisdom, but he had none.

Dillon closed his eyes. It was hard enough to seek out the

living, but finding the dead? He wasn't even sure if they died in the rubble of the dam, or somewhere else. "We'll look for them," Dillon said. "And if we ever find their bodies, we'll decide what to do then."

From here on in, Dillon knew, his decisions would only get harder. In the days since Okoya's departure, tens of thousands had flown in from around the world to bathe in the healing waters of the Colorado and Columbia Rivers, and to witness Dillon's miracle of the Backwash. People whispered his name, from the humblest to the most elite of circles, as their alliances realigned toward him. Okoya was right about one thing: It was too late to stop it. How long until everyone in the world knew his name? Twenty-four days and counting, whether he liked it or not.

"Come on, we'd better get out of here," said Winston. "This isn't a good place to stand for too long, if you know what I mean."

Dillon looked around, and knew exactly what Winston meant. Thanks to Dillon, all the dead flowers gracing the neighboring stones had become fresh again—and thanks to Winston, they were all growing new buds. Even more worrisome was Dillon's sense that the rows of the dead were ever so slowly being coaxed back toward life by his own healing presence. It was everywhere around them—growth and rejuvenation, old life and new. It was a wonderful thing, and yet terrible all at once, for this world was not ready for their brand of talents, and they were not ready to wield them.

"Come on, Dillon. Can't let grass grow beneath our feet," said Winston with a wry smile, because in fact it was.

Dillon had to smile as well. He couldn't read all the patterns ahead; there were too many variables now, too many gaping unknowns. But then he could never predict the future, could he? He could only see the directions that chance and design were *supposed* to take, as they moved toward an unseen future. But things change; and no pattern can ever be cast in stone. It frightened him to know that even with his remarkable vision, so much in the world was out of his control and unknowable. It was that fear of the unknown that bound him to what he was; never a god, and always human. There was comfort in that, and as they left the dead behind, Dillon took strength in the knowledge that so many things were still unknown.